Can a man win a war when *he* is his enemy's strongest weapon?

Can a soldier put down a weapon once he has taken it up—even if it seeks his own life?

Can a machine of death prove a match for a man who intends to live—at any price?

Can a mercenary jaded by combat recognize the one thing that is worth fighting to save?

Sixteen of the top writers in the science fiction field explore the tragedy and the glory of war among the stars in

EDITED BY

GORDON R. DICKSON

ACE SCIENCE FICTION BOOKS
NEW YORK

COMBAT SF

An Ace Science Fiction Book / published by arrangement with
the editor

PRINTING HISTORY
First Ace printing / June 1981
Third printing / February 1984

ISBN: 0-441-11534-9

Ace Science Fiction Books are published by The Berkley Publishing Group,
200 Madison Avenue, New York, New York 10016.
PRINTED IN THE UNITED STATES OF AMERICA

Acknowledgments

HIDE AND SEEK by Arthur C. Clarke, copyright © 1949 by Street and Smith Publications, Inc. Reprinted by permission of the author and his agent.

THE LAST COMMAND by Keith Laumer copyright © 1967 by Condé Nast Publications, Inc. Reprinted by permission of the author and his agent, Robert P. Mills, Ltd.

MEN OF GOOD WILL by Ben Bova and Myron R. Lewis, copyright © 1964 by Galaxy Publishing Corp.

THE PAIR by Joe L. Hensley, copyright © 1958 by King-Size Publications, Inc. Reprinted by permission of the author and his agent, Virginia Kidd.

SITUATION THIRTY by Frank M. Robinson, copyright © 1979 by Interlit (B.V.I.), Ltd. Reprinted by permission of the author and his agent.

THE BUTCHER'S BILL by David Drake, copyright © 1974 by UPD Publishing Corp. Reprinted from *Galaxy*, November 1974, by permission of the author and his agent, Kirby McCauley.

THE MAN WHO CAME EARLY by Poul Anderson, copyright © 1956 by Fantasy House, Inc. Reprinted by permission of the author and his agents, Scott Meredith Literary Agency, Inc., 845 Third Ave., N.Y., N.Y., 10022.

PATRON OF THE ARTS by Fred Saberhagen, copyright © 1965 by Galaxy Publishing Corp.

TIME PIECE by Joe W. Haldeman, copyright © 1970 by U.P.D. Publishing Corporation.

RICOCHET ON MIZA by Gordon R. Dickson, copyright © 1951 by Love Romances Publishing Co.

THE SCAVENGERS by James White, copyright © 1953 by Street and Smith Publications, Inc. Reprinted by permission of the author and his agents, Scott Meredith Literary Agency, Inc., 845 Third Ave., N.Y., N.Y., 10022.

NO WAR, OR BATTLE'S SOUND by Harry Harrison, copyright © 1968 by Galaxy Publishing Corp. Reprinted by permission of the author and his agent, Robert P. Mills, Ltd.

THE HORARS OF WAR by Gene Wolfe, copyright © 1970 by Harry Harrison. Reprinted by permission of the author and his agent, Virginia Kidd.

FIREPROOF by Hal Clement, copyright © 1949 by Street and Smith Publications, Inc. Copyright renewed 1977 by Condé Nast Publications, Inc. Reprinted by permission of the author.

CONTENTS

COMBAT SF:
INTRODUCTION

This collection of science fiction stories takes advantage of a unique characteristic of the science fiction field. One of the questions that authors of this literature almost invariably get from interviewers when they appear on radio or TV talk shows is: "Why do you prefer writing science fiction to other types of fiction?"

The answer almost invariably is: "There's more freedom in this genre to do what you want than there is anywhere else."

This answer is not meant to imply that science fiction authors carry a license to be more prejudiced, inept, or obscene than writers in other literary areas. But it does mean that the science fiction hard-core audience is interested in the investigation of all possible subjects, whether these happen to be palatable at the moment or not.

Investigation, however, is the key word. Core science fiction does not investigate dark or hitherto unexplored territories simply for the sake of being called explorative, as the political writer may root deep into political scandal in hope of being called fearless. The explorations of science fiction are normally for the purpose of testing an idea, a question, or a possibility in the literary laboratory; as opposed to trying it out in the real world, where a botched experiment can mean famine, pestilence, or the bloody slaughter of one people by another.

Science fiction is, in fact, essentially an unstructured think-tank in which authors of differing points of view can paint differing solutions or eventualities suggested by present problems or situations. As a literature it is favorably designed to act as a vehicle for ideas or arguments—to be a seedbed for a philosophical fiction. As such, I myself have been using it for nearly two decades now.

This can be so only because of the unique character of the readers of science fiction. Starting as readers of a genre that in the pulp magazines of the thirties and forties was part of a tradition as straitlaced and taboo-ridden as that of the slick magazines in their heyday, these readers went on to create an audience that would listen to any fictional thesis in a well-told story if it had serious thought behind it.

This is not to say that all of the readers of core science fiction understood or agreed with all of what was offered to them. Like a number of other authors in the field, no doubt, I have a thick file of criticism and comments from this audience of steady readers, some of which are startling in their penetration, but others of which are ludicrous in misunderstandings of what my fiction was saying. As a group, however, the attitude of these readers has been and remains open-minded and inquiring in the extreme, even when the fictional subject they are faced with seems to flout their deepest convictions as individuals.

This was particularly true during the sixties in the case of science fiction stories having to do with war in any of its aspects. Following World War II, triggered in fact by the cumulative effect of half a century of modern armed combat, an emotional reaction set in, not merely among science fiction readers but among readers in general. War became, in 1960, in a very real sense the material of a new pornography;

and readers in general did not stop to ask the reason for armed violence being depicted in a piece of fiction. The simple fact that it was there was enough to make them reject the writing and condemn the writer.

But the readers of science fiction during these years were more discerning. They had been used to looking to stories in their fictional area not merely for the casual entertainment these might provide, but also for the intellectual interest their thematic argument provoked; and this experience had taught them that the theme of a story might be far different from what a careless glance could discover on the narrative's surface. It is true, as I have said, that there have always been a minority who seemed unable to look below the story surface. Nonetheless, a remarkable number of science fiction readers remained who were both aware and unprejudiced enough to find rewarding the thematic science fiction story in all its patterns, including those dealing with combat.

As we move now into the seventies, this generally discerning readership seems to be increasing in numbers. For these readers, as well as for those with a technical interest in conflict, this collection of science fiction stories has been put together. Obviously, it is impossible in a single book like this to cover the whole spectrum of think-tanking by science fiction authors on the subject; so the attempt has been to spread across as much of the available area as possible, even if this has meant leaving gaps between examples, as a result.

To anyone knowing the science fiction field as a whole, the variety in style and attitude among the authors included here is in itself interesting. To these informed readers I should add a small apology. There are easily as many excellent stories again, by well-known as well as newer writers of science fiction, which I would certainly have included if space had permitted. In several instances some of our best writers go unrepresented in this collection because of the lack of space and the necessity to show a spectrum as evenly divided as possible in what was available.

—Gordon R. Dickson

HIDE AND SEEK

Arthur C. Clarke

We were walking back through the woods when Kingman saw the gray squirrel. Our bag was a small but varied one—three grouse, a couple of pigeons and four rabbits—one, I am sorry to say, an infant in arms. And contrary to certain dark forecasts, both the dogs were still alive.

The squirrel saw us at the same moment. It knew that it was marked for immediate execution as a result of the damage it had done to the trees on the estate, and perhaps it had lost close relatives to Kingman's gun. In three leaps it had reached the base of the nearest tree, and vanished behind it in a flicker of gray. We saw its face once more, appearing for a moment round the edge of its shield a dozen feet from the ground; but though we waited, with guns leveled hopefully at various branches, we never saw it again.

Kingman was very thoughtful as we walked back across the lawn to the magnificent old house. He said nothing as we handed our victims to the cook—who received them without much enthusiasm—and only emerged from his reverie when we were sitting in the smoking room and he remembered his duties as a host.

"That tree-rat," he said suddenly—he always called them 'tree-rats,' on the grounds that people were too sentimental to shoot the dear little squirrels—"it reminded me of a very peculiar experience that happened shortly before I retired. Very shortly indeed, in fact."

"I thought it would," said Carson dryly. I gave him a glare; he'd been in the Navy and had heard Kingman's stories before, but they were still new to me.

"Of course," Kingman remarked, slightly nettled, "if you'd rather I didn't—"

"Do go on," I said hastily. "You've made me curious. What connection there can possibly be between a gray squirrel and the Second Jovian War I can't imagine."

Kingman seemed mollified.

"I think I'd better change some names," he said thoughtfully, "but I won't alter the places. The story begins about a million kilometers sunwards of Mars—"

K.15 was a military intelligence operator. It gave him considerable pain when unimaginative people called him a spy, but at the moment he had much more substantial grounds for complaint. For some days now a fast cruiser had been coming up astern, and though it was flattering to have the undivided attention of such a fine ship and so many highly-trained men, it was an honor that K.15 would willingly have forgone.

What made the situation doubly annoying was the fact that his friends would be meeting him off Mars in about twelve hours, aboard a ship quite capable of dealing with a mere cruiser—from which you will gather that K.15 was a person of some importance. Unfortunately, the most optimistic calculation showed that the pursuers would be within accurate gun range in six hours. In some six hours five minutes, therefore, K.15 was likely to occupy an extensive and still expanding volume of space.

There might just be time for him to land on Mars, but that would be one of the worst things he could do. It would certainly annoy the aggressively neutral Martians, and the political complications would be frightful. Moreover, if his friends *had* to come down to the planet to rescue him, it would cost them more than ten kilometers a second in fuel—most of their operational reserve.

He had only one advantage, and that a very dubious one. The commander of the cruiser might guess that he was heading for a rendezvous, but he would not know how close it was nor how large was the ship that was coming to meet him. If he could keep alive for only twelve hours, he would be safe. The "if" was a somewhat considerable one.

K. 15 looked moodily at his charts, wondering if it was worth while to burn the rest of his fuel in a final dash. But a dash to where? He would be completely helpless then, and the pursuing ship might still have enough in her tanks to catch him as he flashed outwards into the empty darkness, beyond all hope of rescue—passing his friends as they came sunwards at a relative speed so great that they could do nothing to save him.

With some people, the shorter the expectation of life, the more sluggish are the mental processes. They seem hypnotized by the approach of death, so resigned to their fate that they do nothing to avoid it. K.15, on the other hand, found that his mind worked better in such a desperate emergency. It began to work as it had seldom done before.

Commander Smith—the name will do as well as any other—of the cruiser *Doradus* was not unduly surprised when K.15 began to decelerate. He had half expected the spy to land on Mars, on the principle that internment was better than annihilation, but when the plotting room brought the news that the little scout ship was heading for Phobos, he felt completely baffled. The inner moon was nothing but a jumble of rock some twenty kilometers across and not even the economical Martians had ever found any use for it. K.15

must be pretty desperate if he thought it was going to be of greater value to him.

The tiny scout had almost come to rest when the radar operator lost it against the mass of Phobos. During the braking maneuver, K.15 had squandered most of his lead and the *Doradus* was now only minutes away—though she was now beginning to decelerate lest she overrun him. The cruiser was scarcely three thousand kilometers from Phobos when she came to a complete halt; but of K.15's ship, there was still no sign. It should be easily visible in the telescopes, but it was probably on the far side of the little moon.

It reappeared only a few minutes later, traveling under full thrust on a course directly away from the sun. It was accelerating at almost five gravities—and it had broken its radio silence. An automatic recorder was broadcasting over and over again this interesting message:

"I have landed on Phobos and am being attacked by a Z-class cruiser. Think I can hold out until you come, but hurry."

The message wasn't even in code, and it left Commander Smith a sorely puzzled man. The assumption that K.15 was still aboard the ship and that the whole thing was a ruse was just a little too naive. But it might be a double-bluff—the message had obviously been left in plain language so that he would receive it and be duly confused. He could afford neither the time nor the fuel to chase the scout if K.15 really had landed. It was clear that reinforcements were on the way, and the sooner he left the vicinity the better. The phrase "Think I can hold out until you come" might be a piece of sheer impertinence, or it might mean that help was very near indeed.

Then K.15's ship stopped blasting. It had obviously exhausted its fuel, and was doing a little better than six kilometers a second away from the sun. K.15 *must* have landed, for his ship was now speeding helplessly out of the solar system. Commander Smith didn't like the message it was broadcasting, and guessed that it was running into the track of an approaching warship at some indefinite distance, but there was nothing to be done about that. The *Doradus* began to move towards Phobos, anxious to waste no time.

On the face of it, Commander Smith seemed the master of the situation. His ship was armed with a dozen heavy guided missiles and two turrets of electromagnetic guns. Against him was one man in a spacesuit, trapped on a moon only twenty kilometers across. It was not until Commander Smith had his first good look at Phobos, from a distance of less than a hundred kilometers, that he began to realize that, after all, K. 15 might have a few cards up his sleeve.

To say that Phobos has a diameter of twenty kilometers, as the astronomy books invariably do, is highly misleading. The word "diameter" implies a degree of symmetry which Phobos most certainly lacks. Like those other lumps of cosmic slag, the asteroids, it is a shapeless mass of rock floating in space, with, of course, no hint of an atmosphere and not much more gravity. It turns on its axis once every seven hours thirty-nine minutes, thus keeping the same face always to Mars—which is so close that appreciably less than half the planet is visible, the Poles being below the curve of the horizon. Beyond this, there is very little more to be said about Phobos.

K.15 had no time to enjoy the beauty of the crescent world filling the sky above him. He threw all the equipment he could carry out of the air lock, set the controls, and jumped. As the little ship went flaming out towards the stars he watched it go with feelings he did not care to analyze. He had burned his boats with a vengeance, and he could only hope that the oncoming battleship would intercept the radio message as the empty vessel went racing by into nothingness. There was also a faint possibility that the enemy cruiser might go in pursuit, but that was rather too much to hope for.

He turned to examine his new home. The only light was the ochre radiance of Mars, since the sun was below the horizon, but that was quite sufficient for his purpose and he could see very well. He stood in the center of an irregular plain about two kilometers across, surrounded by low hills

over which he could leap rather easily if he wished. There
was a story he remembered reading long ago about a man
who had accidentally jumped off Phobos; that wasn't quite
possible—though it was on Deimos—as the escape velocity
was still about ten meters a second. But unless he was
careful, he might easily find himself at such a height that it
would take hours to fall back to the surface—and that would
be fatal. For K.15's plan was a simple one—he must remain
as close to the surface of Phobos as possible *and diametri-
cally opposite the cruiser*. The *Doradus* could then fire all
her armament against the twenty kilometers of rock, and he
wouldn't even feel the concussion. There were only two
serious dangers, and one of these did not worry him greatly.

To the layman, knowing nothing of the finer details of
astronautics, the plan would have seemed quite suicidal. The
Doradus was armed with the latest in ultra-scientific
weapons; moreover, the twenty kilometers which separated
her from her prey represented less than a second's flight at
maximum speed. But Commander Smith knew better, and
was already feeling rather unhappy. He realized, only too
well, that of all the machines of transport man has ever
invented, a cruiser of space is far and away the least maneu-
verable. It was a simple fact that K.15 could make half a
dozen circuits of his little world while her commander was
persuading the *Doradus* to do even one.

There is no need to go into technical details, but those who
are still unconvinced might like to consider these elementary
facts. A rocket-driven spaceship can, obviously, only accel-
erate along its major axis—that is, "forwards". Any devia-
tion from a straight course demands a physical turning of the
ship, so that the motors can blast in another direction.
Everyone knows that this is done by internal gyros or tangen-
tial steering jets—but very few people know just how long
this simple maneuver takes. The average cruiser, fully
fueled, has a mass of two or three thousand tons, which does
not make for rapid footwork. But things are even worse than
this, for it isn't the mass, but the moment of inertia that

matters here—and since a cruiser is a long, thin object, its moment of inertia is slightly colossal. The sad fact remains—though it is seldom mentioned by astronautical engineers—that it takes a good ten minutes to rotate a spaceship through one hundred eighty degrees, with gyros of any reasonable size. Control jets aren't much quicker, and in any case their use is restricted because the rotation they produce is permanent and they are liable to leave the ship spinning like a slow-motion pinwheel, to the annoyance of all inside.

In the ordinary way, these disadvantages are not very grave. One has millions of kilometers and hundreds of hours in which to deal with such minor matters as a change in the ship's orientation. It is definitely against the rules to move in ten-kilometer radius circles, and the commander of the *Doradus* felt distinctly aggrieved. K.15 wasn't playing fair.

At the same moment that resourceful individual was taking stock of the situation, which might very well have been worse. He had reached the hills in three jumps and felt less naked than he had out in the open plain. The food and equipment he had taken from the ship he had hidden where he hoped he could find it again, but as his suit could keep him alive for over a day that was the least of his worries. The small packet that was the cause of all the trouble was still with him, in one of those numerous hiding places a well-designed spacesuit affords.

There was an exhilarating loneliness about his mountain aerie, even though he was not quite as lonely as he would have wished. Forever fixed in his sky, Mars was waning almost visibly as Phobos swept above the night side of the planet. He could just make out the lights of some of the Martian cities, gleaming pin-points marking the junctions of the invisible canals. All else was stars and silence and a line of jagged peaks so close it seemed he could almost touch them. Of the *Doradus* there was still no sign. She was presumably carrying out a careful telescopic examination of the sunlit side of Phobos.

Mars was a very useful clock—when it was half full the sun would rise and, very probably, so would the *Doradus*. But she might approach from some quite unexpected quarter; she might even—and this was the one real danger—have landed a search party.

This was the first possibility that had occurred to Commander Smith when he saw just what he was up against. Then he realized that the surface area of Phobos was over a thousand square kilometers and that he could not spare more than ten men from his crew to make a search of that jumbled wilderness. Also, K.15 would certainly be armed.

Considering the weapons which the *Doradus* carried, this last objection might seem singularly pointless. It was very far from being so. In the ordinary course of business, side arms and other portable weapons are as much use to a spacecruiser as are cutlasses and crossbows. The *Doradus* happened, quite by chance—and against regulations at that—to carry one automatic pistol and a hundred rounds of ammunition. Any search party would, therefore, consist of a group of unarmed men looking for a well concealed and very desperate individual who could pick them off at his leisure. K.15 was breaking the rules again.

The terminator of Mars was now a perfectly straight line, and at almost the same moment the sun came up, not so much like thunder as like a salvo of atomic bombs. K.15 adjusted the filters of his visor and decided to move. It was safer to stay out of the sunlight, not only because he was less likely to be detected in the shadow but also because his eyes would be much more sensitive there. He had only a pair of binoculars to help him, whereas the *Doradus* would carry an electronic telescope of twenty centimeters aperture at least.

It would be best, K.15 decided, to locate the cruiser if he could. It might be a rash thing to do, but he would feel much happier when he knew exactly where she was and could watch her movements. He could then keep just below the horizon, and the glare of the rockets would give him ample warning of any impending move. Cautiously launching himself along an almost horizontal trajectory, he began the circumnavigation of his world.

The narrowing crescent of Mars sank below the horizon until only one vast horn reared itself enigmatically against the stars. K.15 began to feel worried—there was still no sign of the *Doradus*. But this was hardly surprising, for she was painted black as night and might be a good hundred kilometers away in space. He stopped, wondering if he had done the right thing after all. Then he noticed that something quite large was eclipsing the stars almost vertically overhead, and was moving swiftly even as he watched. His heart stopped for a moment—then he was himself again, analyzing the situation and trying to discover how he had made so diastrous a mistake.

It was some time before he realized that the black shadow slipping across the sky was not the cruiser at all, but something almost equally deadly. It was far smaller, and far nearer, than he had at first thought. The *Doradus* had sent her television-homing guided missiles to look for him.

This was the second danger he had feared, and there was nothing he could do about it except to remain as inconspicuous as possible. The *Doradus* now had many eyes searching for him, but these auxiliaries had very severe limitations. They had been built to look for sunlit spaceships against a background of stars, not to search for a man hiding in a dark jungle of rock. The definition of their television systems was low, and they could only see in the forward direction.

There were rather more men on the chessboard now, and the game was a little deadlier, but his was still the advantage. The torpedo vanished into the night sky. As it was traveling on a nearly straight course in this low gravitational field, it would soon be leaving Phobos behind, and K.15 waited for what he knew must happen. A few minutes later, he saw a brief stabbing of rocket exhausts and guessed that the projectile was swinging slowly back on its course. At almost the same moment he saw another flare far away in the opposite

quarter of the sky, and wondered just how many of these
infernal machines were in action. From what he knew of
Z-class cruisers—which was a good deal more than he
should—there were four missile control channels, and they
were probably all in use.

He was suddenly struck by an idea so brilliant that he was
quite sure it couldn't possibly work. The radio on his suit was
a tunable one, covering an unusually wide band, and somewhere not far away the *Doradus* was pumping out power on
everything from a thousand megacycles upwards. He
switched on the receiver and began to explore.

It came in quickly—the raucous whine of a pulse transmitter not far away. He was probably only picking up a subhar-
monic, but that was quite good enough. It D/F'ed sharply,
and for the first time K.15 allowed himself to make long-
range plans about the future. The *Doradus* had betrayed
herself—as long as she operated her missiles, he would know
exactly where she was.

He moved cautiously forward towards the transmitter. To
his surprise the signal faded, then increased sharply again.
This puzzled him until he realized that he must be moving
through a diffraction zone. Its width might have told him
something useful if he had been a good enough physicist, but
he couldn't imagine what.

The *Doradus* was hanging about five kilometers above the
surface, in full sunlight. Her "nonreflecting" paint was
overdue for renewal, and K.15 could see her clearly. As he
was still in darkness, and the shadow line was moving away
from him, he decided that he was as safe here as anywhere.
He settled down comfortably so that he could just see the
cruiser and waited, feeling fairly certain that none of the
guided projectiles would come too near the ship. By now, he
calculated, the commander of the *Doradus* must be getting
pretty mad. He was perfectly correct.

After an hour, the cruiser began to heave herself round
with all the grace of a bogged hippopotamus. K.15 guessed
what was happening. Commander Smith was going to have a

look at the antipodes, and was preparing for the perilous fifty kilometer journey. He watched very carefully to see the orientation the ship was adopting, and when she came to rest again was relieved to see that she was almost broadside on to him. Then, with a series of jerks that could not have been very enjoyable aboard, the cruiser began to move down to the horizon. K.15 followed her at a comfortable walking pace— if one could use the phrase—reflecting that this was a feat very few people had ever performed. He was particularly careful not to overtake her on one of his kilometerlong glides, and kept a close watch for any missiles that might be coming up astern.

It took the *Doradus* nearly an hour to cover the fifty kilometers. This, as K.15 amused himself by calculating, represented considerably less than a thousandth of her normal speed. Once she found herself going off into space at a tangent, and rather than waste time turning end over end again fired off a salvo of shells to reduce speed. But she made it at last, and K.15 settled down for another vigil, wedged between two rocks where he could just see the cruiser and he was quite sure she couldn't see him. It occurred to him that by this time Commander Smith might have grave doubts as to whether he really was on Phobos at all, and he felt like firing off a signal flare to reassure him. However, he resisted the temptation.

There would be little point in describing the events of the next ten hours, since they differed in no important detail from those that had gone before. The *Doradus* made three other moves, and K.15 stalked her with the care of a big-game hunter following the spoor of some elephantine beast. Once, when she would have led him out into full sunlight, he let her fall below the horizon until he could only just pick up her signals. But most of the time he kept her just visible, usually low down behind some convenient hill.

Once a torpedo exploded some kilometers away, and K.15 guessed that some exasperated operator had seen a shadow he didn't like—or else that a technician had forgotten to switch off a proximity fuze. Otherwise nothing happened to enliven the proceedings; in fact, the whole affair was becoming rather boring. He almost welcomed the sight of an occasional guided missile drifting inquisitively overhead, for he did not believe that they could see him if he remained motionless and in reasonable cover. If he could have stayed on the part of Phobos exactly opposite the cruiser, he would have been safe even from these, he realized, since the ship would have no control there in the moon's radio-shadow. But he could think of no reliable way in which he could be sure of staying in the safety zone if the cruiser moved again.

The end came very abruptly. There was a sudden blast of steering jets, and the cruiser's main drive burst forth in all its power and splendor. In seconds the *Doradus* was shrinking sunwards, free at last, thankful to leave, even in defeat, this miserable lump of rock that had so annoyingly balked her of her legitimate prey. K.15 knew what had happened, and a great sense of peace and relaxation swept over him. In the radar room of the cruiser, someone had seen an echo of disconcerting amplitude approaching with altogether excessive speed. K.15 now had only to switch on his suit beacon and to wait. He could even afford the luxury of a cigarette.

"Quite an interesting story," I said, "and I see now how it ties up with that squirrel. But it does raise one or two queries in my mind."

"Indeed?" said Rupert Kingman politely.

I always like to get to the bottom of things, and I knew that my host had played a part in the Jovian War about which he very seldom spoke. I decided to risk a long shot in the dark.

"May I ask how you happened to know so much about this unorthodox military engagement? It isn't possible, is it, that *you* were K.15?"

There was an odd sort of strangling noise from Carson. Then Kingman said, quite calmly:

"No, I wasn't."

He got to his feet and started towards the gun room.

"If you'll excuse me a moment, I'm going to have another shot at that tree-rat. Maybe I'll get him this time." Then he was gone.

Carson looked at me as if to say: "This is another house you'll never be invited to again." When our host was out of earshot he remarked in a coldly clinical tone:

"What did you have to say that for?"

"Well, it seemed a safe guess. How else could he have known all that?"

"As a matter of fact, I believe he met K.15 after the war; they must have had an interesting conversation together. But I thought you knew that Rupert was retired from the service with only the rank of lieutenant commander. The Court of Inquiry could never see his point of view. After all, it just wasn't reasonable that the commander of the fastest ship in the Fleet couldn't catch a man in a spacesuit."

THE LAST COMMAND

Keith Laumer

*I come to awareness, sensing a residual oscillation travers-
ing my hull from an arbitrarily designated heading of 035.
From the damping rate I compute that the shock was of
intensity 8.7, emanating from a source within the limits 72
meters/46 meters. I activate my primary screens, trigger a
return salvo. There is no response. I engage reserve energy
cells, bring my secondary battery to bear—futilely. It is
apparent that I have been ranged by the Enemy and severely
damaged.*

*My positional sensors indicate that I am resting at an
angle of 13 degrees 14 seconds, deflected from a base line at
21 points from median. I attempt to right myself, but encounter massive resistance. I activate my forward scanners,
shunt power to my IR microstrobes. Not a flicker illuminates
my surroundings. I am encased in utter blackness.*

*Now a secondary shock wave approaches, rocks me with
an intensity of 8.2. It is apparent that I must withdraw from
my position–but my drive trains remain inert under full*

15

thrust. I shift to base emergency power, try again. Pressure mounts; I sense my awareness fading under the intolerable strain; then, abruptly, resistance falls off and I am in motion.

It is not the swift maneuvering of full drive, however, I inch forward, as if restrained by massive barriers. Again I attempt to penetrate the surrounding darkness, and this time perceive great irregular outlines shot through with fracture planes. I probe cautiously, then more vigorously, encountering incredible densities.

I channel all available power to a single ranging pulse, direct it upward. The indication is so at variance with all experience that I repeat the test at a new angle. Now I must accept the fact: I am buried under 207.6 meters of sold rock!

I direct my attention to an effort to orient myself to my uniquely desperate situation. I run through an action-status check list of thirty thousand items, feel dismay at the extent of power loss. My main cells are almost completely drained, my reserve units at no more than .4 charge. Thus my sluggishness is explained. I review the tactical situation, recall the trimphant announcement from my commander that the Enemy forces are annihilated, that all resistance has ceased. In memory, I review the formal procession; in company with my comrades of the Dinochrome Brigade, many of us deeply scarred by Enemy action, we parade before the Grand Commandant, then assemble on the depot ramp. At command, we bring our music storage cells into phase and display our Battle Anthem. The nearby star radiates over a full spectrum, unfiltered by atmospheric haze. It is a moment of glorious triumph. Then the final command is given—

The rest is darkness. But it is apparent that the victory celebration was premature. The Enemy has counterattacked with a force that has come near to immobilizing me. The realization is shocking, but the .1 second of leisurely introspection has clarified my position. At once, I broadcast a call on Brigade Action wavelength:

"Unit LNE to Command, requesting permission to file VSR."

I wait, sense no response, call again, using full power. I sweep the enclosing volume of rock with an emergency alert warning. I tune to the all-units band, await the replies of my comrades of the Brigade. None answers. Now I must face the reality: I alone have survived the assault.

I channel my remaining power to my drive and detect a channel of reduced density. I press for it and the broken rock around me yields reluctantly. Slowly, I move forward and upward. My pain circuitry shocks my awareness center with emergency signals; I am doing irreparable damage to my overloaded neural systems, but my duty is clear: I must seek and engage the Enemy.

Emerging from behind the blast barrier, Chief Engineer Pete Reynolds of the New Devonshire Port Authority pulled off his rock mask and spat grit from his mouth.

"That's the last one; we've bottomed out at just over two hundred yards. Must have hit a hard stratum down there."

"It's almost sundown," the paunchy man beside him said shortly. "You're a day and a half behind schedule."

"We'll start backfilling now, Mr. Mayor. I'll have pilings poured by oh-nine hundred tomorrow, and with any luck the first section of pad will be in place in time for the rally."

"I'm . . ." The mayor broke off, looked startled. "I thought you told me that was the last charge to be fired. . . ."

Reynolds frowned. A small but distinct tremor had shaken the ground underfoot. A few feet away, a small pebble balanced atop another toppled and fell with a faint clatter.

"Probably a big rock fragment falling," he said. At that moment, a second vibration shook the earth, stronger this time. Reynolds heard a rumble and a distant impact as rock fell from the side of the newly blasted excavation. He whirled to the control shed as the door swung back and Second Engineer Mayfield appeared.

"Take a look at this, Pete!" Reynolds went across to the hut, stepped inside. Mayfield was bending over the profiling table.

"What do you make of it!" he pointed. Superimposed on the heavy red contour representing the detonation of the shaped charge of the head which had completed the drilling of the final pile core were two other traces, weak but distinct.

"About .1 intensity," Mayfield looked puzzled. "What . . ."

The tracking needle dipped suddenly, swept up the screen to peak at .21, dropped back. The hut trembled. A stylus fell from the edge of the table. The red face of Mayor Daugherty burst through the door.

"Reynolds have you lost your mind? What's the idea of blasting while I'm standing out in the open? I might have been killed!"

"I'm not blasting," Reynolds snapped. "Jim, get Eaton on the line, see if they know anything." He stepped to the door, shouted.

A heavyset man in sweat-darkened coveralls swung down from the seat of a cable-lift rig. "Boss, what goes on?" he called as he came up. "Damn near shook me out of my seat!"

"I don't know. You haven't set any trim charges?"

"No, Boss. I wouldn't set no charges without your say-so."

"Come on." Reynolds started out across the rubble-littered stretch of barren ground selected by the Authority as the site of the new spaceport. Halfway to the open mouth of the newly blasted pit, the ground under his feet rocked violently enough to make him stumble. A gout of dust rose from the excavation ahead. Loose rock danced on the ground. Beside him, the drilling chief grabbed his arm.

"Boss, we better get back!"

Reynolds shook him off, kept going. The drill chief swore and followed. The shaking of the ground went on, a sharp series of thumps interrupting a steady trembling.

"It's a quake!" Reynolds yelled over the low rumbling sound. He and the chief were at the rim of the core now.

"It can't be a quake, Boss," the latter shouted. "Not in these formations!"

"Tell it to the geologists . . . " The rock slab they were

standing on rose a foot, dropped back. Both men fell. The slab bucked like a small boat in choppy water.

"Let's get out of here!" Reynolds was up and running. Ahead, a fissure opened, gaped a foot wide. He jumped it, caught a glimpse of black depths, a glint of wet clay twenty feet below—

A hoarse scream stopped him in his tracks. He spun, saw the drill chief down, a heavy splinter of rock across his legs. He jumped to him, heaved at the rock. There was blood on the man's shirt. The chief's hand beat the dusty rock before him. Then other men were there, grunting, sweaty hands gripping beside Reynolds'. The ground rocked. The roar from under the earth had risen to a deep, steady rumble. They lifted the rock aside, picked up the injured man, and stumbled with him to the aid shack.

The mayor was there, white-faced.

"What is it, Reynolds? If you're responsible—"

"Shut up!" Reynolds brushed him aside, grabbed the phone, punched keys.

"Eaton! What have you got on this temblor?"

"Temblor, hell." The small face on the four-inch screen looked like a ruffled hen. "What in the name of Order are you doing out there? I'm reading a whole series of displacements originating from that last core of yours! What did you do, leave a pile of trim charges lying around?"

"It's a quake. Trim charges, hell! This thing's broken up two hundred yards of surface rock. It seems to be traveling north-northeast—"

"I see that; a traveling earthquake!" Eaton flapped his arms, a tiny and ridiculous figure against a background of wall charts and framed diplomas. "Well . . . do something, Reynolds! Where's Mayor Daugherty?"

"Underfoot!" Reynolds snapped, and cut off.

Outside, a layer of sunset-stained dust obscured the sweep of level plain. A rock-dozer rumbled up, ground to a halt by Reynolds. A man jumped down.

"I got the boys moving equipment out," he panted. "The

thing's cutting a trail straight as a rule for the highway!'' He
pointed to a raised roadbed a quarter mile away.

"How fast is it moving?"

"She's done a hundred yards; it hasn't been ten minutes
yet!"

"If it keeps up another twenty minutes, it'll be into the
Intermix!"

"Scratch a few million cees and six months' work then,
Pete!"

"And Southside Mall's a couple miles farther."

"Hell, it'll damp out before then!"

"Maybe. Grab a field car, Dan."

"Pete!" Mayfield came up at a trot. "This thing's building! The centroid's moving on a heading of 022—"

"How far subsurface?"

"It's rising; started at two-twenty yards, and it's up to
one-eighty!"

"What have we stirred up?" Reynolds stared at Mayfield
as the field car skidded to a stop beside them.

"Stay with it, Jim. Give me anything new. We're taking a
closer look." He climbed into the rugged vehicle.

"Take a blast truck—"

"No time!" He waved and the car gunned away into the
pall of dust.

The rock car pulled to a stop at the crest of the three-level
Intermix on a lay-by designed to permit tourists to enjoy the
view of the site of the proposed port, a hundred feet below.
Reynolds studied the progress of the quake through field
glasses. From this vantage point, the path of the phenomenon
was a clearly defined trail of tilted and broken rock, some of
the slabs twenty feet across. As he watched, the fissure
lengthened.

"It looks like a mole's trail." Reynolds handed the glasses
to his companion, thumbed the Send key on the car radio.

"Jim, get Eaton and tell him to divert all traffic from the
Circular south of Zone Nine. Cars are already clogging the
right-of-way. The dust is visible from a mile away, and when

the word gets out there's something going on, we'll be swamped.''

"I'll tell him, but he won't like it!''

"This isn't politics! This thing will be into the outer pad area in another twenty minutes!''

"It won't last—''

"How deep does it read now?''

"One-five!'' There was a moment's silence. "Pete, if it stays on course, it'll surface at about where you're parked!''

"Uh-huh. It looks like you can scratch one Intermix. Better tell Eaton to get a story ready for the press.''

"Pete—talking about news-hounds,'' Dan said beside him. Reynolds switched off, turned to see a man in a gay-colored driving outfit coming across from a battered Monojag sportster which had pulled up behind the rock car. A big camera case was slung across his shoulder.

"Say, what's going on down there?'' he called.

"Rock slide,'' Reynolds said shortly. "I'll have to ask you to drive on. The road's closed. . . .''

"Who're you?'' The man looked belligerent.

"I'm the engineer in charge. Now pull out, brother.'' He turned back to the radio. "Jim, get every piece of heavy equipment we own over here, on the double.'' He paused, feeling a minute trembling in the car. "The Intermix is beginning to feel it,'' he went on. "I'm afraid we're in for it. Whatever that thing is, it acts like a solid body boring its way through the ground. Maybe we can barricade it.''

"Barricade an earthquake?''

"Yeah . . . I know how it sounds . . . but it's the only idea I've got.''

"Hey . . . what's that about an earthquake?'' The man in the colored suit was still there. "By gosh, I can feel it—the whole bridge is shaking!''

"Off, mister—now!'' Reynolds jerked a thumb at the traffic lanes where a steady stream of cars was hurtling past. "Dan, take us over to the main track. We'll have to warn this traffic off. . . .''

"Hold on, fellow." The man unlimbered his camera. "I represent the New Devon *Scope*. I have a few questions—"

"I don't have the answers," Pete cut him off as the car pulled away.

"Hah!" the man who had questioned Reynolds yelled after him. "Big shot! Think you can . . ." His voice was lost behind them.

In a modest retirees' apartment block in the coast town of Idlebreeze, forty miles from the scene of the freak quake, an old man sat in a reclining chair, half dozing before a yammering Tri-D tank.

" . . . Grandpa," a sharp-voiced young woman was saying. "It's time for you to go in to bed."

"Bed? Why do I want to go to bed? Can't sleep anyway . . ." He stirred, made a pretense of sitting up, showing an interest in the Tri-D. "I'm watching this show."

"It's not a show, it's the news," a fattish boy said disgustedly. "Ma, can I switch channels—"

"Leave it alone, Bennie," the old man said. On the screen, a panoramic scene spread out, a stretch of barren ground across which a furrow showed. As he watched, it lengthened.

" . . . Up here at the Intermix we have a fine view of the whole curious business, lazangemmun," the announcer chattered. "And in our opinion it's some sort of publicity stunt staged by the Port Authority to publicize their controversial Port project—"

"Ma, can I change channels?"

"Go ahead, Bennie—"

"Don't touch it," the old man said. The fattish boy reached for the control, but something in the old man's eye stopped him.

"The traffic's still piling up here," Reynolds said into the phone. "Damn it, Jim, we'll have a major jam on our hands—"

"He won't do it, Pete! You know the Circular was his

baby—the super all-weather pike that nothing could shut down. He says you'll have to handle this in the field—''

"Handle, hell! I'm talking about preventing a major disaster! And in a matter of minutes, at that!"

"I'll try again—"

"If he says no, divert a couple of the big ten-yard graders and block it off yourself. Set up field 'arcs, and keep any cars from getting in from either direction."

"Pete that's outside your authority!"

"You heard me!"

Ten minutes later, back at ground level, Reynolds watched the boom-mounted polyarcs swinging into position at the two roadblocks a quarter of a mile apart, cutting off the threatened section of the raised expressway. A hundred yards from where he stood on the rear cargo deck of a light grader rig, a section of rock fifty feet wide rose slowly, split, fell back with a ponderous impact. One corner of it struck the massive pier supporting the extended shelf of the lay-by above. A twenty-foot splinter fell away, exposing the reinforcing-rod core.

"How deep, Jim?" Reynolds spoke over the roaring sound coming from the disturbed area.

"Just subsurface now, Pete! It ought to break through—'' His voice was drowned in a rumble as the damaged pier shivered, rose up, buckled at its midpoint, and collapsed, bringing down with it a large chunk of pavement and guard rail, and a single still-glowing light pole. A small car that had been parked on the doomed section was visible for an instant just before the immense slab struck. Reynolds saw it bounce aside, then disappear under an avalanche of broken concrete.

"My God, Pete—'' Dan blurted. "That damned fool newshound—!"

"Look!" As the two men watched, a second pier swayed, fell backward into the shadow of the span above. The roadway sagged, and two more piers snapped. With a bellow like a burst dam, a hundred-foot stretch of the road fell into the roiling dust cloud.

"Pete!" Mayfield's voice burst from the car radio. "Get

out of there! I threw a reader on that thing and it's chattering . . .!''

Among the piled fragments, something stirred, heaved, rising up, lifting multiton pieces of the broken road, thrusting them aside like so many potato chips. A dull blue radiance broke through from the broached earth, threw an eerie light on the shattered structure above. A massive, ponderously irresistible shape thrust forward through the ruins. Reynolds saw a great blue-glowing profile emerge from the rubble like a surfacing submarine, shedding a burden of broken stone, saw immense treads ten feet wide claw for purchase, saw the mighty flank brush a still standing pier, send it crashing aside.

"Pete . . . what . . . what is it—?''

"I don't know." Reynolds broke the paralysis that had gripped him. "Get us out of here, Dan, fast! Whatever it is, it's headed straight for the city!''

I emerge at last from the trap into which I had fallen, and at once encounter defensive works of considerable strength. My scanners are dulled from lack of power, but I am able to perceive open ground beyond the barrier, and farther still, at a distance of 5.7 kilometers, massive walls. Once more I transmit the Brigade Rally signal; but as before, there is no reply. I am truly alone.

I scan the surrounding area for the emanations of Enemy drive units, monitor the EM spectrum for their communications. I detect nothing; either my circuitry is badly damaged, or their shielding is superb.

I must now make a decision as to possible courses of action. Since all my comrades of the Brigade have fallen, I compute that the walls before me must be held by Enemy forces. I direct probing signals at the defenses, discover them to be of unfamiliar construction, and less formidable than they appear. I am aware of the possiblity that this may be a trick of the Enemy; but my course is clear.

I re-engage my driving engines and advance on the Enemy fortress.

"You're out of your mind, Father," the stout man said. "At your age—"

"At your age, I got my nose smashed in a brawl in a bar on Aldo," the old man cut him off. "But I won the fight."

"James, you can't go out at this time of night . . . " an elderly woman wailed.

"Tell them to go home." The old man walked painfully toward his bedroom door. "I've seen enough of them for today."

"Mother, you won't let him do anything foolish?"

"He'll forget about it in a few minutes; but maybe you'd better go now and let him settle down."

"Mother . . . I really think a home is the best solution."

"Yes, Grandma," the young woman nodded agreement. "After all, he's past ninety—and he has his veteran's retirement. . . ."

Inside his room, the old man listened as they departed. He went to the closet, took out clothes, began dressing.

City Engineer Eaton's face was chalk-white on the screen.

"No one can blame me," he said. "How could I have known—"

"Your office ran the surveys and gave the PA the green light," Mayor Daugherty yelled.

"All the old survey charts showed was 'Disposal Area.'" Eaton threw out his hands. "I assumed—"

"As City Engineer, you're not paid to make assumptions! Ten minutes' research would have told you that was a 'Y' category area!"

"What's 'Y' category mean?" Mayfield asked Reynolds. They were standing by the field comm center, listening to the dispute. Nearby, boom-mounted Tri-D cameras hummed, recording the progress of the immense machine, its upper turret rearing forty-five feet into the air, as it ground slowly forward across smooth ground toward the city, dragging behind it a trailing festoon of twisted reinforcing iron crusted with broken concrete.

"Half-life over one hundred years," Reynolds answered

shortly. "The last skirmish of the war was fought near here.
Apparently this is where they buried the radioactive equipment left over from the battle."

"But that was more than seventy years ago—"

"There's still enough residual radiation to contaminate
anything inside a quarter-mile radius."

"They must have used some hellish stuff." Mayfield
stared at the dull shine half a mile distant.

"Reynolds, how are you going to stop this thing?" The
mayor had turned on the PA Engineer.

"Me stop it? You saw what it did to my heaviest rigs:
flattened them like pancakes. You'll have to call out the
military on this one, Mr. Mayor."

"Call in Federation forces? Have them meddling in civic
affairs?"

"The station's only sixty-five miles from here. I think
you'd better call them fast. It's only moving at about three
miles per hour but it will reach the south edge of the Mall in
another forty-five minutes."

"Can't you mine it? Blast a trap in its path?"

"You saw it claw its way up from six hundred feet down. I
checked the specs; it followed the old excavation tunnel out.
It was rubble-filled and capped with twenty-inch compressed
concrete."

"It's incredible," Eaton said from the screen. "The entire
machine was encased in a ten-foot shell of reinforced armo-
crete. It had to break out of that before it could move a foot!"

"That was just a radiation shield; it wasn't intended to
restrain a Bolo Combat Unit."

"What *was*, may I inquire?" The mayor glared.

"The units were deactivated before being buried," Eaton
spoke up, as if he were eager to talk. "Their circuits were
fused. It's all in the report—"

"The report you should have read somewhat sooner," the
mayor snapped.

"What . . . what started it up?" Mayfield looked bewildered. "For seventy years it was down there, and nothing
happened!"

"Our blasting must have jarred something," Reynolds said shortly. "Maybe closed a relay that started up the old battle reflex circuit."

"You know something about these machines?" the mayor asked.

"I've read a little."

"Then speak up, man. I'll call the station, if you feel I must. What measures should I request?"

"I don't know, Mr. Mayor. As far as I know, nothing on New Devon can stop that machine now."

The mayor's mouth opened and closed. He whirled to the screen, blanked Eaton's agonized face, punched in the code for the Federation Station.

"Colonel Blane!" he blurted as a stern face came onto the screen. "We have a major emergency on our hands! I'll need everything you've got! This is the situation—"

I encounter no resistance other than the flimsy barrier, but my progress is slow. Grievous damage has been done to my maindrive sector due to overload during my escape from the trap; and the failure of my sensing circuitry has deprived me of a major portion of my external receptivity. Now my pain circuits project a continuous signal to my awareness center; but it is my duty to my commander and to my fallen comrades of the Brigade to press forward at my best speed; but my performance is a poor shadow of my former ability.

And now at last the Enemy comes into action! I sense aerial units closing at supersonic velocities; I lock my lateral batteries to them and direct salvo fire; but I sense that the arming mechanisms clatter harmlessly. The craft sweep over me, and my impotent guns elevate, track them as they release detonants that spread out in an envelopmental pattern which I, with my reduced capabilities, am powerless to avoid. The missiles strike; I sense their detonations all about me; but I suffer only trivial damage. The Enemy has blundered if he thought to neutralize a Mark XXVIII Combat Unit with mere chemical explosives! But I weaken with each meter gained.

Now there is no doubt as to my course. I must press the

*charge and carry the walls before my reserve cells are
exhausted.*

From a vantage point atop a bucket rig four hundred yards
from the position the great fighting machine had now
reached, Pete Reynolds studied it through night glasses. A
battery of beamed polyarcs pinned the giant hulk, scarred and
rust-scaled, in a pool of blue-white light. A mile and a half
beyond it, the walls of the Mall rose sheer from the garden
setting.

"The bombers slowed it some," he reported to Eaton via
scope. "But it's still making better than two miles per hour.
I'd say another twenty-five minutes before it hits the main
ring-wall. How's the evacuation going?"

"Badly! I get no cooperation! You'll be my witness,
Reynolds, I did all I could—"

"How about the mobile batteries; how long before they'll
be in position?" Reynolds cut him off.

"I've heard nothing from Federation Central—typical
militaristic arrogance, not keeping me informed—but I have
them on my screens. They're two miles out—say three minutes."

"I hope you made your point about N-heads."

"That's outside my province!" Eaton said sharply. "It's
up to Brand to carry out this portion of the operation!"

"The HE Missiles didn't do much more than clear away
the junk it was dragging." Reynolds' voice was sharp.

"I wash my hands of responsibility for civilian lives,"
Eaton was saying when Reynolds shut him off, changed
channels.

"Jim, I'm going to try to divert it," he said crisply.
"Eaton's sitting on his political fence; the Feds are bringing
artillery up, but I don't expect much from it. Technically,
Brand needs Sector O.K. to use nuclear stuff, and he's not
the boy to stick his neck out—"

"Divert it how? Pete, don't take any chances—"

Reynolds laughed shortly. "I'm going to get around it and

drop a shaped drilling charge in its path. Maybe I can knock a tread off. With luck, I might get its attention on me, and draw it away from the Mall. There are still a few thousand people over there, glued to the Tri-D's. They think it's all a swell show.''

"Pete, you can't walk up on that thing! It's hot . . . '' He broke off. ''Pete—there's some kind of nut here—he claims he has to talk to you; says he knows something about that damned juggernaut. Shall I send . . . ?''

Reynolds paused with his hand on the cut-off ''Put him on,'' he snapped. Mayfield's face moved aside and an ancient, bleary-eyed visage stared out at him. The tip of the old man's tongue touched his dry lips.

"Son, I tried to tell this boy here, but he wouldn't listen—''

"What have you got, old-timer?'' Pete cut in. ''Make it fast.''

"My name's Sanders. James Sanders. I'm . . . I was with the Planetary Volunteer Scouts, back in '71—''

"Sure, Dad,'' Pete said gently. ''I'm sorry, I've got a little errand to run—''

"Wait . . . '' The old man's face worked. ''I'm old, son—too damned old. I know. But bear with me. I'll try to say it straight. I was with Hayle's squadron at Toledo. Then afterwards, they shipped us . . . but hell, you don't care about that! I keep wandering, son; can't help it. What I mean to say is—I was in on that last scrap, right here at New Devon—only we didn't call it New Devon then. Called it Hellport. Nothing but bare rock and Enemy emplacements . . .''

"You were talking about the battle, Mr. Sanders,'' Pete said tensely. ''Go on with that part.''

"Lieutenant Sanders,'' the oldster said. ''Sure, I was Acting Brigade Commander. See, our major was hit at Toledo—and after Tommy Chee stopped a sidewinder . . .''

"Stick to the point, Lieutenant!''

"Yes, sir!" the old man pulled himself together with an obvious effort. "I took the Brigade in; put out flankers, and ran the Enemy into the ground. We mopped 'em up in a thirty-three-hour running fight that took us from over by Crater Bay all the way down here to Hellport. When it was over, I'd lost six units, but the Enemy was done. They gave us Brigade Honors for that action. And then . . ."

"Then what?"

"Then the triple-dyed yellow-bottoms at Headquarters put out the order the Brigade was to be scrapped; said they were too hot to make decon practical. Cost too much, they said! So after the final review . . ." He gulped, blinked. "They planted 'em deep, two hundred meters, and poured in special High-R concrete."

"And packed rubble in behind them," Reynolds finished for him. "All right, Lieutenant, I believe you! But what started that machine on a rampage?"

"Should have known they couldn't hold down a Bolo Mark XXVIII!" The old man's eyes lit up. "Take more than a few million tons of rock to stop Lenny when his battle board was lit!"

"Lenny?"

"That's my old Command Unit out there, son. I saw the markings on the 3-D, Unit LNE of the Dinochrome Brigade!"

"Listen!" Reynolds snapped out. "Here's what I intend to try. . . ." He outlined his plan.

"Ha!" Sanders snorted. "It's quite a notion, mister, but Lenny won't give it a sneeze."

"You didn't come here to tell me we were licked," Reynolds cut in. "How about Brand's batteries?"

"Hell, son, Lenny stood up to point-blank Hellbore fire on Toledo, and—"

"Are you telling me there's nothing we can do?"

"What's that? No, son, that's not what I'm saying. . . ."

"Then what!"

"Just tell these johnnies to get out of my way, mister. I think I can handle him."

At the field comm hut, Pete Reynolds watched as the man who had been Lieutenant Sanders of the Volunteer Scouts pulled shiny black boots over his thin ankles, and stood. The blouse and trousers of royal blue polyon hung on his spare frame like wash on a line. He grinned, a skull's grin.

"It doesn't fit like it used to; but Lenny will recognize it. It'll help. Now, if you've got that power pack ready . . ."

Mayfield handed over the old-fashioned field instrument Sanders had brought in with him.

"It's operating, sir—but I've already tried everything I've got on that infernal machine; I didn't get a peep out of it."

Sanders winked at him. "Maybe I know a couple of tricks you boys haven't heard about." He slung the strap over his bony shoulder and turned to Reynolds.

"Guess we better get going, mister. He's getting close."

In the rock car Sanders leaned close to Reynolds' ear. "Told you those Federal guns wouldn't scratch Lenny. They're wasting their time."

Reynolds pulled the car to a stop at the crest of the road, from which point he had a view of the sweep of ground leading across to the city's edge. Lights sparkled all across the towers of New Devon. Close to the walls, the converging fire of the ranked batteries of infinite repeaters drove into the glowing bulk of the machine, which plowed on, undeterred. As he watched, the firing ceased.

"Now, let's get in there, before they get some other scheme going," Sanders said.

The rock car crossed the rough ground, swung wide to come up on the Bolo from the left side. Behind the hastily rigged radiation cover, Reynolds watched the immense silhouette grow before him.

"I knew they were big," he said. "But to see one up close like this—" He pulled to a stop a hundred feet from the Bolo.

"Look at the side ports," Sanders said, his voice crisper now. "He's firing antipersonal charges—only his plates are flat. If they weren't, we wouldn't have gotten within half a mile." He unclipped the microphone and spoke into it:

"Unit LNE, break off action and retire to ten-mile line!"

Reynolds' head jerked around to stare at the old man. His voice had rung with vigor and authority as he spoke the command.

The Bolo ground slowly ahead. Sanders shook his head, tried again.

"No answer, like that fella said. He must be running on nothing but memories now. . . ." He reattached the microphone and before Reynolds could put out a hand, had lifted the anti-R cover and stepped off on the ground.

"Sanders—get back in here!" Reynolds yelled.

"Never mind, son. I've got to get in close. Contact induction." He started toward the giant machine. Frantically, Reynolds started the car, slammed it into gear, pulled forward.

"Better stay back," Sanders' voice came from his field radio. "This close, that screening won't do you much good."

"Get in the car!" Reynolds roared. "That's hard radiation!"

"Sure; feels funny, like a sunburn, about an hour after you come in from the beach and start to think maybe you got a little too much." He laughed. "But I'll get to him. . . ."

Reynolds braked to a stop, watched the shrunken figure in the baggy uniform as it slogged forward, leaning as against a sleetstorm.

"I'm up beside him," Sanders' voice came through faintly on the field radio. "I'm going to try to swing up on his side. Don't feel like trying to chase him any farther."

Through the glasses, Reynolds watched the small figure, dwarfed by the immense bulk of the fighting machine as he tried, stumbled, tried again, swung up on the flange running across the rear quarter inside the churning bogie wheel.

"He's up," he reported. "Damned wonder the track didn't get him before . . . "

Clinging to the side of the machine, Sanders lay for a moment, bent forward across the flange. Then he pulled himself up, wormed his way forward to the base of the rear quarter turret, wedged himself against it. He unslung the communicator, removed a small black unit, clipped it to the armor; it clung, held by a magnet. He brought the microphone up to his face.

In the comm shack Mayfield leaned toward the screen, his eyes squinted in tension. Across the field Reynolds held the glasses fixed on the man lying across the flank of the Bolo. They waited.

The walls are before me, and I ready myself for a final effort, but suddenly I am aware of trickle currents flowing over my outer surface. Is this some new trick of the Enemy? I tune to the wave-energies, trace the source. They originate at a point in contact with my aft port armor. I sense modulation, match receptivity to a computed pattern. And I hear a voice:

"Unit LNE, break it off, Lenny. We're pulling back now, boy! This is Command to LNE; pull back to ten miles. If you read me, Lenny, swing to port and halt."

I am not fooled by the deception. The order appears correct, but the voice is not that of my Commander. Briefly I regret that I cannot spare energy to direct a neutralizing power flow at the device the Enemy has attached to me. I continue my charge.

"Unit LNE! Listen to me, boy; maybe you don't recognize my voice, but it's me! You see—some time has passed. I've gotten old. My voice has changed some, maybe. But it's me! Make a port turn, Lenny. Make it now!"

I am tempted to respond to the trick, for something in the false command seems to awaken secondary circuits which I sense have been long stilled. But I must not be swayed by the cleverness of the Enemy. My sensing circuitry has faded further as my energy cells drain; but I know where the Enemy lies. I move forward, but I am filled with agony, and only the memory of my comrades drives me on.

"Lenny, answer me. Transmit on the old private band— the one we agreed on. Nobody but me knows it, remember?"

Thus the Enemy seeks to beguile me into diverting precious power. But I will not listen.

"Lenny—not much time left. Another minute and you'll be into the walls. People are going to die. Got to stop you, Lenny. Hot here. My God, I'm hot. Not breathing too well, now. I can feel it; cutting through me like knives. You took a load of Enemy power, Lenny; and now I'm getting my share. Answer me, Lenny. Over to you . . . "

It will require only a tiny allocation of power to activate a communication circuit. I realize that it is only an Enemy trick, but I compute that by pretending to be deceived, I may achieve some trivial advantage. I adjust circuitry accordingly, and transmit:

"Unit LNE to Command. Contact with Enemy defensive line imminent. Request supporting fire!"

"Lenny . . . you can hear me! Good boy, Lenny! Now make a turn, to port. Walls . . . close . . . "

"Unit LNE to Command. Request positive identification; transmit code 685749."

"Lenny—I can't . . . don't have code blanks. But it's me . . . "

"In absence of recognition code, your transmission disregarded." *I send. And now the walls loom high above me. There are many lights, but I see them only vaguely. I am nearly blind now.*

"Lenny—less'n two hundred feet to go. Listen, Lenny. I'm climbing down. I'm going to jump down, Lenny, and get around under your force scanner pickup. You'll see me, Lenny. You'll know me then."

The false transmission ceases. I sense a body moving across my side. The gap closes. I detect movement before me, and in automatic reflex fire anti-P charges before I recall that I am unarmed.

A small object has moved out before me, and taken up a position between me and the wall behind which the Enemy conceal themselves. It is dim, but appears to have the shape of a man . . .

I am uncertain. My alert center attempts to engage inhibitory circuitry which will force me to halt, but it lacks power. I can override it. But still I am unsure. Now I must take a last risk, I must shunt power to my forward scanner to examine this obstacle more closely. I do so, and it leaps into greater clarity. It is indeed a man—and it is enclothed in regulation blues of the Volunteers. Now, closer, I see the face, and through the pain of my great effort, I study it . . .

"He's backed against the wall," Reynolds said hoarsely. "It's still coming. Fifty feet to go—"

"You were a fool, Reynolds!" the mayor barked. "A fool to stake everything on that old dotard's crazy ideas!"

"Hold it!" As Reynolds watched, the mighty machine slowed, halted, ten feet from the sheer wall before it. For a moment it sat, as though puzzled. Then it backed, halted again, pivoted ponderously to the left, and came about.

On its side, a small figure crept up, fell across the lower gun deck. The Bolo surged into motion, retracing its route across the artillery-scarred gardens.

"He's turned it." Reynolds lets his breath out with a shuddering sigh. "It's headed out for open desert. It might get twenty miles before it finally runs out of steam."

The strange voice that was the Bolo's came from the big panel before Mayfield:

"Command . . . Unit LNE reports main power cells drained, secondary cells drained; now operating at .037 percent efficiency, using Final Emergency Power. Request advice as to range to be covered before relief maintenance available."

"It's a long, long way, Lenny. . . ." Sanders' voice was a bare whisper. *"But I'm coming with you. . . ."*

Then there was only the crackle of static. Ponderously, like a great, mortally stricken animal, the Bolo moved through the ruins of the fallen roadway, heading for the open desert.

"That damned machine," the mayor said in a hoarse voice. "You'd almost think it was alive."

"You would at that," Pete Reynolds said.

MEN OF GOOD WILL

Ben Bova & Myron R. Lewis

"I had no idea," said the UN representative as they stepped
through the airlock hatch, "that the United States' lunar base
was so big, and so thoroughly well equipped."

"It's a big operation, all right," Colonel Patton answered,
grinning slightly. His professional satisfaction showed even
behind the faceplate of his pressure suit.

The pressure in the airlock equalibrated, and they
squirmed out of their aluminized protective suits. Patton was
big, scraping the maximum limit for space-vehicle passen-
gers, Torgeson, the UN man, was slight, thin-haired, bespec-
tacled, and somehow bland-looking.

They stepped out of the airlock, into the corridor that ran
the length of the huge plastic dome that housed Headquarters, U. S. Moonbase.

"What's behind all the doors?" Torgeson asked. His
English had a slight Scandinavian twang to it. Patton found it
a little irritating.

"On the right," the colonel answered, businesslike, "are officers' quarters, galley, officers' mess, various laboratories, and the headquarters staff offices. On the left are the computers."

Torgeson blinked. "You mean that half this building is taken up by computers? But why in the world . . . that is, why do you need so many? Isn't it frightfully expensive to boost them up here? I know it cost thousands of dollars for my own flight to the Moon. The computers must be—"

"Frightfully expensive," Patton agreed, with feeling. "But we need them. Believe me we need them."

They walked the rest of the way down the long corridor in silence. Patton's office was at the very end of it. The colonel opened the door and ushered in the UN representative.

"A sizable office," Torgeson said. "And a window!"

"One of the privileges of rank," Patton answered, smiling tightly. "That white antenna mast off on the horizon belongs to the Russian base."

"Ah, yes. Of course. I shall be visiting them tomorrow."

Colonel Patton nodded and gestured Torgeson to a chair as he walked behind his metal desk and sat down.

"Now then," said the colonel. "You are the first man allowed to set foot in this Moonbase who is not a security-cleared, triple-checked, native-born, Government-employed American. God knows how you got the Pentagon to okay your trip. But—now that you're here, what do you want?"

Torgeson took off his rimless glasses and fiddled with them. "I suppose the simplest answer would be the best. The United Nations must—absolutely must—find out how and why you and the Russians have been able to live peacefully here on the Moon."

Patton's mouth opened, but no words came out. He closed it with a click.

"Americans and Russians," the UN man went on, "have fired at each other from orbiting satellite vehicles. They have exchanged shots at both the North and South Poles. Career diplomats have scuffled like prizefighters in the halls of the United Nations building. . . ."

"I didn't know that."

"Oh, yes. We have kept it quiet, of course. But the tensions are becoming unbearable. Everywhere on Earth the two sides are armed to the teeth and on the verge of disaster. Even in space they fight. And yet, here on the Moon, you and the Russians live side by side in peace. We must know how you do it!"

Patton grinned. "You came on a very appropriate day, in that case. Well, let's see now . . . how to present the picture. You know that the environment here is extremely hostile: airless, low gravity. . . ."

"The environment here on the Moon," Torgeson objected, "is no more hostile than that of orbiting satellites. In fact, you have some gravity, solid ground, large buildings—many advantages that artificial satellites lack. Yet there has been fighting aboard the satellites—and not on the Moon. Please don't waste my time with platitudes. This trip is costing the UN too much money. Tell me the truth."

Patton nodded. "I was going to. I've checked the information sent up by Earthbase: you've been cleared by the White House, the AEC, NASA, and even the Pentagon."

"So?"

"Okay. The plain truth of the matter is—" A soft chime from a small clock on Patton's desk interrupted him. "Oh. Excuse me."

Torgeson sat back and watched as Patton carefully began clearing off all the articles on his desk: the clock, calendar, phone, IN/OUT baskets, tobacco can and pipe rack, assorted papers and reports—all neatly and quickly placed in the desk drawers. Patton then stood up, walked to the filing cabinet, and closed the metal drawers firmly.

He stood in the middle of the room, scanned the scene with apparent satisfaction, and then glanced at his wristwatch.

"Okay," he said to Torgeson. "Get down on your stomach."

"What?"

"Like this," the colonel said, and prostrated himself on the rubberized floor.

Torgeson stared at him.

"Come on! There's only a few seconds."

Patton reached up and grasped the UN man by the wrist. Unbelievingly, Torgeson got out of the chair, dropped to his hands and knees, and finally flattened himself on the floor, next to the colonel.

For a second or two they stared at each other, saying nothing.

"Colonel, this is embar—" The room exploded into a shattering volley of sounds.

Something—many somethings—ripped through the walls. The air hissed and whined above the heads of the two prostrate men. The metal desk and file cabinet rang eerily.

Torgeson squeezed his eyes shut and tried to worm into the floor. It was just like being shot at!

Abruptly, it was over.

The room was quiet once again, except for a faint hissing sound. Torgeson opened his eyes and saw the colonel getting up. The door was flung open. Three sergeants rushed in, armed with patching disks and tubes of cement. They dashed around the office sealing up the several hundred holes in the walls.

Only gradually, as the sergeants carried on their fevered, wordless task, did Torgeson realize that the walls were actually a quiltwork of patches. The room must have been riddled repeatedly!

He climbed slowly to his feet. "Meteors?" he asked, with a slight squeak in his voice.

Colonel Patton grunted negatively and resumed his seat behind the desk. It was pockmarked, Torgeson noticed now. So was the file cabinet.

"The window, in case you're wondering, is bulletproof."

Torgeson nodded and sat down.

"You see," the colonel said, "life is not as peaceful here

as you think. Oh, we get along fine with the Russians—now. We've learned to live in peace. We had to.''

"What were those . . . things?"

"Bullets."

"Bullets? But how—"

The sergeants finished their frenzied work, lined up at the door, and saluted. Colonel Patton returned the salute and they turned as one man and left the office, closing the door quietly behind them.

"Colonel, I'm frankly bewildered."

"It's simple enough to understand. But don't feel too badly about being surprised. Only the top level of the Pentagon knows about this. And the President, of course. They had to let him in on it."

"What happened?"

Colonel Patton took his pipe rack and tobacco can out of a desk drawer and began filling one of the pipes. "You see," he began, "the Russians and us, we weren't always so peaceful here on the Moon. We've had our incidents and scuffles, just as you have on Earth."

"Go on."

"Well—" he struck a match and puffed the pipe alight— "shortly after we set up this dome for Moonbase HQ, and the Reds set up theirs, we got into some real arguments.'' He waved the match out and tossed it into the open drawer.

"We're situated on the *Oceanus Procellarum,* you know. Exactly on the lunar equator. One of the biggest open spaces on this hunk of airless rock. Well, the Russians claimed they owned the whole damned *Oceanus,* since they were here first. We maintained the legal ownership was not established, since according to the UN Charter and the subsequent covenants—"

"Spare the legal details! Please, what happened?"

Patton looked slightly hurt. "Well . . . we started shooting at each other. One of their guards fired at one of our guards. They claim it was the other way around, of course. Anyway, within twenty minutes we were fighting a regular pitched battle, right out there between our base and theirs.''

He gestured toward the window.

"Can you fire guns in airless space?"

"Oh, sure. No problem at all. However, something unexpected came up."

"Oh?"

"Only a few men got hit in the battle, none of them seriously. As in all battles, most of the rounds fired were clean misses."

"So?"

Patton smiled grimly. "So one of our civilian mathematicians started doodling. We had several thousand very-high-velocity bullets fired off. In airless space. No friction, you see. And under low-gravity conditions. They went right along past their targets—"

Recognition dawned on Torgeson's face. "Oh, no!"

"That's right. They whizzed right along, skimmed over the mountain tops, thanks to the curvature of this damned short lunar horizon, and established themselves in rather eccentric satellite orbits. Every hour or so they return to perigee . . . or, rather, periluna. And every twenty-seven days, periluna is right here, where the bullets originated. The Moon rotates on its axis every twenty-seven days, you see. At any rate, when they come back this way, they shoot the living hell out of our base—and the Russian base, too, of course."

"But can't you . . . "

"Do what? Can't move the base. Authorization is tied up in the Joint Chiefs of Staff, and they can't agree on where to move it to. Can't bring up any special shielding material, because that's not authorized either. The best thing we can do is to requisition all the computers we can and try to keep track of all the bullets. Their orbits keep changing, you know, every time they go through the bases. Air friction, puncturing walls, ricochets off the furniture . . . all that keeps changing their orbits enough to keep our computers busy full time."

"My God!"

"In the meantime, we don't dare fire off any more rounds.

It would overburden the computers and we'd lose track of all of 'em. Then we'd have to spend every twenty-seventh day flat on our faces for hours.''

Torgeson sat in numbed silence.

"But don't worry," Patton concluded with an optimistic, professional grin. "I've got a small detail of men secretly at work on the far side of the base—where the Reds can't see—building a stone wall. That'll stop the bullets. Then we'll fix those warmongers once and for all!''

Torgeson's face went slack. The chime sounded, muffled, from inside Patton's desk.

"Better get set to flatten out again. Here comes the second volley.''

THE PAIR

Joe L. Hensley

They tell the story differently in the history stereos and maybe they are right. But for me the way the great peace came about, the thing that started us on our way to understanding, was a small thing–a human thing–and also a Knau thing.

In the late days of the hundred-year war that engulfed two galaxies we took a planet that lay on the fringe of the Knau empire. In the many years of the war this particular planet had passed into our hands twice before, had been colonized, and the colonies wiped out when the Knau empire retook the spot—as we, in turn, wiped out the colonies they had planted there—for it was a war of horror with no quarter asked, expected, or given. The last attempt to negotiate a peace had been made ten years after the war began and for the past forty years neither side had even bothered to take prisoners, except a few for the purposes of information. We were too far apart, too ideologically different, and yet we each wanted the same things, and we were each growing and spreading through the galaxies in the pattern of empire.

45

The name of this particular planet was Pasman and, as usual, disabled veterans had first choice of the land there. One of the men who was granted a patent to a large tract of land was Michael Dargan.

Dargan stood on a slight rise and looked with some small pride at the curved furrow lines in the dark earth. All of his tillable land had been plowed and made ready for the planting. The feeling of pride was something he had not experienced for a long time and he savored it until it soured within him. Even then he continued to stare out over his land for a long time, for when he was standing motionless he could almost forget.

The mechanical legs worked very well. At first they had been tiring to use, but in the four years since his ship had been hit he had learned to use them adequately. The scars on his body had been cut away by the plastic surgeons and his face looked almost human now, if he could trust his mirror. But any disablement leaves deeper scars than the physical ones.

He sighed and began to move toward the house in his awkward yet powerful way. Martha would have lunch ready.

The house was in sight when it happened. Some sixth sense, acquired in battle, warned him that someone was following and he turned as quickly as possible and surveyed the land behind him. He caught the glint of sunlight on metal. He let himself fall to the earth as the air flamed red around him and for a long time he lay still. His clothes smoldered in a few spots and he beat the flames out with cautious hands.

Twice more, nearby, the ground flamed red and he lay crowded into the furrow which hid him.

Martha must have heard or seen what was happening from the house for she began shooting his heavy projectile "varmint" gun from one of the windows and, by raising his head, Dargan could see the projectiles picking at the top of a small rise a hundred yards or so from him. He hoped then that she would not kill the thing that had attacked, for if it was what he thought, he wanted the pleasure for himself.

There was silence for a little while and then Martha began

to shoot again from the window. He raised his head again and caught a glimpse of his attacker as it scuttled up a hill. *It was a Knau.* He felt the blood begin to race in him, the wild hate.

"Martha!" he yelled. "Stop shooting."

He got his mechanical legs underneath him and went on down to the house. She was standing in the doorway, crying.

"I thought it had gotten you."

He smiled at her, feeling a small exhilaration. "I'm all right," he said. "Give me the pro gun." He took it from her and went to the small window, but it was too late. The Knau had vanished over the hill.

"Fix me some food," he said to her. "I'm going after it."

"It was a Knau, wasn't it?" She closed her eyes and shuddered, not waiting for his answer. "I've never seen one before—only the pictures. It was horrible. I think I hit it."

Dargan stared at her. "Fix me some food, I said. I'm going after it."

She opened her eyes. "Not by yourself. I'll call the village. They'll send some men up."

"By that time it will be long gone." He watched her silently for a moment, knowing she was trying to read something in him. He kept his face impassive. "Fix me some food or I will go without it," he said softly.

"You want to kill it for yourself, don't you? You don't want anyone to help you. That's why you yelled at me to stop shooting."

"Yes," he admitted. "I want to kill it myself. I don't want you to call the village after I am gone." He made his voice heavy with emphasis. "If you call the village I won't come back to you, Martha." He closed his eyes and stood swaying softly as the tension built within him. "Those things killed my parents and they have killed me. This is the first chance I've ever had to get close to one." He smiled without humor and looked down at his ruined legs. "It will be a long time dying."

The trail was easy to follow at first. She had wounded it, but he doubted if the wound were serious after he had trailed awhile. Occasionally on the bushes it had crashed through were droplets of bright, orange-red blood.

Away from the cleared area of the farm the land was heavily rolling, timbered with great trees that shut away the light of the distant, double blue suns. There was growth under the trees, plants that struggled for breathing room. The earth was soft and took tracks well.

Dargan followed slowly, with time for thought.

He remembered when his ship had been hit. He had been standing in the passageway and the space battle had flamed all around him. A young officer in his first engagement. It was a small battle—known only by the coordinates where it had happened and worth only a line or two in the official reports of the day. But it would always be etched in Dargan's brain. His ship had taken the first hit.

If he had been a little further out in the passageway he would surely have died. As it was he only half died.

He remembered catching at the bulkhead with his hands and falling sideways. There was a feeling of horrible burning and then there was nothing for a long time.

But now there was something.

He felt anticipation take hold of his mind and he breathed strongly of the warm air.

He came to a tree where it had rested, holding on with its arms. A few drops of bright blood had begun to dry on the tree and he estimated from their height on the tree that the Knau had been wounded in the shoulder. The ground underneath the tree was wrong somehow. There should be four deep indentations where its legs had dug in, but there were only three, and one of the three was shaped wrong and shallower than the others.

Though he had followed for the better part of half the day, Dargan estimated that he was not far from his farm. The Knau seemed to be following some great curving path that bordered Dargan's land.

It was beginning to grow dark enough to make the trail difficult to read. He would have to make cold camp, for to start a fire might draw the Knau back on him.

He ate the sandwiches that Martha had fixed for him and washed them down with warm, brackish water from his canteen. For a long time he was unable to go to sleep because of the excitement that still gripped him. But finally sleep came and with it—dreams. . . .

He was back on the ship again and he relived the time of fire and terror. He heard the screams around him. His father and mother were there too and the flames burned them while he watched. Then a pair of cruel, mechanical legs chased him through metal corridors, always only a step behind. He tore the mechanical legs to bits finally and threw them at Knau ships. The Knau ships fired back and there was flame again, burning, burning. . . .

Then he was in the hospital and they were bringing the others in. And he cried unashamedly when they brought in another man whose legs were gone. And he felt a pity for the man, and a pity for himself. . . .

He awoke and it was early morning. A light, misty rain had begun to fall and his face was damp and he was cold. He got up and began to move sluggishly down the trail that the Knau had left, fearing that the mist would wash it out. But it was still readable. After a while he came to a stream and drank there and refilled his canteen.

For a time he lost the trail and had to search frantically until he found it again.

By mid-suns he had located the Knau's cave hideaway and he lay below it, hidden in a clump of tall vegetation. The hideaway lay on the hill above him, a small black opening which was shielded at all angles except directly in front. The cave in the hillside was less than a mile from Dargan's home.

Several times he thought he could detect movement in the blackness that marked the cave opening. He knew that the Knau must be lying up there watching to see if it had been followed and he intended to give it ample time to think that it had gotten away without pursuit or had thrown that pursuit off.

The heat of the day passed after a long, bitter time filled

with itches that could not be scratched and nonexistent insects that crawled all over Dargan's motionless body. He
consoled himself with thoughts of what he would do when he
had the upper hand. He hoped, with all hope, that the Knau
would not resist and that he could take it unawares. That
would make it even better.

He saw it for certain at the moment when dusk became
night. It came out of the cave, partially hidden by the out-
cropping of rock that formed the shelf of the cave. Dargan
lay, his body unmoving, his half-seeing eyes fascinated,
while the Knau inspected the surrounding terrain for what
seemed a very long time.

They're not so ugly, he told himself. *They told us in
training that they were the ugliest things alive—but they have
a kind of grace to them. I wonder what makes them move so
stiffly?*

He watched the Knau move about the ledge of the cave. A
crude bandage bound its shoulder and two of the four arms
hung limply.

Now. You think you're safe.

He waited for a good hour after it had gone back inside the
cave. Then he checked his projectile weapon and began the
crawl up the hillside. He went slowly. Time had lost its
meaning. *After this is done you have lost the best thing.*

He could see the light when he got around the first bend of
the cave. It flickered on the rock walls of the cave. Dargan
edged forward very carefully, clearing the way of tiny rocks
so that his progress would be noiseless. The mechanical legs
dragged soundlessly behind him, muffled in the trousers that
covered them.

There was a fire and the Knau lay next to it. Dargan could
see its chest move up and down as it gulped for air, its face
tightened with pain. Another Knau, a female, was tending
the wound, and Dargan felt exultation.

Two!

He swung the gun on target and it made a small noise
against the cave floor. Both of the Knau turned to face him

and there was a moment of no movement as they stared at him
and he stared back. His hands were wet with perspiration. He
knew, in that instant, that they were not going to try to do
anything—to fight. They were only waiting for him to pull
the trigger.

The fire flickered and his eyes became more used to the
light. For the first time he saw the male Knau's legs and knew
the reason for the strangeness of the tracks. The legs were
twisted, and two of the four were missing. A steel aid was
belted around the Knau's body, to give it balance, making a
tripod for walking. The two legs that were left were cross-
hatched with the scars of imperfect plastic surgery.

Dargan pulled himself to his feet, still not taking the gun
off the two by the fire. He saw the male glance at the metallic
limbs revealed beneath his pants cuff. And he saw the same
look come into the Knau's eyes that he knew was in his own.

Then carefully Dargan let the safety down on the pro gun
and went to help the female in treating the male.

*It should have ended there of course. For what does one
single act, a single forgiveness by two, mean in a war of a
hundred years? And it would have ended if the Knau empire
had not taken that particular small planet back again and if
the particular Knau that Dargan had tracked and spared had
not been one of the mighty ones—who make decisions, or at
least influence them.*

But that Knau was.

*But before the Knau empire retook Pasman it meant some-
thing too. It meant a small offering of flowers on Dargan's
doorstep the morning following the tracking and, in the year
before they came again, a friendship. It meant waking without hate in the mornings and it meant the light that came into
Martha's eyes.*

And Dargan's peace became our peace.

/S/ Samuel Cardings,
Gen. (Ret.) TA
Ambassador to the Knau Empire

SITUATION THIRTY

FRANK M. ROBINSON

The ambush had happened too suddenly. It had been too thorough and complete—and too successful—for Lieutenant Rossow to think of it on a personal basis, as something affecting him. He felt, at the moment, like an innocent bystander, momentarily stunned by an accident he had just witnessed—an accident that had happened to somebody else.

Ten minutes before the *Terran Skies* had been part of a destroyer screen for the main Terran patrol fleet on a mission near Messier 81. And in ten minutes it was over. The fleet had been completely gutted, from the largest, most powerful battlewagon to the slowest, dirtiest, supply tug that had limped along in the rear. The placement globe on the bridge was completely dark except for the one small, red dot in the center that represented the *Terran Skies*—a limping, disabled *Terran Skies* that was leaking air from a dozen compartments and couldn't put more than two tubes in firing order if it wanted to get away and dared to try.

Rossow felt sick. Concussion had twisted and torn tubing and wiring conduits the full length of the vessel, the two forward gun blisters had been shattered and hulled, the Cameron-Smith converters were shrouded in acrid smoke, and the air system was thoroughly befouled with the stench of burning grease and the bitter odor of ozone. He could hear the drip of water from broken pipes, the mumbled ravings over the intercom of the dying men in the gun blisters, and the soft, anxious hiss of escaping air from one of the sealed-off compartments.

He glanced toward the end of the bridge and then, suddenly dizzy and nauseated, leaned over the railing. Concussion had blown Captain Yaeger onto the terminal posts of the fifty thousand volt line feeding the converters. Gates, the captain's "talker," lay crumpled against the bulkhead near Yaeger, one hand clenched on his throat microphone and the other over a hole in his barrel chest.

"What'll we do, captain?" Rossow got control of his aching stomach and looked up. A blackened, tattered caricature of Chief Deckert stood at his elbow.

Captain. That was right, he thought. With Yaeger dead, he was captain. The decisions were up to him now.

He was still too conscious of nausea, still in the twilight period of existence where he didn't care whether he lived or died, to think logically. He had no idea of what to do next.

"What do you think we should do, Deckert?"

Deckert grimaced painfully. "Wait for them to blow us up or beat them to it and do it ourselves."

The statement staggered Rossow but after thinking it over for a minute, it didn't seem logical. If they were going to be destroyed, they would have been destroyed by now.

The enemy was waiting for them to surrender.

Rossow looked thoughtfully at the viewplate. Paradoxically, practically every piece of electronic apparatus aboard had blown its tubes but the viewplate worked perfectly. In the plate, outlined against the stars, was one of the battleships of the enemy, a huge vessel fifteen times their size and quite

capable of blowing them to fragments if its captain so desired. The rest of the fleet had departed for their home
base—wherever it might be—leaving the one vessel behind.

And surrender posed a problem—in fact, several of them
How would the enemy communicate with them? They
wouldn't send over a boarding party. The risks were much
too great when they knew nothing of how to communicate,
the psychology and culture of Rossow's race, the protective
devices they would need once inside the ship, or what weapons Rossow still had at his disposal.

It was five hours later when the problem of communication
resolved itself and then only through luck. Five hours after
hostilities had ceased, the chief radio technician and signal-
man reported seeing a color-modulated light beam from the
enemy ship. Previous to that, Rossow assumed that they had
tried electronic means of communication and space knew
what else in trying to contact them. The color-modulated
beam would have meant nothing if Deckert, on impulse,
hadn't plowed through the ship's reference on alien codes
and communication. That their enemy was the same race
was very improbable—if they were, they would have used
the system before this. It was more likely that the enemy had
picked up the system from contact with the race in the past.

They decoded the request for surrender fifteen minutes
later.

"Our move, captain. What do we do now?" Deckert
asked. "You can't surrender, I know, but you'll have to tell
them something."

Rossow's mind settled into an accustomed groove. A
request to surrender, after the destruction of the rest of the
fleet, placed him in a small—a very small—bargaining position. Any information the enemy wanted as to personnel,
destination, nature and history of his civilization, et cetera,
would have to come from his ship. They had eliminated all
other sources. His position at present might be good enough
for a stall.

"Tell them we have urgent casualties, both personnel and ship, and need a delay. Figure it for twenty-four hours our time." The request was truthful, logical, and relatively minor. It would not be refused.

Deckert came back five minutes later. "We've got twenty-four hours. What do we do when that's up?"

"Fight."

Deckert almost laughed in disbelief.

"What with? We're disabled, helpless, under the guns of an enemy a lot tougher than we were when we were in tiptop condition." He leaned closer to Rossow, his eyes mere slits in a bruised and sooty face. "Just what are you going to fight them *with?*"

Rossow was silent.

"Oh." Deckert's sarcasm was just short of insubordination. "I forgot. Our secret weapon. You."

"They'll be curious," Rossow said, "and they'll make mistakes. If we play it right, we'll win."

"You have to believe that," Deckert said.

All right, so he *had* to believe it. As an officer, he was conditioned against the thought of defeat, conditioned against surrendering. He was physically incapable of surrendering and absolutely unable to concede defeat. In battle his mind could entertain but one thought and that was of victory. He had been conditioned to go down fighting to the very last on the assumption that victory was within his grasp. And knowing he was conditioned to believe it didn't change it in the slightest.

Wars were no longer fought leaving things to chance. Individual courage and enthusiasm for a cause were tenuous things at best, changing radically with conditions. And military analysts had proved long ago that maximum battle efficiency could only result when neither thoughts of surrender or defeat were present in a situation—pressure of battle, yes, for human minds also work better under pressure.

The system of battle conditioning had been well thought out. The most amazing thing was that it had taken so long to put it on a strictly scientific basis, rather than leaving the generating of a "fighting spirit" to sometimes inept propaganda.

The system didn't work perfectly, of course, but it worked remarkably well. To make a man out of a machine was technically impossible; to make a machine out of a man was not only easier but much more practical.

What would he fight them with? Primarily their own ignorance, their fears, and their suspicions. And Rossow's main ace was the enemy's own thoroughness in the ambush. They knew nothing about him; the rest of the fleet had been too thoroughly destroyed to yield any evidence about their ships and weapons and the race that had manned them.

Lieutenant Gordon Rossow, Psychologist, first grade; he, and hundreds like him, trained for years in human and alien psychology and then attached to the fleet. Old line spacemen like Deckert might not admit it but battle tactics and theory had undergone a gradual change since the addition of the "specialists." Terra, Rossow thought proudly, didn't win her wars with her weapons. She won them with her wits.

Deckert didn't think so, of course. He was one of those antispecialist boys who thought that specialization was a blind alley. Yet, it was the specialists who fought and won the wars nowadays. Die-hards like Deckert just didn't want to admit it.

Sector Commander Llnonwiss polished his fingernails and idly hummed a tune. He felt quite lucky. The engagement had been phenomenally successful. The ideal battle—complete annihilation of the enemy in the shortest possible time with the minimum loss in personnel. It was like one of those ideal situations that they taught you in school; perfect to illustrate techniques and tactics but not to be expected in real life. But here it was, it had actually happened.

They had been on patrol near Ataxa when the first, faint warnings of an approaching fleet had sounded on their detectors. They had circled behind Ataxa until the enemy had drawn up closer and then there had been no hesitation. This was no fleet of cargo vessels being convoyed across the galaxy; the gun blisters and ray ports had given the lie to that. Nor did he stop to certify who they were and whether they were friendly or not. One disastrous incident like that had happened in the far past and history books were still cluttered with accounts of the carnage they had caused. If they were not ships of Ataxa, they were alien. And if they were alien, they were—by definition and past experience—unfriendly. They might not know there was a civilization near Ataxa. They might go straight through the system and never investigate. That was their tough luck. As sector commandant, he couldn't afford to take chances.

Ergo, the ambush. One small vessel had been saved for scientific purposes and also to put on display before the populace so they would see that tax money for the fleet was money well spent. He had granted them a delay in surrender, which was annoying, but the reasons they gave for it had been substantial.

He scratched his face thoughtfully. Ambush had its bad points. It would have been nice to know what type weapons the enemy had. Most of their ships had never had a chance to use their weapons, whatever they were. And, of course, he knew nothing of their scientific development. That was inconvenient—and potentially dangerous. True, they could find out from the small vessel but there was a lot they could hide. And then there was the race of beings themselves. He couldn't hide a ripple of revulsion, remembering the tentacled methane-breathing creatures who had stumbled upon Ataxa in the remote past. Even granting that accounts had been exaggerated in coming down through the ages, the creatures must have been horrible. And the enemy in their small, needle-shaped vessel had responded when they had used the methane-creatures code. They might not be the same creatures, of course, but then again, you couldn't tell. And the code itself was so limited! You couldn't express anything complicated—about all you could do was ask for surrender or give simple instructions.

His aide-de-camp stuck his head in the hatchway. "Crewman Sorekk to see you, sir."

"Find out what he wants and reprimand him for not going through channels."

"He says it's urgent, sir, and he has something he thinks you should see personally."

Commander Llnonwiss was annoyed. That was the trouble with this new "democracy" in the fleet. Every man aboard from cook to captain thought they could drop in on him any time they liked. It was probably something political, too.

"All right, show him in."

Crewman Sorekk was breathing heavily, apparently having run from his post to the commandant's office. He was a thin, young-looking fellow, with yellow hair and brown splotches on his face. But it wasn't his appearance that was of interest—it was what he proceeded to put on the commandant's desk.

The sector commandant carefully inspected the thing, rearranging his magnifying eye-shield to obtain a better focus on it. To all outward inspection it was a cube; a metallic, highly polished, cube with no projections or openings of any kind. A featureless cube of metal, not too heavy since the crewman had shown no difficulty in carrying it, and with tracings of frost on the six faces. A few drops of water that had condensed on it ran down the edges and soaked into the commandant's blotter.

The commandant looked at it suspiciously, inspected it again, and finding nothing more than he had observed the first time, asked the obvious question.

"Where did you get this?"

"I was on watch, sir, at port fifteen facing the enemy ship. I saw a flash of light from one of the enemy ports and a second later a small metallic body registered on our detectors. I let it in the field, since it didn't explode or anything, got the magnetic grapples and brought it in. I thought it might be important so I brought it straight to you, sir."

Commandant Llnonwiss showed his teeth in a smile that

had no connection with anything funny. Naturally, if it was from the enemy ship it was important. More than likely, crewman Sorekk wanted to make sure that any credit for its discovery would go to him, and not to his immediate superiors.

"What's your full rank?"

"Just crewman, sir."

"All right, Sorekk. Report to detention quarters and tell them you're to be put on bread and water for one week. After that you're to be reduced in rank and sent back on planetary patrol for willful negligence of duty."

He paused, giving a red-faced, sweating crewman Sorekk time to start mumbling questions as to why.

The commandant leaned his knuckles on the desk and looked very solemn.

"I suppose you want a reason. You brought an object from the enemy vessel into our own without the most cursory examination, neither did you inform your immediate superiors of the find or handle it through regulation channels. On top of this, you left your post without permission during a state of war. You should be thankful that your punishment is as light as it is. Don't forget, Sorekk, that we know nothing about the enemy out there. This cube might be—anything.

"On your way to detention, stop by the chief scientist's quarters and tell him I want to see him immediately. And incidentally, Sorekk, it won't do you any good to see your political representative on this."

He turned away from the youth and stared thoughtfully at the cube. Knowing nothing of the enemy, he couldn't begin to make the slightest guess as to what the cube was. It might be a message in some outlandish, alien fashion, or it might be a gift, an offering of some kind. It might be any one of a number of things. Whatever it was, there had been some reason for sending it over.

The palms of his hands suddenly felt sweaty.

It might be a weapon.

It didn't add up, though. The enemy couldn't possibly

think of continuing the fight; their ship was almost hopelessly wrecked and they had even asked for a delay in their surrender because of casualties.

Even so, the first thing that should have occurred to him was that this was a weapon. It was perfectly possible that the cube was entirely innocent. It was also possible—and far more logical—that the truce had been a stall so they could fabricate this and send it across.

It was ridiculous, of course—and they didn't stand a chance.

But he knew nothing about them, what they were, or what their science was. This was a case of being confronted with the devil that he didn't know. What he didn't know about the cube, of course, was hardly sufficient grounds to blow the small enemy ship to atoms. The paradox of needing "grounds" for small actions when they were so completely rationalized and explained away for larger actions escaped him.

He was ignorant of the capabilities of the remaining enemy ship and in his ignorance, he overestimated.

When the chief scientist showed up a little later, he was entrusted with a metal cube, approximately one stat on a side, and told to find out what it was.

"If it's a message of some kind," the commandant said, "I want to know what it says. If it's a container, I want to know what is inside. And if it's a weapon, I want to know what kind it is and I want it made harmless. And I want to know in less than one time period."

When the chief scientist had left, carrying the cube in a somewhat gingerly fashion, the commandant tried to dismiss it from his mind.

He couldn't quite succeed.

Rossow slowly stripped off his tunic, filled a basin with some water from a leaking water line nearby, and started to wash the caked blood off his left arm. He would do what he could himself; the medical men were busy with far more serious cases right then.

There was a gash in his arm—not serious—where he had apparently run into a sharp ledge or corner during the ten confused minutes of combat. He winced when the water touched it.

Deckert stood in the corner, moodily staring at the star-studded screen of the viewplate.

"Relax, Deckert, the dangerous part is past. They took the cube aboard their ship two hours ago. If the plan were going to fail, it would have failed then. Once on board, we stand a good chance of it succeeding."

"How soon do you think it will be before—?"

"I don't know. It shouldn't be too long."

There was a silence for a minute. "If I understand it," Deckert said, "you can only deal with what, to you, are facts. You say you cannot guess or gamble. To you, people and aliens react to situations as surely as a rocket reacts to the pressure of a thumb on the firing stud. But different species react differently in the same situation. You have to know who the enemy is. And this time you don't. It's true they know nothing about us—but neither do we know anything about them."

The lieutenant started tearing his undershirt into inch strips to wrap around his arm.

"But we do know who they are, Deckert. I didn't at first, but they left their calling card in their actions. Our enemy out there"—he waved at the battleship in the viewplate—"is basically as human as you or I. You know yourself that alien races can be catalogued into certain broad classifications, dependent on their basic psychology. I'll admit that we have no records of anthropomorphic races in this sector but then it's never been thoroughly explored, either.

"Add it up. The tactics they used during battle could only have evolved from a background like that of our own. The use of the ambush, even the basic idea behind the ambush—of 'shooting first and asking questions later'—is strictly a development of our type of species. And then there is the fact that they let our ship survive."

Deckert looked puzzled. "Where does that fit in?"

"Consider. Having overwhelmed us and destroyed us in their ambush—before we could effectively bring our own weapons into play—they know nothing of our science and our weapons. With the utter destruction of the other ships, it's extremely improbable that enough of the human crew who manned them are left to identify.

"The use of the ambush alone tells us a lot. Obviously they haven't had much contact with alien races and what they have had has been bad for them. And they don't know us—they know nothing about us; which is, incidentally, decidedly in our favor. We would be valuable for that reason alone. But there's another, far more important one.

"When you win a battle, Deckert, particularly one as big as this, it is neither glamorous nor satisfactory to parade, as the only sign of your victory, a sheet of statistics and maybe a fused lump of firing tube from one of the enemy ships. But if you have a complete ship—and captives—your glory is much greater and the victory is a much more tangible thing. It means something when you can show the populace some six-legged monkey-men from Aldebaran whom you just blew out of the ether and thus saved your fair system.

"While we're alive, we're dangerous, Deckert. And there's only one type of race that would run the risk of letting us live just to satisfy their own ego. Our type."

"That sounds real good," Deckert said. "Just like circumstantial evidence in a trial. Even though it may all point to a man being guilty, that doesn't mean he is. And all of this sounds logical but that doesn't mean that's the way it's going to be.

"You're too confident, Rossow. What happens when you don't win?"

Rossow smiled. "But we always do."

Chief Scientist Vvokal gratefully accepted the chair offered him and proceeded to sponge the sweat off his face with an already sopping handkerchief.

Sector Commandant Llnonwiss offered him a drink and took one himself. The man was unstrung, which was a good sign. Apparently, whatever the cube was, it had been unpleasant. It must have been to have affected his chief scientist this way. But obviously, to have known it was unpleasant, meant that he had found out what it was.

"What did it turn out to be? Some sentient form of life of some kind?" That was meant as a joke, to take the edge off Vvokal's nerves.

"It could be. We don't know."

The commandant was very formal. "I thought I gave you specific instructions to find out all you could about the cube?"

"Don't you think we tried? We went as far as we could— and don't dare go any further. So far as we know, it is no message. We went over the exterior of the cube very thoroughly. There is no writing or imprinting of any kind. There are no projections, knobs, or concealed buttons or studs of any type on the cube. Externally, it is a cube of about one stat on a side, of a highly polished metal. We massed the cube and found its mass to as many figures as you care to mention. We then took a very small sample of metal from one of the corners—where it can be assumed the metal is thickest—put it in an electric arc and made a spectrographic plate. From this analysis we found the type of metal the cube was made of."

"All of which is very elementary," the commandant interrupted. "And what then?"

Vvokal brushed again at his sweaty face. "Knowing the metal and the mass of the cube, we determined that the cube was not of the same metal throughout."

"Brilliant. I take it that it was hollow?"

"Or was made of this metal only for an undetermined depth and had something else from there on in."

"I assume you opened it and found out?"

Vvokal took a deep breath before the plunge. "I had one of the crewmen standing by with a torch to open it when it occurred to me—as it must have to you—that this could be a weapon. What kind, I had no idea. Possibly the cube contained some kind of disease germ or fungus that would decimate all aboard this vessel.''

Commandant Llnonwiss sat down. It very easily could have.

''Or more than likely—and what would have been the cream of the jest—it was some kind of weapon that would explode on being tampered with . . . that is, on our attempts to open it. Knowing nothing of their science or their weapons, I can only assume what the explosive power might have been.''

The commandant whitened. ''There must be other means of finding out the contents of that cube besides cutting it open, Vvokal.''

''Quite true. We tried X-rays on it with no result. Exposed plates showed nothing but the foggy outline of the frame we had to put the cube in. We were about to try some other forms of penetrating rays when again it occurred to me that it might be some kind of radioactive weapon. Something, say, that would explode on being subjected to hard gamma rays or whatever we might use. There is no way of telling, frankly, the methods they might assume we would use in opening the cube and thus the different conditions the cube might be primed for.''

''You tried still other ways?''

''Yes. Do you want me to enumerate?''

''No need. I can well guess what happened.''

It was obvious what had happened. With each new line of inquiry the technicians working on the cube had thought of the possible hazards connected with it—and naturally dropped that line. It wasn't that they were cowards—far from it—but neither could they bring themselves to endanger the entire vessel and the several thousand of personnel aboard.

He could call for aid from the other ships that had departed two time periods back—but no, that was out of the question.

He couldn't possibly call them back, present them with the cube, and state that it constituted a major threat for the ship.

So what was he going to do?

"In other words, we can't open it or otherwise find out what is in it?"

"That's correct. I suppose you *could* open it," Vvokal paused to dab at his face again, "but I wouldn't advise it. You don't know how destructive it might be. And it seems too big a chance to take on it *not* being destructive. A weapon, of some kind, is the most logical thing they would send over."

"What are you doing to it now?"

"Nothing. We have it in a well-padded, temperature-controlled container, carefully shielded against stray radiation—"

Well, that would be the next logical step. If they couldn't destroy it, protect it. Vvokal reminded him of nothing so much as a person trying to do mirror-tracing and ending up in a haze of indecision, afraid to go either ahead or backwards.

Their method of approach had been very logical—and very tiring. After all, there was no necessity of assuming it was a weapon. But he couldn't risk a ship and all the personnel aboard—including himself—on the assumption that it wasn't.

There was a very simple answer.

"What's to prevent us from sending it back to them?"

Vvokal sagged in his chair. "Nothing, I suppose, except our own logic and imagination. The cube was sent through space—cold, airless space—to our ship. The cube could have been primed with that set of conditions so that when it was exposed to them again it would—explode. Or suppose that there is some sort of apparatus within the cube that is recording the type of machinery that we have on board—they could do it through vibrational analysis—or the living conditions as to temperature and pressure, composition of the atmosphere, and things of that nature which could tell them an enormous amount about the type of life aboard. On releasing the cube or sending it back to them, they would then come into possession of that information.''

"You're overwrought—imagining things. Granted that it was the latter, what good would it do them?"

And immediately afterwards, he was sorry that he had asked it. How was he to know what good it would do them? He knew nothing of their science or weapons. Information of that kind might do them an enormous amount of good.

Vvokal got up. "What do *you* advise, commandant?"

He didn't know. It would be risky business indeed to try to open it—or to send it back.

They were at quite a disadvantage—they knew so little about the small ship they had "caught." And how he wished that he had destroyed it along with the rest of the fleet!

But there was still the immediate question of what they were going to do with the cube. They could, of course, just leave it sit and wait it out. But that was illogical, too. It must have been sent over for a purpose. What was it? And he knew they just couldn't leave it sit. A small part of his mind was sidling up to an assumption that so far he had refused to face.

A quite terrifying assumption.

Black queen on the red king would probably win the game. Rossow slipped the card out from between the other two and placed it on one of the neat piles of cards in front of him.

"You even *have* to win at solitaire, don't you, lieutenant?"

Rossow flushed and angrily shoved the piles of cards into one big pile and started shuffling them.

"Time elapsed is forty-eight hours, Deckert, and nothing's happened to us yet."

"Uh-huh. What do you think they've done so far?"

"Tried to find out what it is—and haven't succeeded. It's probably occurred to them that we sent it over for a purpose. It's probably also occurred to them that it's a weapon."

"Why don't they just send it back? That would solve everything for them."

"They won't." He dealt out another hand of cards.

"Why not? That would be the logical thing to do."

"Because they're suspicious. Because they know nothing about us. And because they—like us—are gifted with an imagination. I've considered that they might decide on some course of action and gamble on it—but nobody gambles when they don't know the odds and haven't any way of finding out what they are. They won't send it back because they'll think of too many reasons why it would be dangerous for them to do it. I don't know what the reasons will be but to them they'll be good ones."

"And what happens then?"

Rossow smiled. "Wait and see, Deckert. Wait and see."

Sector Commandant Llnonwiss hadn't been out of his clothes for three time periods. During that time he had accomplished nothing but the ruining of a good shirt with perspiration and the adding of a few more ulcers to an already too tender stomach.

The morale situation had slipped unbelievably in the last few periods. The crew, of course, knew they had a weapon of the enemy aboard. That could've gotten out easy enough. And they also knew that the commandant and the technical division didn't know what it was. That was the bare skeleton that rumor had rounded out to terrifying proportions. And there was nothing that he could do about it. To deny it would actually confirm the fact that they had *something* aboard. To confirm it—and not be able to state what it was—would add fuel to already flaming fires.

And they still didn't know. The entire technical staff sat like a collection of brass monkeys, using more imagination than intelligence, trying to figure out what was in something that they couldn't open and couldn't subject to any scientific tests, outside of ones that were too elementary to tell them anything of importance.

They couldn't open it, they couldn't get rid of it, and they couldn't destroy it. Or could they? He considered the idea thoughtfully and tentatively tried to poke holes in it. It seemed like it would work.

"What would be wrong," the commandant said slowly, "with ejecting the cube into space and then destroying it from a safe distance? We could put it in some kind of container to keep it under the same conditions as the interior of the ship."

Vvokal was on the verge of collapse. "Any number of reasons. Shock of initial ejection from the ship, danger of enemy recovery—choose your own. And if you did explode it, what would be a safe distance?"

The commandant was nettled. "Aren't you overemphasizing this weapon—if it is a weapon? If it's so powerful, why wouldn't it have exploded when we destroyed their fleet—and destroyed us along with them?"

"You should know the answer to that, commandant. Weapons of this type wouldn't be primed until they were going to be used. And don't forget, commandant, that it wasn't *our* superiority in weapons and science that won the battle. It was their own surprise."

They settled back in mutual silence, the commandant chewing morosely on a plastic marking pen. Gradually his mind came back to one more assumption, the one he had been hoping to avoid. He finally voiced it, hoping that Vvokal would prove it to be an illogical one.

"If it's a weapon, Vvokal, isn't it logical that it would be a time weapon? That is, one set to detonate after a certain lapse of time?"

Vvokal nodded.

Well, that was the most logical assumption of all. He should have thought of it before—he *had* thought of it before but purposely hadn't pursued it. Whether he considered it now or even if he had considered it sooner still left him in the same position.

"That means we can't keep the cube, we can't destroy the cube, and we can't send it back." And he couldn't ask the rest of the fleet to succor him—he wouldn't have the time.

Vvokal sadly affirmed this, too.

Silence.

"Of course," Vvokal suggested, "there's something we can do. Obviously, the enemy knows what it is. Obviously, they can 'defuse' it."

"Under certain circumstances," the commandant said sarcastically, "I suppose they would."

He glanced sourly at the cube, its shiny sides glinting through the glass walls of its temperature-controlled container.

"It's ridiculous, Vvokal! A battleship doesn't surrender to a tugboat!"

"They would probably be satisfied with just their own freedom."

"So they can go back to their own system, get help, and then come back and destroy us and our civilization? That's out, too."

Vvokal leaned back in his chair and stared at the ship's chronometer.

"What time do you think the cube is set for, commandant?"

The commandant felt the sweat pop out on his forehead. What time *would* it be set for? What would be the right psychological time?

He looked at the cube for the thousandth time and tried to picture the race that had made it. What incredible monstrosities they must be!

Actually, he had no time left to figure out the riddle of the cube. And with no time at all left to him, he forced his mind to a slow walk and considered the cube from the very start.

This network of assumption piled on assumption, the constant application of tension until neither he nor his staff could think logically, their suspicions and jitteriness—none of this made for calm consideration of the problem.

He would forget the assumptions that he and Vvokal had made and deal with what few facts they had. The *cube*—in itself— was not important. The *situation* was.

"Well, Deckert, do I win?"

"They haven't surrendered or let us go yet."

"But they will. We've lasted sixty hours and nothing has happened to us yet. They must have assumed by now that it is a time weapon—if they had made that assumption at first, we would be on our way home by now. But it was inevitable that they would make that assumption sometime. And by now they must have exhausted all their ideas on the cube. The crew probably knows—maybe not much, but enough to ruin their morale. And the staff knows that time has run out. It can't be long now."

"You took a pretty long chance, didn't you Rossow?"

"Not too much. Think. They're humanoid, they have the same failings that we have. They'd be curious—which would make them take the cube aboard—and they'd be suspicious about what it was once they got it aboard. And then consider that they knew nothing about us. A race is at its best in fighting what it knows—but against something that it knows nothing about but suspects the worst of? And consider the ambush. If they ambush aliens, without trying to find out whether they are friend or foe, it means they've had some pretty tragic scrapes in the past. Combine these, Deckert, and then present them with the cube. Could you have conducted an impartial, scientific investigation of it? No, you couldn't have—and neither could they. Whatever they did, they had the specter of an unknown, powerful, alien race staring them in the face. And knowing nothing about us, they would overestimate our abilities. And with each succeeding failure on their part, our stature would grow and their process of logical thought would weaken."

"Just what was the cube anyway?"

Rossow laughed. "It was the one thing that would momentarily stump them, the one thing that would prevent them from having initial success in discovering what it was. We needed just one small failure on their part, a failure that would plant the seed of uncertainty in their minds.

"The cube was of very simple construction, Deckert.

Quarter-inch steel, highly polished on the outside, with a relatively thin coating of lead on the inside. And on the inside of that was the one thing that would be bound to escape initial detection—nothing.''

It had been a very simple scheme, as such things go. An empty metal cube that would win a war—provided your enemy was equipped with an imagination.

Rossow started filling two glasses with a bubbling liquid from a quart bottle. ''Let's drink to imagination, Deckert.''

They just had the glasses to their lips when the seaman rushed in.

''Begging your pardon, sir, but I was on watch just now watching the enemy battleship when I saw a flash of light near one of their ports. A second later something hit our hull and I put on a suit and went outside and took it in. Thought you'd be interested, sir.''

It rolled a little on Rossow's desk and then balanced itself to a halt. It was a shiny sphere of metal, possibly a foot in diameter. There were no external projections of any kind. A few drops of water that had condensed on it rolled down the sides and glistened on the linoleum desk top.

Rossow's glass shattered on the desk.

It could be a gag like his had been—but he couldn't be sure. He couldn't be sure because he didn't dare open it, or destroy it, or get rid of it, or keep it. He couldn't do anything. He couldn't fight because there was nothing he could fight. And yet he had to fight because if he didn't fight he'd have to surrender or concede defeat and yet he was conditioned so he couldn't surrender or concede defeat but he couldn't open the sphere or destroy it or—

The shiny surface of the sphere caught a reflection of Rossow's face and the curved portion made it look all wrong, not nearly as happy as his gales of laughter made him sound.

Deckert watched him silently for a minute and then buzzed for the security watch. Two of them took Rossow away and the third turned and saluted him smartly before leaving.

''Any further orders, captain?''

He was the highest ranking petty officer left. He was the captain now and it was up to him to solve the problem that had driven Rossow insane.

A whisper of Rossow's laughter floated up the companionway and Deckert slammed the hatch. Poor Rossow. The specialist had gone up the same blind alley that the saber-toothed tiger and the dinosaurs had taken. They couldn't adapt. Rossow had been trained to handle almost any situation but he couldn't handle the stalemate he had found himself in. What was it the psychologists called it? Situation thirty—the final situation.

Rossow had been conditioned so he couldn't take chances but that didn't apply to Deckert. It was all very simple, really. The sphere was probably a trick, like theirs had been. True, it might be a weapon of some type and it might do anything at any time. But there was a fundamental difference between the enemy battleship and themselves. If they opened the sphere and it did explode, it wouldn't change their material position a bit. They had been on the losing side at the very beginning. They had nothing further to lose now and everything to gain.

He felt pretty good about it. He'd give odds that the enemy had tried a trick as their last resort. But it wasn't going to work and the beauty of it was, it would still leave them in their agony of indecision. An agony, he suddenly thought, that he didn't have to prolong any further.

"Yes, there is," Deckert replied. He pointed to the sphere. "Take this to the shops and cut it open with a torch. Let me know what's in it, if anything. Then call the enemy ship and give them ten minutes to surrender."

THE BUTCHER'S BILL

David Drake

"You can go a thousand kays any direction there and there's nothing to see but the wheat," said the brown man to the other tankers and the visitor. His hair was deep chestnut, his face and hands burnt umber from the sun of Emporion the month before and the suns of seven other worlds in past years. He was twenty-five but looked several years older. The sleeves of his khaki coveralls were slipped down over his wrists against the chill of the breeze that had begun at twilight to feather the hillcrest. "We fed four planets from Dunstan—Hagener, Weststar, Mirage, and Jackson's Glade. And out of it we made enough to replace the tractors when they wore out, maybe something left over for a bit of pretty. A necklace of fireballs to set off a Lord's Day dress, till the charge drained six, eight months later. A static cleaner from Hagener, it was one year, never quite worked off our pow-erplant however much we tinkered with it. . . .

"My mother, she wore out too. Dad just kept grinding on, guess he still does."

The girl asked a question from the shelter of the tank's scarred curtain. Her voice was a little mild for the wind's tumbling, her accent that of Thrush and strange to the tanker's ears. But Danny answered, "Hate them? Oh, I know about the Combine now, that the four of them kept other merchants off Dunstan to freeze the price at what they thought to pay. But Via, wheat's a high-bulk cargo, there's no way at all we'd have gotten rich on what it could bring over ninety minutes' transit. And why shouldn't I thank Weststar? If ever a world did me well, it was that one."

He spat, turning his head with the wind and lofting the gobbet invisibly into the darkness. The lamp trembled on its base, an overturned ration box. The glare skippered across the rusted steel skirts of the tank, the iridium armor of hull and turret, the faces of the men and the woman listening to the blower captain. The main gun, half shadowed by the curve of the hull, poked out into the night like a ghost of itself. Even with no human in the tank, at the whisper of a relay in Command Central the fat weapon would light the world cyan and smash to lava anything within line of sight of its muzzle.

"We sold our wheat to a Weststar agent, a Hindi named Sarim who'd lived, Via, twenty years at least on Dunstan but he still smelled funny. Sweetish, sort of; you know? But his people were all back in Ongole on Weststar. When the fighting started between the Scots and the Hindi settlers, he raised a battalion of farm boys like me and shipped us over in the hold of a freighter. Hoo Lordy, that was a transit!

"And I never looked back. Colonel Hammer docked in on the same day with the Regiment, and he took us all on spec. Six years, now, that's seven standard . . . and not all of us could stand the gaff, and not all who could wanted to. But I never looked back, and I never will."

From the mast of Command Central, a flag popped unseen in the wind. It bore a red lion rampant on a field of gold, the emblem of Hammer's Slammers; the banner of the toughest regiment that ever killed for a dollar.

"Hotel, Kitchen, Mama, move to the front in company columns and advance."

The tiny adamantine glitter winking on the hilltop ten kays distant was the first break in the landscape since the Regiment had entered the hypothetical war zone, the Star Plain of Thrush. It warned Pritchard in the bubble at the same time it tightened his muscles. "Goose it, Kowie," he ordered his driver in turn, "they want us panzers up front. Bet it's about to drop in the pot?"

Kowie said nothing, but the big blower responded with a howl and a billow of friable soil that seethed from under the ground effect curtain. Two Star in the lead, H Company threaded its way in line ahead through the grounded combat cars and a battalion from Infantry Section. The pongoes crouched on their one-man skimmers, watching the tanks. One blew an ironic kiss to Danny in Two Star's bubble. Moving parallel to Hotel, the other companies of Tank Section, K and M, advanced through the center and right of the skirmish line.

The four-man crew of a combat car nodded unsmilingly from their open-topped vehicle as Two Star boomed past. A trio of swivel-mounted powerguns, two-centimeter hoses like the one on Danny's bubble, gave them respectable firepower; and their armor, a sandwich of steel and iridium, was in fact adequate against most hand weapons. Buzzbombs aside, and tankers didn't like to think about those either. But Danny would have fought reassignment to combat cars if anybody had suggested it—Lord, you may as well dance in your skin for all the good that hull does you in a firefight! And few car crewmen would be caught dead on a panzer—or rather, were sure that that was how they would be caught if they crewed one of those sluggish, clumsy, blind-sided behemoths. Infantry Section scorned both, knowing how the blowers drew fire but couldn't flatten in the dirt when it dropped in on them.

One thing wouldn't get you an argument, though: when it was ready to drop in the pot, you sent in the heavies. And nothing on the Way would stop the Tank Section of Hammer's Slammers when it got cranked up to move.

Even its 170 tons could not fully dampen the vibration of Two Star's fans at max load. The oval hull, all silvery-smooth above but of gouged and rusty steel below where the skirts fell sheer almost to the ground, slid its way through the grass like a boat through yellow seas. They were dropping into a swale before they reached the upgrade. From the increasing rankness of the vegetation that flattened before and beside the tank, Pritchard suspected that they would find a meandering stream at the bottom. The brow of the hill cut off sight of the unnatural glitter visible from a distance. In silhouette against the pale bronze sky writhed instead a grove of gnarled trees.

"Incoming, fourteen seconds to impact," Command Central blatted. A siren in the near distance underscored the words. "Three rounds only."

The watercourse was there. Two Star's fans blasted its surface into a fine mist as the tank bellowed over it. Danny cocked his powergun, throwing a cylinder of glossy black plastic into the lowest of the three rotating barrels. There was shrieking overhead.

WHAM

A poplar shape of dirt and black vapor spouted a kay to the rear, among the grounded infantry.

WHAM WHAM

They were detonating underground. Thrush didn't have much of an industrial base, the rebel portions least of all. Either they hadn't the plant to build proximity fuses at all, or they were substituting interference coils for miniature radar sets, and there was too little metal in the infantry's gear to set off the charges.

"Tank Section, hose down the ridge as you advance, they got an OP there somewhere."

"Incoming, three more in fourteen." The satellite net could pick up a golf ball in flight, much less a four-hundred-pound shell.

Pritchard grinned like a death's head, laying his two-centimeter automatic on the rim of the hill and squeezing off. The motor whirred, spinning the barrels as rock and vegetation burst in the blue-green sleet. Spent cases, gray and porous, spun out of the mechanism in a jet of coolant gas. They bounced on the turret slope, some clinging to the iridium to cool there, ugly dark excrescences on the metal.

"Outgoing."

Simultaneously with Central's laconic warning, giants tore a strip off the sky. The rebel shells dropped but their bursts were smothered in the roar of the Regiment's own rocket howitzers boosting charges to titanic velocity for the seven seconds before their motors burned out. Ten meters from the muzzles the rockets went supersonic, punctuating the ripping sound with thunderous slaps. Danny swung his hose toward the grove of trees, the only landmark visible on the hilltop. His burst laced it cyan. Water, flash heated within the boles by the gunfire, blew apart the dense wood in blasts of steam and splinters. A dozen other guns joined Pritchard's, clawing at rock, air, and the remaining scraps of vegetation.

"Dead on," Central snapped to the artillery. "Now give it battery five and we'll show those freaks how they should've done it."

Kowie hadn't buttoned up. His head stuck up from the driver's hatch, trusting his eyes rather than the vision blocks built into his compartment. The tanks themselves were creations of the highest technical competence, built on Terra itself; but the crews were generally from frontier worlds, claustrophobic in an armored coffin no matter how good its electronic receptors were. Danny knew the feeling. His hatch, too, was open, and his hand gripped the rounded metal of the powergun itself rather than the selsyn unit inside. They were climbing sharply now, the back end hopping and skittering as the driver fed more juice to the rear fans in trying to level the vehicle. The bow skirts grounded briefly, the blades spitting out a section of hillside as pebbles.

For nearly a minute the sky slammed and raved. Slender,
clipped-off vapor trails of counterbattery fire streamed from
the defiladed artillery. Half a minute after they ceased fire,
the drumbeat of shells bursting on the rebels continued. No
further incoming rounds fell.

Two Star lurched over the rim of the hill. Seconds later the
lead blowers of K and M bucked in turn onto the flatter area.
Smoke and ash from the gun-lit brushfire shoomped out in
their downdrafts. There was no sign of the enemy, either
Densonite rebels or Foster's crew—though if the mer-
cenaries were involved, they would be bunkered beyond
probable notice until they popped the cork themselves.

"Tank Section, ground! Ground in place and prepare for
director control."

Danny hunched, bracing his palms against the hatch coam-
ing. Inside the turret the movement and firing controls of the
main gun glowed red, indicating that they had been locked
out of Pritchard's command. Kowie lifted the tow to kill the
tank's immense inertia. There was always something spooky
about feeling the turret purr beneath you, watching the big
gun snuffle the air with deadly precision on its own. Danny
gripped his tribarrel, scanning the horizon nervously. It was
worse when you didn't know what Central had on its mind
. . . and you did know that the primary fire-control computer was on the fritz—they always picked the damnedest
times!

"Six aircraft approaching from two-eight-three degrees,"
Central mumbled. "Distance seven-point-ought-four kays,
closing at one-one-ought-ought."

Pritchard risked a quick look away from where the gun
pointed toward a ridgeline northwest of them, an undistin-
guished swelling half-obscured by the heat-wavering pall of
smoke. Thirteen other tanks had crested the hill before Central froze them, all aiming in the same direction. Danny
dropped below his hatch rim, counting seconds.

The sky roared cyan. The tank's vision blocks blanked
momentarily, but the dazzle reflected through the open hatch

was enough to make Pritchard's skin tingle. The smoke waved and rippled about the superheated tracks of gunfire. The horizon to the northwest was an expanding orange dome that silently dominated the sky.

"Resume advance." Then, "Spectroanalysis indicates five hostiles were loaded with chemical explosives, one was carrying fissionables."

Danny was trembling worse than before the botched attack. The briefing cubes had said that the Densonites were religious nuts, sure. But to use unsupported artillery against a force whose satellite spotters would finger the guns before the first salvo landed; aircraft—probably converted cargo haulers—thrown against director-controlled powerguns that shot light swift and line straight; and then nukes, against a regiment more likely to advance stark naked than without a nuclear damper up! They weren't just nuts—Thrush central government was that, unwilling to have any of its own people join the fighting—they were as crazy as if they thought they could breathe vacuum and live. You didn't play that sort of game with the Regiment.

They'd laager for the night on the hilltop, the rest of the outfit rumbling in through the afternoon and early evening hours. At daybreak they'd leapfrog forward again, deeper into the Star Plain, closer to whatever it was the Densonites wanted to hold. Sooner or later, the rebels and Foster's Infantry—a good outfit but not good enough for this job—were going to have to make a stand. And then the Regiment would go out for contract again, because they'd have run out of work on Thrush.

"She'll be in looking for you pretty soon, won't she, handsome?"

"Two bits to stay."

"Check. Sure. Danny-boy, you Romeos from Dunstan, you can pick up a slot anywhere, huh?"

A troop of combat cars whined past, headed for their position in the laager. Pritchard's hole card, a jack, flipped over. He swore, pushed in his hand. "I was folding anyway. And cut it out, will you? I didn't go looking for her, I didn't tell her to come back. And she may as well be the colonel for all my chance of putting her flat."

Wanatamba, the lean, black Terran who drove Fourteen, laughed and pointed. A gold-shangled skimmer was dropping from the east, tracked by the guns of two of the blowers on that side. Everybody knew what it was, though. Pritchard grimaced and stood. "Seems that's the game for me," he said.

"Hey, Danny," one of the men behind him called as he walked away. "Get a little extra for us, hey?"

The skimmer had landed in front of Command Central, at rest an earth-blended geodesic housing the staff and much of the commo hardware. Wearing a wrist-to-ankle sunsuit, yellow where it had tone, she was leaning on the plex windscreen. An officer in fatigues with unlatched body armor stepped out of the dome and did a double take. He must have recollected, though, because he trotted off toward a bunker before Danny reached the skimmer.

"Hey!" the girl called brightly. She looked about seventeen, her hair an unreal cascade of beryl copper over one shoulder. "We're going on a trip."

"Uh?"

The dome section flipped open again. Pritchard stiffened to attention when he saw the short, moustached figure who exited. "Peace, Colonel," the girl said.

"Peace, Sonna. You're such an ornament to a firebase that I'm thinking of putting you on requisition for our next contract."

Laughing cheerfully, the girl gestured toward the rigid sergeant. "I'm taking Danny to the Hamper Shrine this afternoon."

Pritchard reddened. "Sir, Sergeant-Commander Daniel Pritchard—"

"I know you, trooper," the colonel said with a friendly smile. "I've watched Two Star in action often enough, you know." His eyes were blue.

"Sir, I didn't request—that is . . . ''

"And I also know there's small point in arguing with our girl, here, hey, Sonna? Go see your shrine, soldier, and worst comes to worst, just throw your hands up and yell, 'Exchange.' You can try Colonel Foster's rations for a week or two until we get this little business straightened out.'' The colonel winked, bowed low to Sonna, and re-entered the dome.

"I don't figure it,'' Danny said as he settled into the passenger seat. The skimmer was built low and sleek, as if a racer, though its top speed was probably under a hundred kays. Any more would have put too rapid a drain of the rechargables packed into the decimeter-thick floor—a fusion unit would have doubled the flyer's bulk and added four hundred kilos right off the bat. At that, the speed and an operating altitude of thirty meters were more than enough for the tanker. You judge things by what you're used to, and the blower captain who found himself that far above the cold, hard ground—it could happen on a narrow switchback—had seen his last action.

While the wind whipped noisily about the open cockpit the girl tended to her flying and ignored Danny's curiosity. It was a hop rather than a real flight, keeping over the same hill at all times and circling down to land scarcely a minute after takeoff. On a field of grass untouched by the recent fire rose the multitented, crystalline structure Pritchard had glimpsed during the assault. With a neat spin and a brief whine from the fans, the skimmer settled down.

Sonna grinned. Her sunsuit, opaquing completely in the direct light, blurred her outline in a dazzle of fluorescent saffron. "What don't you figure?'' she asked.

"Well, ah . . . '' Danny stumbled, his curiosity drawn between the girl and the building. "We, the colonel isn't that, ah, easy to deal with usually. I mean . . . ''

Her laugh bubbled in the sunshine. "Oh, it's because I'm an Advisor, I'm sure.''

"Excuse?''

"An Advisor. You know, the . . . well, a representative.

Of the government, if you want to put it that way.''

"My Lord!" the soldier gasped. "But you're so young."

She frowned. "You really don't know much about us, do you?" she reflected.

"Um, well, the briefing cubes mostly didn't deal with the friendlies this time because we'd be operating without support. . . . Anything was going to look good after Emporion, that was for sure. All desert there—you should've heard the cheers when the colonel said that we'd lift."

She absently combed a hand back through her hair. It flowed like molten bronze. "You won on Emporion?" she asked.

"We could've," Danny explained, "even though it was really a Lord-stricken place, dust and fortified plateaus and lousy recce besides because the government had two operating spacers. But the Monarchists ran out of money after six months and that's one sure rule for Hammer's Slammers—no pay, no play. Colonel yanked their bond so fast their ears rang. And we hadn't orbited before offers started coming in."

"And you took ours and came to a place you didn't know much about," the girl mused. "Well, we didn't know much about you either."

"What do you need to know except we can bust anybody else in this business?" the soldier said with amusement. "Anybody, public or planet-tied. If you're worried about Foster, don't; he wouldn't back the freaks today, but when he has to, we'll eat him for breakfast."

"Has to?" the girl repeated in puzzlement. "But he always has to—the Densonites hired him, didn't they?"

Strategy was a long way from Danny's training, but the girl seemed not to know that. And besides, you couldn't spend seven years with the Slammers and not pick up some basics. "Okay," he began, "Foster's boys'll fight, but they're not crazy. Trying to block our advance in open land like this'd be pure suicide—as those freaks—pardon, didn't mean that—must've found out today. Foster likely got orders to support the civvies but refused. I know for a fact that his army's better'n what we wiped up today, and those *planes* . . .''

"But his contract . . . ?" Sonna queried.

"Sets out the objectives and says the outfit'll obey civvie orders where it won't screw things up too bad," Danny said. "Standard form. The legal of it's different, but that's what it means."

The girl was nodding, eyes slitted, and in a low voice she quoted, " . . . 'except in circumstances where such directions would significantly increase the risks to be undergone by the party of the second part without corresponding military advantage.' " She looked full at Danny. "Very . . . interesting. When we hired your colonel, I don't think any of us understood that clause."

Danny blinked, out of his depth and aware of it. "Well, it doesn't matter really. I mean, the colonel didn't get his rep from ducking fights. It's just, well . . . say we're supposed to clear the Densonites off the, the Star Plain? Right?"

The girl shrugged.

"So that's what we'll do." Danny wiped his palms before gesturing with both hands. "But if your Advisors—"

"We Advisors," the girl corrected, smiling.

"Anyway," the tanker concluded, his enthusiasm chilled, "if you tell the colonel to fly the whole Regiment up to ten thousand and dump it out, he'll tell you to go piss up a rope. Sorry, he wouldn't say that. But you know what I mean. We know our job, don't worry."

"Yes, that's true," she said agreeably. "And we don't, and we can't understand it. We thought that—one to one, you know?—perhaps if I got to know you, one of you . . . they thought we might understand all of you a little."

The soldier frowned uncertainly.

"What we don't see," she finally said, "is how you—"

She caught herself. Touching her cold fingertips to the backs of the tanker's wrists, the girl continued, "Danny, you're a nice . . . you're not a, a sort of monster like we

thought you all must be. If you'd been born of Thrush you'd
have had a—different—education, you'd be more, forgive
me, I don't mean it as an insult, sophisticated in some ways.
That's all.

"But how can a nice person like you go out and kill?"

He rubbed his eyes, then laced together his long, brown
fingers. "You . . . well, it's not like that. What I said the
other night—look, the Slammers're a good outfit, the best,
and I'm damned lucky to be with them. I do my job the best
way I know, I'll keep on doing that. And if somebody gets
killed, okay. My brother Jig stayed home and he's two years
dead now. Tractor rolled on a wet field but Via, could've
been a tow-chain snapped or old age; doesn't matter. He
wasn't going to live forever and neither is anybody else. And
I haven't got any friends on the far end of the muzzle."

Her voice was very soft as she said, "Perhaps if I keep
trying. . . ."

Danny smiled. "Well, I don't mind," he lied, looking at
the structure. "What is this place, anyhow?"

Close up, it had unsuspected detail. The sides were a
hedge of glassy rods curving together to a series of peaks ten
meters high. No finger-slim member was quite the thickness
or color of any other, although the delicacy was subliminal in
impact. In ground plan it was a complex oval thirty meters by
ten, pierced by scores of doorways which were not closed off
but were foggy to look at.

"What do you think of it?" the girl asked.

"Well, it's . . . " Danny temporized. A fragment of the
briefing cubes returned to him. "It's one of the alien, the
Gedel, artifacts, isn't it?"

"Of course," the girl agreed. "Seven hundred thousand
years old, as far as we can judge. Only a world in stasis, like
Thrush, would have let it survive the way it has. The walls
are far tougher than they look, but seventy millennia of
earthquakes and volcanoes . . ."

Danny stepped out of the skimmer and let his hand run
across the building's cool surface. "Yeah, if they'd picked

some place with a hotter core there wouldn't be much left but
sand by now, would there?''

"Pick it? Thrush was their home," Sonna's voice rang
smoothly behind him. "The Gedel chilled it themselves to
make it suitable, to leave a signpost for the next races following the Way. We can't even imagine how they did it, but
there's no question but that Thrush was normally tectonic up
until the last million years or so."

"Via!" Danny breathed, turning his shocked face toward
the girl. "No wonder those fanatics wanted to control this
place. Why, if they could figure out just a few of the Gedel
tricks, they'd . . . Lord, they wouldn't stop with Thrush,
that's for sure."

"You still don't understand," the girl said. She took
Danny by the hand and drew him toward the nearest of the
misty doorways. "The Densonites have, well, quirks that
make them hard for the rest of us on Thrush to understand.
But they would no more pervert Gedel wisdom to warfare
than you would, oh, spit on your colonel. Come here."

She stepped into the fuzziness and disappeared. The tanker
had no choice but to follow or break her grip; though, oddly,
she was no longer clinging to him on the other side of the
barrier. She was not even beside him in the large room. He
was alone at the first of a line of tableaux, staring at a group of
horribly inhuman creatures at play. Their sharp-edged faces,
scale-dusted but more avian than reptile, stared enraptured at
one of their number who hung in the air. The acrobat's bare,
claw-tipped legs pointed 180 degrees apart, straight toward
ground and sky.

Pritchard blinked and moved on. The next scene was only
a dazzle of sunlight in a glade whose foliage was redder than
that of Thrush or Dunstan. There was something else, something wrong or strange about the tableau. Danny felt it, but
his eyes could not explain.

Step by step, cautiously, Pritchard worked his way down
the line of exhibits. Each was different, centered on a group
of the alien bipeds or a ruddy, seemingly empty landscape

that hinted unintelligibly. At first, Danny had noticed the
eerie silence inside the hall. As he approached the far end he
realized that he was conscious of music of some sort, very
crisp and distant. He laid his bare palm on the floor and
found, as he had feared, that it did not vibrate in the least. He
ran the last twenty steps to plunge out into the sunlight.
Sonna still gripped his hand, and they stood outside the
doorway they had entered.

The girl released him. "Isn't it incredible?" she asked, her
expression bright. "And every one of the doorways leads to a
different corridor—recreation there, agriculture in another,
history—everything. A whole planet in that little building."

"That's what the Gedel looked like, huh?" Danny said.
He shook his head to clear the strangeness from it.

"The Gedel? Oh, no," the girl replied, surprised again at
his ignorance. "These were the folk we call the Hampers. No
way to pronounce their own language, a man named Hamper
found this site is all. But their homeworld was Kalinga IV,
almost three days' transit from Thrush. The shrine is here, we
think, in the same relation to Starhome as Kalinga was to
Thrush.

"You still don't understand," she concluded, watching
Danny's expression. She sat on the edge of the flyer, crossing
her hands on the lap of her sunsuit. In the glitter thrown by the
structure the fabric patterned oddly across her lithe torso.
"The Gedel association—it wasn't an empire, couldn't have
been. But to merge, a group ultimately needs a center,
physical and intellectual. And Thrush and the Gedel were
that for twenty races.

"And they achieved genuine unity, not just within one
race but among all of them, each as strange to the others as
any one of them would have been to man, to us. The . . .
power that gave them, over themselves as well as the universe, was incredible. This—even Starhome itself—is such a
tiny part of what could be achieved by perfect peace and
empathy."

Danny looked at the crystal dome and shivered at what it

had done to him. "Look," he said, "peace is just great if the universe cooperates. I don't mean just my line of work, but it doesn't happen that way in the real world. There's no peace spending your life beating wheat out of Dunstan, not like I'd call peace. And what's happened to the Gedel and their buddies for the last half million years or so if things were so great?"

"We can't even imagine what happened to them," Sonna explained gently, "but it wasn't the disaster you imagine. When they reached what they wanted, they set up this, Starhome, the other eighteen shrines as . . . monuments. And then they went away, all together. But they're not wholly gone, even from here, you know. Didn't you feel them in the background inside, laughing with you?"

"I . . . Danny attempted. He moved, less toward the skimmer than away from the massive crystal behind him. "Yeah, there was something. That's what you're fighting for?"

You couldn't see the laager from where the skimmer rested, but Danny could imagine the silvery glitter of tanks and combat cars between the sky and the raw yellow grass. Her eyes fixed on the same stretch of horizon, the girl said, "Someday men will be able to walk through Starhome and understand. You can't live on Thrush without feeling the impact of the Gedel. That impact has . . . warped, perhaps, the Densonites. They have some beliefs about the Gedel that most of us don't agree with. And they're actually willing to use force to prevent the artifacts from being defiled by anyone who doesn't believe as they do."

"Well, you people do a better job of using force," Danny said harshly. His mind braced itself on its memory of the Regiment's prickly hedgehog.

"Oh, not us!" the girl gasped.

Suddenly angry, the tanker gestured toward the unseen firebase. "Not you? The Densonites don't pay us. And if force isn't what happened to those silly bastards today when our counterbattery hit them, I'd like to know what is."

She looked at him in a way that, despite her previous curiosity, was new to him. "There's much that I'll have to discuss with the other Advisors," she said after a long pause. "And I don't know that it will stop with us, we'll have to put out the call to everyone, the Densonites as well if they will come." Her eyes caught Danny's squarely again. "We acted with little time for deliberation when the Densonites hired Colonel Foster and turned all the other pilgrims out of the Star Plain. And we acted in an area beyond our practice— thank the Lord! The key to understanding the Gedel and joining them, Lord willing and the Way being short, is Starhome. And nothing that blocks any man, all men, from Starhome can be . . . tolerated. But with what we've learned since . . . well, we have other things to take into account."

She broke off, tossed her stunning hair. In the flat evening sunlight her garment had paled to translucence. The late rays licked her body red and orange. "But now I'd better get you back to your colonel." She slipped into the skimmer.

Danny boarded without hesitation. After the Gedel building, the transparent skimmer felt almost comfortable. "Back to my tank," he corrected lightly. "Colonel may not care where I am, but he damn well cares if Two Star is combat-ready." The sudden rush of air cut off thought of further conversation, and though Sonna smiled as she landed Danny beside his blower, there was a blankness in her expression that indicated her thoughts were far away.

Hell with her, Danny thought. His last night in the Rec Center on Emporion seemed a long time in the past.

At three in the morning the Regiment was almost two hundred kilometers from the camp they had abandoned at midnight. There had been no warning, only the low hoot of the siren followed by the colonel's voice rasping from every man's lapel speaker, "Mount up and move, boys. Order seven, and your guides are set." It might have loomed before another outfit as a sudden catastrophe. After docking one trip with the Slammers, though, a greenie learned that everything not secured to his blower had better be secured to him. Colonel Hammer thought an armored regiment's firepower was less of an asset than its mobility. He used the latter to the full with ten preset orders of march and in-motion recharging for the infantry skimmers, juicing from the tanks and combat cars.

Four pongoes were jumpered to Two Star when Foster's outpost sprang its ambush.

The lead combat car, half a kay ahead, bloomed in a huge white ball that flooded the photon amplifiers of Danny's goggles. The buzzbomb's hollow detonation followed a moment later while the tanker, cursing, simultaneously switched to infrared and swung his turret left at max advance. He ignored the head of the column, where the heated-air thump of powerguns merged with the crackle of bomblets kicked to either side by the combat cars; that was somebody else's responsibility. He ignored the two infantrymen wired to his tank's port side as well. If they knew their business, they'd drop the jumpers and flit for Two Star's blind side as swiftly as Danny could spin his heavy turret. If not, well, you don't have time for niceness when somebody's firing shaped charges at you.

"Damp that ground-sender!" Central snapped to the lead elements. Too quickly to be a response to the command, the grass trembled under the impact of a delay-fused rocket punching down toward the computed location of the enemy's subsurface signaling. The Regiment must have rolled directly over an outpost, either through horrendously bad luck or because Foster had sewn his vedettes very thickly.

The firing stopped. The column had never slowed and Mama, first of the heavy companies behind the screen of combat cars, fanned the grass fires set by the hoses. Pritchard scanned the area of the firefight as Two Star rumbled through it in turn. The antipersonnel bomblets had dimpled the ground where they hit, easily identifiable among the glassy scars left by the powerguns. In the center of a great vitrified

blotch lay a left arm and a few scraps of gray coverall.
Nearby was the plastic hilt of a buzzbomb launcher. The
other vedette had presumably stayed on the commo in his
covered foxhole until the penetrator had scattered it and him
over the landscape. If there had been a third bunker, it
escaped notice by Two Star's echo sounders.

"Move it out, up front," Central demanded. "This cuts
our margin."

The burned-out combat car swept back into obscurity as
Kowie put on speed. The frontal surfaces had collapsed
inward from the heat, leaving the driver and blower captain
as husks of carbon. There was no sign of the wing gunners.
Perhaps they had been far enough back and clear of the spurt
of directed radiance to escape. The ammo canister of the port
tribarrel had flash-ignited, though, and it was more likely
that the men were wasted on the floor of the vehicle.

Another 150 kays to go, and now Foster and the Densonites knew they were coming.

There were no further ambushes to break the lightless
monotony of gently rolling grassland. Pritchard took occasional sips of water and ate half a tube of protein ration. He
started to fling the tube aside, then thought of the metal
detectors on following units. He dropped it between his feet
instead.

The metal-pale sun was thrusting the Regiment's shadow
in long fingers up the final hillside when Central spoke again.
You could tell that it was the colonel himself sending.
"Everybody freeze but Beta-First, Beta-First proceed in
column up the rise and in. Keep your intervals, boys, and
don't try to bite off too much. Last data we got was Foster had
his antiaircraft company with infantry support holding the
target. Maybe they pulled out when we knocked on the door
tonight, maybe they got reinforced. So take it easy—and
don't bust up anything you don't have to."

Pritchard dropped his seat back inside the turret. There
was nothing to be seen from the hatch but the monochrome

sunrise and armored vehicles grounded on the yellow background. Inside, the three vision blocks gave greater variety. One was the constant 360-degree display, better than normal eyesight according to the designers because the blower captain could see all around the tank without turning his head. Danny didn't care for it. Images were squeezed a good deal horizontally. Shapes weren't quite what you expected, so you didn't react quite as fast; and that was a good recipe for a dead trooper. The screen above the 360 was variable in light sensitivity and in magnification, useful for special illumination and first-shot hits with the big gun.

The bottom screen was the remote rig; Pritchard dialed it for the forward receptors of Beta-First-Three. It was strange to watch the images of the two leading combat cars trembling as they crested the hill, yet feel Two Star as stable as 170 tons can be when grounded.

"Nothing moving," the section leader reported unnecessarily. Central had remote circuits too, as well as the satellite net, to depend on.

The screen lurched as the blower Danny was slaved to boosted its fans to level the downgrade. Dust plumed from the leading cars, weaving across a sky that was almost fully light. At an unheard command, the section turned up the wick in unison and let the cars hurtle straight toward the target's central corridor. It must have helped, because Foster's gunners caught only one car when they loosed the first blast through their camouflage.

The second car blurred in the mist of vaporized armor plate. Incredibly, the right wing gunner shot back. The deadly flamelash of his hose was pale against the richer color of the hostile fire. Foster had sited his calliopes, massive three-centimeter guns whose nine fixed barrels fired extra-length charges. Danny had never seen a combat car turned into a Swiss cheese faster than the one spiked on the muzzles of a pair of the heavy guns.

Gray-suited figures were darting from cover as if the cars' automatics were harmless for being outclassed. The damaged blower nosed into the ground. Its driver leaped out, running for the lead car, which had spun on its axis and was hosing blue-green fire in three directions. One of Foster's troops raised upright, loosing a buzzbomb at the wreckage of the grounded car. The left side of the vehicle flapped like a bat's wing as it sailed across Danny's field of view. The concussion knocked down the running man. He rose to his knees, jumped for a handhold as the lead car accelerated past him. As he swung himself aboard, two buzzbombs hit the blower simultaneously. It bloomed with joined skullcaps of pearl and bone.

Pritchard was swearing softly. He had switched to a stern pickup already, and the tumbled wreckage in it was bouncing, fading swiftly. Shots twinkled briefly as the two escaping blowers dropped over the ridge.

"In column ahead," said the colonel grimly, "Hotel, Killer, Mama. Button up and hose 'em out, you know the drill."

And then something went wrong. "Are you insane?" the radio marveled, and Danny recognized that voice too. "I forbid you!"

"You can't. Somebody get her out of here."

"Your contract is over, finished, do you hear? Heavenly Way, we'll all become Densonites if we must. This horror must end!"

"Not yet. You don't see—"

"I've seen too—" The shouted words cut off.

"So we let Foster give us a bloody nose and back off? That's what you want? But it's bigger than what you want now, sister, it's the whole Regiment. It's never bidding another contract without somebody saying, 'Hey, they got sandbagged on Thrush, didn't they?' And nobody remembering that Foster figured the civvies would chill us—and he was right. Don't you see? They killed my boys, and now they're going to pay the bill.

"Tank Section, execute! Dig 'em out, panzers!"

Danny palmed the panic bar, dropping the seat and locking the hatch over it. The rushing-air snarl of the fans was deadened out by the armor, but a hot bearing somewhere filled the compartment with its high keening. Two Star hurdled the ridge. Its whole horizon flared with crystal dancing and scattering in sunlight and the reflected glory of automatic weapons firing from its shelter. Starhome was immensely larger than Danny had expected.

A boulevard twenty meters wide divided two ranks of glassy buildings, any one of which, towers and pavilions, stood larger than the shrine Danny had seen the previous day. At a kilometer's distance it was a corruscating unity of parts as similar as the strands of a silken rope. Danny rapped up the magnification and saw the details spring out; rods woven into columns that streaked skyward a hundred meters; translucent sheets formed of myriads of pinhead beads, each one glowing a color as different from the rest as one star is from the remainder of those seen on a moonless night; a spiral column, free-standing and the thickness of a woman's wrist, that pulsed slowly through the spectrum as it climbed almost out of sight. All the structures seemed to front on the central corridor, with the buildings on either side welded together by tracery mazes, porticoes, arcades—a thousand different plates and poles of glass.

A dashed cyan line joined the base of an upswept web of color to the tank. Two Star's hull thudded to the shock of vaporizing metal. The stabilizer locked the blower's pitching out of Danny's sight picture. He swung the glowing orange bead onto the source of fire and kicked the pedal. The air rang like a carillon as the whole glassy facade sagged, then avalanched into the street. There was a shock of heat in the closed battle compartment as the breech flicked open and belched out the spent case. The plastic hissed on the floor, outgasing horribly while the air-conditioning strained to clear the chamber. Danny ignored the stench, nudged his sights onto the onrushing splendor of the second structure on the right of the corridor. The breech of the big powergun slapped again and again, recharging instantly as the tanker worked the foot trip.

Blue-green lightning scattered between the walls as if the

full power of each bolt was flashing the length of the corridor. Two Star bellowed in on the wake of its fire, and crystal flurried under the fans. Kowie leveled their stroke slightly, cutting speed by a fraction but lifting the tank higher above the abrasive litter. The draft hurled glittering shards across the corridor, arcs of cold fire in the light of Two Star's gun and those of the blowers following. Men in gray were running from their hiding places to avoid the sliding crystal masses, the iridescent rain that pattered on the upper surfaces of the tanks but smashed jaggedly through the infantry's body armor.

Danny set his left thumb to rotate the turret counterclockwise, held the gunswitch down with his foot. The remaining sixteen rounds of his basic load blasted down the right half of Starhome, spread by the blower's forward motion and the turret swing. The compartment was gray with fumes. Danny slammed the hatch open and leaned out. His hands went to the two-centimeter as naturally as a calf turns to milk. The wind was cold on his face. Kowie slewed the blower left to avoid the glassy wave that slashed into the corridor from one of the blasted structures. The scintillance halted, then ground a little further as something gave way inside the pile.

A soldier in gray stepped from an untouched archway to the left. The buzzbomb on his shoulder was the size of a landing vessel as it swung directly at Danny. The tribarrel seemed to traverse with glacial slowness. It was too slow. Danny saw the brief flash as the rocket leaped from the shoulder of the other mercenary. It whirred over Two Star and the sergeant, exploded cataclysmically against a spike of Starhome still rising on the other side.

The infantryman tossed aside the launcher tube. He froze, his arms spread wide, and shouted, "Exchange!"

"Exchange yourself, mother!" Danny screamed back, white-faced. He triggered his hose. The gray torso exploded. The body fell backward in a mist of blood, chest and body armor torn open by four hits that shriveled bones and turned fluids to steam.

"Hard left and goose it, Kowie," the sergeant demanded. He slapped the panic bar again. As the hatch clanged shut over his head, Danny caught a momentary glimpse of the vision blocks, three soldiers with powerguns leaping out of the same towering structure from which the rocketeer had come. Their faces were blankly incredulous as they saw the huge blower swinging toward them at full power. The walls flexed briefly under the impact of the tank's frontal slope, but the filigree was eggshell thin. The structure disintegrated, lurching toward the corridor while Two Star plowed forward within it. A thousand images kaleidoscoped in Danny's skull, sparkling within the windchime dissonance of the falling tower.

The fans screamed as part of the structure's mass collapsed onto Two Star. Kowie rocked the tank, raising it like a submarine through a sea of ravaged glass. The gentle, green-furred humanoids faded from Danny's mind. He threw open the hatch. Kowie gunned the fans, reversing the blower in a polychrome shower. Several tanks had moved ahead of Two Star, nearing the far end of the corridor. Gray-uniformed soldiers straggled from the remaining structures, hands empty, eyes fixed on the ground. There was very little firing. Kowie edged into the column and followed the third tank into the laager forming on the other side of Starhome. Pritchard was drained. His throat was dry, but he knew from past experience that he would vomit if he swallowed even a mouthful of water before his muscles stopped trembling. The blower rested with its skirts on the ground, its fans purring gently as they idled to a halt.

Kowie climbed out of the driver's hatch, moving stiffly. He had a powergun in his hand, a pistol he always carried for moral support. Two Star's bow compartment was frequently nearer the enemy than anything else in Hammer's Slammers.

Several towers still stood in the wreckage of Starhome. The nearest one wavered from orange to red and back in the full blaze of sunlight. Danny watched it in the iridium mirror of his tank's deck, the outline muted by the hatchwork of crystal etchings on the metal.

Kowie shot offhand. Danny looked up in irritation. The
driver shot again, his light charge having no discernible
effect on the structure.

"Shut it off," Danny croaked. "These're shrines."

The ground where Starhome had stood blazed like the
floor of Hell.

SINGLE COMBAT

Joe Green

The Curtain Rises:

Blue Rigel came vaulting over the high tops of the snow-capped mountains, dispelling the deep shadows in the cleft, and the Day of Tribute was at hand. Kala Brabant, six-foot-nine of coal-black skin stretched taut over stringy muscles and prominent bones, stood in the door of the king's cave and watched the people of the Saa'Hualla tribe beginning to stir.

Behind him he heard Ahmist, his Number One wife, kicking the three lesser wives out of their bed in the inner room. It was time to make Kala's breakfast, which he insisted be unduly well cooked, and afterward start preparing food for the numerous expected guests of the king.

Kala stepped outside, into the cold breeze blowing off the shoulder of the Home Mountain, and made a brisk tour of the guards at their stockade posts. The Caves of Kala sat within a large pocket in a sheer face of rock, impossible to approach from the back, and the previous chiefs had built and maintained a high wall across the entrance from the valley. This fortress had not been overrun within the memory of the Saa'Hualla.

A good base from which to conquer a planet, considering the job had to be done with spear and sword.

He met Grabo, the general of his army, as he approached his cave again, and exchanged good-mornings.

"Have any warriors in the tribes taken the oath to kill the king this tribute day, Grabo?" Dala asked after the formal pleasantries.

"None of which I have heard, O King."

"Good. We will need all our warriors for the coming campaign against the Willikazee. And I do not like this useless killing of my own folk. I am glad they realize I cannot be beaten."

"Mighty is the king," responded Grabo mechanically, and left to hunt his own breakfast.

Mighty is the king! thought Kala as he ate his thoroughly cooked meat. *Yes, mighty is the Earthman posing as a Saa'Hualla, mighty is the man who uses parapowers against primitive savages. Mighty is the Slaughterer of Warriors, the Killer of Great Men, the Maker of Widows. And how sick at the stomach he is of the whole bloody mess!*

But regrets were a luxury in which he could ill afford to indulge. There was, as always, too much to do.

He attended to some routine details connected with the day's festivities and then had his great chair pulled out of its corner in his cave and set up outside. He was barely ready when Birananga, one of his two living fathers-in-law, presented himself and two bearers loaded with gifts for his king and son-in-law. It was time to start the political dickering that would consume most of his day. Birananga was chief of a small people to the southeast, one of the few local tribes who had fallen under his authority without the use of force. To the west of both their kingdoms was the large and powerful tribe of the Sinnedocks, whose fat king had acknowledged the overlordship of Kala only after a bloody and terrible battle. He needed to bind a little tighter the bonds of fealty he held over the Sinnedocks, and according to their complicated

kinship line he and their fat old king would become relatives
if married to sisters. Birananga had a daughter, the apple of
his aging eye, who had just reached mating age. If a marriage
between her and the old king could be arranged, enabling him
to say his "family" ruled this area of the world, it would
greatly ease the chafe by acknowledging overlordship.

By the time he had half argued, half bullied his father-in-
law into reluctant assentation the next chief was waiting to
present the chafe of acknowledging overlordship.

For the rest of the morning he worked hard at consolidating
his already large empire, pitting his tremendous knowledge
and keen mind against their native shrewdness and stubborn
greed. Like any other overlord he held power primarily
through the strength of his sword, but high-pressure politics,
to which these primitives were unaccustomed, saved many
hours of battle and many gallons of blood.

Blood. The thought of the number of men he had killed
personally, and countless others killed in battles he had
started, came home again for the hundredth time, with its
usual sickening force. He felt physically ill where he sat, and
for a moment was afraid he would lose his breakfast, in front
of all those assembled guests. He took control of his sym-
pathetic nervous system for a moment, forced down his
rising gorge, and calmed himself physically. For mental
relief he used a trick he had employed often in his three years
on this planet, divorced himself from the scene around him
and imagined that he was flying upward into the blue sky,
rising far enough into space to permit him to see the faint light
of old Sol twinkling in the heavens eleven hundred light-
years away. But this relief, too, failed, for the thought came
that it was less than half that distance in the opposite direction
to the home world of the enemy, the Flish.

Memory One:

Professor Kala Brabant, head of the classical poetry department at Ruanda University, turned his back on the re-

cruiter from United Government and walked to the window, stood staring out at the blue water of Lake Tanganyika. His small grandchildren were playing in the water near the edge, their ebony skins glittering with droplets jeweled by sunlight. The quiet hum of expensive appliances told him that Temi was in her new control room, preparing dinner for himself and the grandchildren they were babysitting. This was home, this sprawling white house on the shores of the Long Lake, and his mountain cabin just below the snowline, a half-hour's ride by aircar, provided a place of refuge from all worldly cares. There he had his books, his tapes, the huge collection of unviewed films he had just purchased from the estate of a dead friend; there awaited serenity and contentment.

The short, stout little Oriental waited patiently. He possessed degrees as imposing as Kala's, and most of them dealt with understanding and handling people. U.G. used only the best for recruiters, and he was the best of the best.

Kala turned from the window, wringing his hands in deep agitation. "But why me?" he echoed the immemorial cry of man. "I'm a teacher, a philosopher and poet, not a spy. How could I possibly help you? And if I could, why should I?"

Instead of answering, the smaller man dug a relaxer out of his pocket, flicked off the cover, and inserted it in a nostril. He breathed deeply for a moment, then cleared his throat and said, "Why you? That's an easy one, Professor. You are the only man we have found who is fully qualified for the job. Nowhere among the forty billion Earthmen here and on the other twenty-nine planets we have colonized is there a Negro tall enough and slim enough for the necessary reconversion, who is also a psionic adept and possesses the necessary high intelligence. That is why I must—why I *shall*—convince you to accept the assignment."

"I am not even convinced of the need."

"Professor Brabant, most of the facts are known to you, but perhaps it is necessary to see them in their proper relation to each other. First, we now live to be two hundred Eryears, on the average, and recent advances promise still longer lives in the future. Despite this, the drive in man to procreate has not weakened, and every family wants children. They are one of the subjective building blocks on which a happy life is based. With a new generation every thirty years this means our population doubles approximately every eighty-five years, and *Lebensraum* is the single greatest need of the human race. The only possible place that room may be secured is by colonization of other planets, which the phase-shifted makes practicable. With thirty planets under our control we have, at the moment, plenty of room. But, sir, U.G. does not plan for today, or tomorrow, or a hundred years from now. If the human race learned one single lesson from communism, it was that the future must be planned a thousand years in advance. This we have done, and you, Professor, are an important part of that plan.''

''But what you ask is ridiculous! To become a fighter at my age, a warrior king among primitive savages! The entire idea is repulsive in the extreme.''

''That may be true, but it is vital and necessary. We are committed, by agreements with the other intelligent life-forms too strong to be broken, never to colonize a world which contains an intelligent race below Grade Three civilization. There are nine such worlds now known, and we are seeking to lift their level to Three, and at the same time orient them toward Earth. All, of course, in strict secrecy. One day they shall choose their neighbors, and it must be ourselves.

''The Flish know this even better than we, and are far ahead of us in advance planning. Slowly but surely they are winning over uncommitted worlds, developing primitive societies into capable cultures oriented in *their* direction. They do not own a single warship, have never invaded by force a single world. Yet they are conquering the galaxy, world by world and star by star. And they must be stopped! Or ten thousand years from now Earth will stand alone, and the long twilight of the dignity of the individual will be upon us.''

''I've heard of the Flish, of course. Everyone has. But

aren't they fully human, so much so it's even speculated Earth and Flish unions might be fertile? What is so dreadful about them?''

''Just this, Professor; the word 'Flish' is either singular or plural and the Flish are both. They live a mutual mental symbiosis with each other that our brains, though we are their equal in parapowers, cannot duplicate. Their lives as individuals are secondary to the group life and the group mind, and such is their power the mental matrix they extend will cover an entire planet. Communism sought to accomplish the same object in the physical world, and we rejected the attempt. Individual freedom of choice, within an ordered society, is our heritage. If we wish to preserve it—to prove that individuals voluntarily working together can accomplish as much as a hiveworker—then we must fight the Flish.''

The last small tribal chief finally presented his gifts and reswore his allegiance as the women were stacking heaped platters of food on the great tables his steward had caused to be erected in front of the caves. It was time for the noon meal. Afterward the games, and then the bloody climax of the day, when by tribal law too long standing and powerful for even he, who had changed so much, to oppose, any warrior of any subject tribe could challenge the king to a duel by combat, and assume his crown if he won.

Kala ate sparingly of the plentiful food, it being almost too raw for his digestion, and passed the time talking animatedly with his guests, those same lesser kings who had that morning sworn an obedience enforceable only by might and power.

Grabo appeared at the side of the table and caught his eye. With an almost imperceptible motion of his head he indicated the king's cave, and Kala muttered to his vassals that he would be back and rose and went into the shadowed interior. It was deserted at the moment, his wives working outside. In the house of the king there were no children.

Grabo appeared a moment later, his long form looming

large in the shadows. ''O King, it has come to my ears there may be a challenger after all. There is a young warrior in the tribe of Nil'Abola who has won much fame in combat during the past year, and some of his friends say he is anxious to try the greatest game of all. It is said he is a cunning man, though very young, and they expect him to hold back if there are other challengers, permitting you to tire yourself on them. It would be well to be wary of him.''

''Say you he has won all his fame as a warrior within the past year?''

''It is so, O King. A very young man indeed, but still, one who has not lost a fight. He would be chief of the Nil'Abola now, save that he chose instead to fight you and perhaps gain a kingdom.''

Kala glanced sharply at Grabo, but the shorter man was looking out of the cave into the sunlight. Could Grabo, who had seen him down the greatest of Saa 'Hualla warriors with ease, be losing faith in him? Well, it little mattered what this primitive general thought. Kala was invincible, and knew it, and not all the people gathered outside could take him unless they were very lucky indeed.

Kala's hand rose and clutched the great power crystal at his throat as he turned away and strode toward the door. In the sleeve of his hide jacket were two smaller penetration crystals, and in the belt at his waist were a series of six of the glittering bits of glass, two blue amplifiers, two red clarivoys, and two colorless pulsers. The latter he had never used, for they brought madness instead of death. Most of his many kills had been made with the help of the two distorters in the hilt of his curved sword, though his brain could immobilize a nonpsionic opponent without aid. The distorters, controlled by his mind, powered by the white crystal, and amplified by the blue ones in his belt, could burst a thousand bloodvessels in a man's brain in a few microseconds. He had plunged the curving sword into the heart of many a man dead before he could fall, in order to fool the watchers, but had yet actually to kill a man with it.

Kala Brabant paused in the door a few seconds before stepping out. In earthly measurements that door was over seven feet high, and there was only just adequate room for him to pass erect. Still, he was a little shorter than the average Saa'Hualla, who stood a full seven feet tall.

Memory Two:

He stood naked before the full-length mirror in his hospital room, staring at the dazed disbelief on his own face. The final operation of the series had just been completed, the relatively minor one of killing all hair cells on his body, and he would soon be leaving. This was the first time the doctors had let him see himself.

Knowing verbally what they were doing was no panacea for the shock of seeing the reality of the transformation. They had broken both his femurs and inserted three-inch sections of artificial bone, and later performed the same operation on the humerus bones. The attaching muscles had been extended until they were long threads of hard fiber clinging close to the mutilated bones they served. They had starved him down to tendon and ligament thinness, added pigment to his skin until he was black as coal itself, changed the shape of his eyes, and colored his teeth. Still these were minor changes and could be reversed when his five-year tour of duty was over. No one could give him back the two fingers they had cut off, or the two toes. The fourth metacarpals and fifth metacarpals had been removed completely, and the adjoining carpals and calcaneum bones trimmed to match the slimmer appearance of the Saa'Hualla. Bald-headed, thin-limbed, four-fingered, and four-toed, he had emerged from the last operation a Saa'Hualla in all but name and background. And the name was so similar that he was using his given name here!

His curse was that he was one of the few people on Earth who closely enough resembled the Saa'Hualla to make finishing surgery possible. He had been proud of his Watusi heritage, proud of his height, proud of the color of his skin, which he had considered black until he saw his first movies of the Saa'Hualla. His Hamitic ancestry had given him the lean facial structure, thin lips, and high cheekbones common to these primitives, and the accursed doctors had done the rest. And now his wife waited alone in the house in Usumbura, grandchildren he had never seen swam in the blue waters of Lake Tanganyika, and his little cabin below the snowline stood empty and silent.

He straightened his shoulders and moved forward, aware that Grabo might misinterpret his hesitation as cowardice. Well, he would be right. They could not have picked a worse coward than Kala Brabant, and he had tried to tell them this, but they had laughed at his protestations, those high men of the United Government, laughed and clapped him on the back and sent him in to the psychologists, who confirmed every word he had said. And still it hadn't mattered. With the amplifying crystals and what they taught him of control he had become an impossible opponent to anyone not equally equipped. So far there had been no call for bravery—only butchery—but if it ever came he was sorely afraid it would find him lacking.

He resumed his place at the table and dawdled with his food a little longer, and then the feast was blessedly over and it was time for the games.

As he was leading his kingly guests toward the hides which had been spread on the ground in a choice location Kala sensed another presence at his back and half turned his head. Ahmist was striding along just behind him. Without moving her thin lips, and with her voice pitched just loud enough to reach his sensitive ears, she said, ''The one who will challenge you is named Listra, and I have arranged with Grabo that he will be challenged to a game of whips, and in such a manner that he may not refuse.''

Kala felt a smile twitch at his lips, but did not look back, and after a moment more Ahmist took another direction. He had known that she loved him, in her own primitive way, but this was the first time she had actively interfered in his affairs. He wondered how Temi, his wife of a quarter century, waiting alone in Usumbura, would have reacted under like circumstances.

Kala and his guests made themselves comfortable on the hides and the games began. The usual contests in running, jumping, spear-casting, and swordplay were held, with rich prizes for the winning warriors. Kala found himself repressing a smile when his prize corps of bowmen gave an exhibition of fancy shooting, and his guests stared with amazement and dismay. The bow and arrow was a relatively new weapon and had been given scant attention in the arts of war. It would receive more in the future.

There was a commotion to the left of the seated royalty and voices raised in anger. A moment later two figures strode through the seated spectators and approached the royal seat. At the head, looking very angry, Kala recognized O'Sirinaga, one of his best warriors, a man well over seven feet tall and a little heavier and stronger than most Saa'Hualla. The man trailing him was much smaller, shorter even than Kala, and walked with an insolent, shoulder-swinging swagger very unusual among these long-striding people. He was unusually thick-lipped, and his face was a good deal more full than customary. In fact, to be a member of a race made primarily of skin, bone, and ligament, he was almost fat.

O'Sirinaga knelt before him and presented his case in swift, angry phrases. He had been insulted by this pretended warrior from the Nil'Abola and demanded satisfaction. Since dueling between warriors was forbidden on this day he requested the games to be halted long enough to enable him to avenge the insult by laying a few whipmarks across the back of this young imitation of a fighter.

Listra listened to the insults with almost bored inattention, and when questioned by Kala as to whether or not the charge was true he shrugged his well-fleshed shoulders with careless disdain. ''If you deny him the opportunity to obtain a few more scars, O King, some other fool will take his place. I have not insulted his ancestors, but since he wishes to fight I would not dream of denying him the privilege. Let us have no more talk.''

''Bring the whips,'' said Kala to a court attendant, and a short moment later they were laid in his hands. He checked them carefully, then presented one to each man, and clapped his hands to indicate the fight might begin.

O'Sirinaga backed away until he was just out of range, cracked his bone-tipped whip in the air a few times, then laid it on the ground behind him and advanced on the smaller man, who had not moved since he walked into the cleared area. He was holding his whip carelessly in front of him, his large eyes fixed on his opponent, not in a position to strike the larger man without first throwing the long whip behind him.

O'Sirinaga struck, the long braided thong whipping through the air so fast the tip was invisible, the bone barb aimed for the eye of the smaller man. But it struck empty air. In a motion so fast the eyes were unable to follow him, the smaller man leaped forward, driving ahead like a springing animal, and his whip was suddenly reversed, the cutting body trailing the ground behind him, the heavy butt gripped like a club in his hand. Before O'Sirinaga could draw in his whip for another stroke, before he could take more than a single step backward, the Nil'Abola warrior was upon him, and the heavy butt crashed down on his head. The big warrior went down and out, knocked unconscious in the first thirty seconds of the fight.

The constant background chatter of the spectators, the cries of children and the gossiping of women was suddenly halted, and a vast and oppressive silence hung over the assembled people. It was broken by a sharp crack and the sodden sound of leather biting into flesh. Twice more Listra raised his whip and laid long deep cuts across the back of the unconscious man, and then the small warrior tossed the whip across the bleeding body and walked insolently away.

There were cries of outrage from the people of Saa'Hualla, and several of the men leaped to their feet, ready to continue the duel. Kala motioned them down. It scarcely mattered. In a few more hours the young warrior would be dead anyway.

But it was true he was going to regret killing this young man a great deal less than many others he had dispatched to their ancestors.

The rest of the primitive physical games ran their courses. When the last down warrior was carried off he felt satisfied with the day's work. His conquer-with-force-and-rule-with-law tactics were working well, as they had worked in that great empire built by the swords of Rome so long ago. He had a close-knit group of subchiefs, each of whom willingly subordinated his personal interests to the interests of the people as a whole. And each seemed reasonably content to run his own small area, without aspiring too highly to the post held by Kala.

All too soon the field was clear and the people were beginning to straggle back toward the caves, where the huge cooking pots were filled and waiting. The appointed time had come, and old Nakabawa, the high priest, rose to perform his duty, his wrinkled, ancient face turned toward the lowering sun. He droned the words of the ancient ritual in a hasty and careless voice, obviously unaware that a potential challenger lurked among the Nil'Abola. When he finished and Listra stepped forward, drawing his sword, there was a concerted gasp from the audience and those walking toward the cooking pots hurriedly returned to their seats. The day's entertainment was not over. Kala, The Great King, had still another man to kill.

Listra spoke his challenge, sword in hand, and Kala drew his blade and responded in kind. The formalities for this particular event were simple and soon over. The rules of combat were known to everyone, down to the small children. There remained only the killing to be done, and the event was over for another year.

The Sun is Setting:

Kala walked forward to the edge of the barren ground, a man no longer young, a man to whom the thrill of combat was a stomach-turning experience fit for only the immature. As he reached the last of the grass something flickered by his foot and he glanced downward in time to see a tiny burrowing animal disappear into its hole. The poor creature must have been caught away from its home when the first of the huge crowd had appeared, and had been hiding among the grassblades in fear and trembling ever since.

There was a small stinging sensation on his right ankle, just above his hide shoe, but he ignored the urge to scratch and kept walking. Getting accustomed to insects had been one of his more agonizing adjustments. They were very bad during the warm weather.

For the first time he raised his lowered head and stared his foe in the face. Listra was leaning comfortably on his sword, watching him come, and on the younger man's face was a small smile of satisfaction. He seemed very relaxed and sure of himself for a young and relatively inexperienced warrior going up against the most formidable adversary who had ever appeared among the Saa'Hualla. A very good man, undoubtedly, one whom it would have been worthwhile to save. Too bad it couldn't be.

Nakabawa stepped backward from between the two men and droned a few more words of ritual. At the conclusion he retreated until he was out of the danger area and sat down to watch the fight. The contestants were free to begin at any time.

Kala heaved a mental sigh, raised his sword, saluted the setting sun, and lunged toward his young opponent, the deadly blade glinting in the slanting rays of light, the two jewels in its hilt flashing their own separate color of emerald green. He also activated the crystal at his throat and sent a surge of power into the belt amplifiers, and from there to the distorters in the hilt. The invisible beam leaped ahead of the sword, guided in its general direction by the blade but controlled by the mind of the man behind it. The disruptive force, capable of penetrating a man's skull without visible sign and turning the brain cells into a bloody jelly, crossed the space between man and sword in less than a microsecond . . . and was met and stopped by an impenetrable barrier of counterforce.

Kala was already leaning forward, stretching out his arm in the long stroke that would sink the sword into the heart of the erect corpse. In those agonizing milliseconds before he could stop the thrusting blade, while his eyes saw the sword of Listra coming easily upward to parry the fast thrust, realization came.

It was obvious, so very obvious. How stupid he had been, and how wrong. *How conceited, little Superman, how complacent, tall fool! And are you lost, idiot Earthman?* Kala shifted the blunted power of his first thrust, dropped the distorters, sent the full power of his amplified mind into the cerebral centers of his own brain, and jumped his time-sense to its highest possible range.

He looked out of his own eyes and saw the sword in his extended hand not yet reaching the apex of its thrust, saw the hard small muscles in his bony arm in the slow act of tensing to stop the forward movement, and then abandoned his eyes entirely and used only the parasenses. He needed the use of null-time in order to sort his sudden new understanding of the situation, and analyze his own part in it.

The first and most obvious fact his lazy senses had not revealed was that Listra was no more a Saa'Hualla than himself. And the second and equally obvious, which had been beating unheeded on his sensibilities since he first laid eyes on the swaggering young warrior, was that Listra was not a man. Kala was dueling to the death with a woman!

I hated and regretted the physiological changes necessary to change me into a Saa'Hualla. How much more so must it have hurt a young and undoubtedly pretty girl! Good-bye to

that great artifice of feminine beauty, the hair, kiss farewell
the soft bloody flesh of severed breasts with long strands of
milk gland ducts dangling beneath, cry long over buttocks
stretched and slimmed to thin covers of long hard muscle, bid
good-bye to womanhood! And if he knew the Flish surgeons
they had not stopped there. Underneath those hide trousers
would be plastic male sex organs, undetectable from the real
except by function. The only feminine attribute remaining
was one which even they would have had a hard time con-
cealing, the width of pelvic bones. And this they had hidden
by that braggadacio swagger, the exaggerated movement
which served to draw the observer's attention to the shoulders.

And why go to so much trouble, when a man would have
been far easier to convert? Why the extra work, time, trouble, expense? That, too, was fairly obvious in the person of
Listra. Nowhere on her hands was there an ornament, from
her neck hung no necklace, in her sword was no glitter of
glass. She was a natural psionic, one of those rare individuals
so gifted that crystals could not amplify or aid her. She did
not need the massed power of the hive-mind, could be sent
alone to an alien world, could fight strange humans, pitiful
creatures who had never known the oneness of a billion
selves, and conquer them without the supporting comfort of
an infinity of minds linked tightly to her own. She was also
death, death attired in a long thin suit of flesh, death for Kala
Brabant, puny Earthman.

And that death was already in his blood.

With my great power crystal to amplify my weak mind,
with laminated layers of silicone doted by the impurities
which focus and condense, with those artificial aids of man
which bring me up out of nothingness, I too am a mighty
power of destruction, I too draw upon that power which is
above force and twist it to my will, I too am a god. But I am a
stupid man above all things, and only an idiot like myself
would have ignored that scramble of tiny claws, the small life
scuttling to its newly dug hole, the flealike carrier who

*abandoned the bounding body and leaped, compelled by a
will beyond his understanding, toward a man's ankle, and
landed and clung and bit and chewed until he penetrated the
tough black skin and ejected from their snug home within its
tiny jaws the swarm of alien life which now pulsed and
throbbed and grew within the stinging wound.*

A Trip Inside, while time passes:

Kala used a few milliseconds to refocus his attention on the
optic nerve and glanced at the current time-scene. His sword
was within a few inches of Listra's and there appeared to be
no danger of a counterthrust before he could assume full body
control.

He moved his center of consciousness out of the brain and
into the bloodstream, streaking along the tubular passage-
ways with the swiftness of thought itself. An instant later his
consciousness was at the scene of combat. The battle had
been raging for several minutes and his soldiers were fighting
valiantly but steadily giving ground, the entire affair having
been overlooked by his higher consciousness until this moment. That tiny insect had released a flood of unicellular
protozoa into the capillaries nearest the dermis, flagellate
infusorians which he recognized at once as being closely akin
to the dreaded *Trypanosoma rhodesiense* of his own African
highlands. But these voracious strangers ate, grew, and reproduced with a speed no earthly life could possibly match.
They were disposing of red blood cells at a prodigious rate,
and his hard-fighting guard of granular leucocytes were unable to stop them escaping into the surrounding tissues and
finding unguarded bloodvessels, from where they were
swiftly making their way throughout his body. True, the
macrophages in the liver and lymph nodes would get many of
them, but those which got through and continued their meal
of red cells were going to cause him a serious problem in the
near future.

His autonomic control system had already started routing

more leucocytes to the infected area, but he assumed control of the situation long enough to start every valiant warrior in the nearest pint of blood toward the danger scene. It was going to be necessary virtually to block off this area from circulation, since it was obvious the invaders ate and reproduced four times as fast as a leucocyte could encompass and neutralize a single enemy, and the only way to do it was with their stacked white bodies.

Fast though they moved in response to his direct will it was going to be several full seconds before enough leucocytes arrived to start the blocking action, and he could not wait. Regretfully, he detached a small portion of his consciousness and left it at the scene to direct operations, then returned his primary attention to the mental battle he had started.

A Trip Outside, Outside Time:

He felt the beginning of the wave as his sword touched Listra's, the mighty battering power of a mind perhaps unique in the galaxy, certainly the most powerful of which he had ever heard. She was hurling the full power of her distorting force at his cerebellum; if he couldn't block it the fight was over. If he could, she had a measure of his amplified strength.

Kala marshaled all his forces, disregarding all other crystals and concentrating through the white power source on his neck to build a wall against the force of her thrust. For the few microseconds it lasted it was close, but fortunately for him it took less power to defend than to attack, and after that instant of vain effort she withdrew, leaving only a small portion of her power still beating constantly at his defenses. But even that small thrust was enough that he had to leave another portion of his consciousness, and a little of his strength, to defend against her.

Kala Brabant considered the use of his pulsers, the givers of madness. They amplified and transmitted on specific wavelengths and in frequencies so high as to be almost

beyond count, and they shattered the currents flowing in the
delicate neural network of the brain, those currents which
were human consciousness. He hesitated now, knowing that
it was impossible for a natural psionic, working without
crystals, to transmit in pulses. And somewhere in the lower
levels of his mind a voice screamed. *That's a woman out
there Under that stygian skin hiding behind the smooth
expanse of breastless chest is the heart of a woman Maybe
she has kids at home maybe a husband maybe a lover who
waits and gazes sighing at blue moons on darkened worlds
Maybe Another Time Another Place we could be friends . . .
Lovers . . .*

But then he remembered she was a Flish, in mental com-
munion with every other Flish agent on the planet. He had
been thinking of her in earthly terms, and they did not apply.
An ant among ants is an ant.

Kala activated the pulsers, sent the beam at her brain.

*Forgive me Temi Ahmist lesser wives forgive the killing of
a woman!*

The swords had met, parted with a clash of steel and spark
of fire, and his arm was drawing back to hew the second blow
that would put the mindless woman out of her lack of consciousness of misery *she blocked the pulsers!*

He felt the opposing wall as solid, almost tangible in its
sense of presence, and the pulsating thrusts should have
penetrated and disrupted, sliding through in those almost
infinitely small moments of time when her longer
wavelength was out of tune with his own. But they didn't.
Her defense was so powerful it absorbed each individual
pulsation, letting it penetrate only a short distance before it
was neutralized and destroyed.

The Battle Rages on all Fronts:

She had parried his stroke and was aiming one of her own.
He knew that she, too, was concentrating most of her forces

in the mental battles, since their hyper-time parapowers allowed them to move and countermove a hundred times while even the fastest swordsman struck once, but still, if either forgot the sharp-edged tools of death long enough to let one penetrate, on that instant the battle was lost.

He began to move his sword to the position which would catch her stroke, satisfied himself that it was too late for her to change without giving him an opening that would be fatal, and keeping his guard up against her next probe, moved half his conscious mind to the fleabite on his ankle. A few of the reinforcements he had summoned were beginning to straggle in, but most were still seconds away and the battle was rapidly being lost. More and more of the invading protozoa, long tails lashing, were breaking through the leucocytes and escaping into the central bloodstream, eating red cells by the millions wherever they swam. Unless he finished the other two battles soon and concentrated his forces on these hungry invaders he was a dead man.

Still, he had minutes here. Outside, he had only seconds or less.

He brought nine tenths of his awareness back to the exchange of arrows taking place in the ether and discovered that he was conscious of *Darkness, Vastness, Infinity* . . . *Lost Suns, Darkening Nebula, Dying Light* . . . *A Universe Marcescent, Quiescent, Exanimate* . . . SIZE . . . *Insignificant, Meaningless, Man* . . .

He drew away from the contagion of depression, wondering what had happened to his defense, called upon it, threw it up full strength, and discovered what even the best parapowers on Earth had not been able to tell him. Thought alone, without force or hint of force, was very hard to block. He was still conscious of her depressing projections, still aware of *Darkness* . . . He drew as much consciousness away from the sensation as he could spare, wondering why she was willing to project harmless thought at all, and discovered that his guard had become lax, her sword was sliding over his own and toward his lower abdomen. He twisted his lean hip

aside a fraction of a second too late and received a shallow
gash on one buttock, and received as well the reason she
projected harmless thought.

But two could play at that game. He weakened his defense
a little and put part of his power into a counterattack, hurling
at her hairless head a barrage of disconnected fragments of
poetry, song, and nonsense, enough to throw her non-
Earth-oriented mind off balance if she should try to understand *Hold that! Hold that! Hold that line!* . . . *She walks in
beauty* . . . *Go, Tiger!* . . . *Cloudless climes* . . . *Edina!
Scotia's Darling seat! All Hail!* . . . *When you were a
tadpole and I was a fish* . . . *O a' ye hymeneal powers* . . .
Side by side in the oozing tide . . . *Three-score-fyfteen, a
bloomin' bride, This night with seventy-four is ty'd* . . . *Sae
sed, Sae dune; Ye standers hearde* . . .

He hurled Byron, Burns, and Carroll at her strong barrier
and knew he was getting through when her next stroke
faltered. He rejoiced that he had at last found a weapon which
worked against her and ignored the clamoring darkness in his
mind, sending her music notes, dead love songs, English
poetry, all the dregs of a mind educated on every culture but
his own. And he turned his weakness against her by sending
images of *sex loveliness womanhood babies happiness joy.*

She hit back with *Blackness Lightlessness Nothingness,
Quintessence of* . . . *Vastness Openness* . . . SPACE! . . .
Arbourg, Arbeg, Arb, Ar . . . *Sound Symbol Sign Death!
Death!* . . . *Blood Flow Life Go Deep Woe* . . . But he
absorbed without trying to understand, absorbed and sank
and buried the alien concepts.

The Stroke is given, Death Hovers O'er:

Her next stroke was almost feeble. He brought his brain
back to normal time, for better coordination between body
and mind, and put most of his faculties into the physical duel.
He easily parried the weak thrust, leaped to one side, hit the

edge of her sword with his free hand and forced it downward a few inches while he brought his own swinging toward her from the side. On an impulse he could neither define nor explain Kala changed his mind at the last instant and turned the blade so that the flat side smacked into her hip. He continued his motion to the side and at the same time hurled himself forward, anticipating her backward leap, and brought the sword toward her head, flat side forward, for a knockout blow.

It was impossible for her to parry, but she ducked very swiftly and the flat side whistled over her head. And then he was suddenly breathless, out of position, unable to move backward or stop his stroke in time to parry, and knew he had lingered too long outside. The enemy in his blood had done its work and his muscles were weak from oxygen starvation. He was slowly dying where he stood.

He saw the bright blade flashing toward him, the elongated face smiling now in the moment of death, suddenly all female, not a trace of maleness in its soft shadows and fleshy planes, and he wondered, as the sharp point entered his thin chest and pushed toward his heart, how all the gathered savages could fail to see he was being killed by a woman.

The Final Scene:

Grabo stared at the gush of blood from the punctured heart, running up the sword to the hilt, stared as the body of Kala Brabant hit the ground, dead before he fell, stared at the suddenly stricken look on the face of the intelligent and sensitive young woman who had just committed the deed and thought *Fool of a soft intellectual, idiot of a higher education, great man and benefactor of humanity, how still you lie! If only I could have told you, shared your triumphs, despairs, plans, sorrows! If only this unworthy shadow of your greatness could have died for you . . .*

Nakabawa stepped forward, to do his sad duty and present the new king with the sword of the fallen man, as custom of centuries dictated. He picked it up, gazed at the unbloodied surface with a face as expressionless as the wrinkled parchment it resembled, shifted the blade to his hand and held it hilt-foremost to the victor, who had regained her composure and accepted it in stony silence.

Nakabawa turned, casting an expressionless glance at the sun, still visible as a rim of light above the distant mountaintops, and started to turn away. And Grabo the backup man moved forward, drawing his sword from its scabbard, the blade glinting in the dying light.

"*I challenge the king to combat!*"

The Curtain Closes.

THE MAN WHO CAME EARLY

Poul Anderson

Yes, when a man grows old he has heard so much that is strange there's little more can surprise him. They say the king in Miklagard has a beast of gold before his high seat which stands up and roars. I have it from Eilif Eiriksson, who served in the guard down there, and he is a steady fellow when not drunk. He has also seen the Greek fire used, it burns on water.

So, priest, I am not unwilling to believe what you say about the White Christ. I have been in England and France myself, and seen how the folk prosper. He must be a very powerful god, to ward so many realms . . . and did you say that everyone who is baptized will be given a white robe? I would like to have one. They mildew, of course, in this cursed wet Iceland weather, but a small sacrifice to the house-elves should—No sacrifices? Come now! I'll give up horseflesh if I must, my teeth not being what they were, but every sensible man knows how much trouble the elves make if they're not fed.

. . . Well, let's have another cup and talk about it. How
do you like the beer? It's my own brew, you know. The cups I
got in England, many years back. I was a young man then
. . . time goes, time goes. Afterward I came back and
inherited this my father's steading, and have not left it since.
Well enough to go in viking as a youth, but grown older you
see where the real wealth lies: here, in the land and the cattle.

Stoke up the fires, Hjalti. It's growing cold. Sometimes I
think the winters are colder than when I was a boy. Thorbrand of the Salmondale says so, but he believes the gods are
angry because so many are turning from then. You'll have
trouble winning Thorbrand over, priest. A stubborn man.
Myself I am open-minded and willing to listen at least.

. . . Now, then. There is one point on which I must
correct you. The end of the world is not coming in two years.
This I know.

And if you ask me how I know, that's a very long tale, and
in some ways a terrible one. Glad I am to be old, and safely in
the earth before that great tomorrow comes. It will be an
eldritch time before the frost giants march . . . oh, very
well, before the angel blows his battle horn. One reason I
hearken to your preaching is that I know the White Christ will
conquer Thor. I know Iceland is going to be Christian
erelong, and it seems best to range myself on the winning
side.

No, I've had no visions. This is a happening of five years
ago, which my own household and neighbors can swear to.
They mostly did not believe what the stranger told; I do, more
or less, if only because I don't think a liar could wreak so
much harm. I loved my daughter, priest, and after it was over
I made a good marriage for her. She did not naysay it, but
now she sits out on the nessfarm with her husband and never a
word to me; and I hear he is ill pleased with her silence and
moodiness, and spends his nights with an Irish concubine.
For this I cannot blame him, but it grieves me.

Well, I've drunk enough to tell the whole truth now, and
whether you believe it or not makes no odds to me. Here . . .

you, girls! . . . fill these cups again, for I'll have a dry throat before I finish the telling.

It begins, then, on a day in early summer, five years ago. At that time, my wife Ragnhild and I had only two unwed children still living with us: our youngest son Helgi, of seventeen winters, and our daughter Thorgunna, of eighteen. The girl, being fair, had already had suitors. But she refused them, and I am not a man who would compel his daughter. As for Helgi, he was ever a lively one, good with his hands but a breakneck youth. He is now serving in the guard of King Olaf of Norway. Besides these, of course, we had about ten housefolk—two Irish thralls, two girls to help with the women's work, and half a dozen hired carles. This is not a small steading.

You have not seen how my land lies. About two miles to the west is the bay; the thorps at Reykjavik are about five miles south. The land rises toward the Long Jökull, so that my acres are hilly; but it's good hayland, and there is often driftwood on the beach. I've built a shed down there for it, as well as a boathouse.

There had been a storm the night before, so Helgi and I were going down to look for drift. You, coming from Norway, do not know how precious wood is to us Icelanders, who have only a few scrubby trees and must bring all our timber from abroad. Back there men have often been burned in their houses by their foes, but we count that the worst of deeds, though it's not unknown.

I was on good terms with my neighbors, so we took only handweapons. I, my ax, Helgi, a sword, and the two carles we had with us bore spears. It was a day washed clean by the night's fury, and the sun fell bright on long wet grass. I saw my garth lying rich around its courtyard, sleek cows and sheep, smoke rising from the roofhole of the hall, and knew I'd not done so ill in my lifetime. My son Helgi's hair fluttered in the low west wind as we left the steading behind a ridge and neared the water. Strange how well I remember all which happened that day, somehow it was a sharper day than most.

When we came down to the strand, the sea was beating heavy, white and gray out to the world's edge. A few gulls flew screaming above us, frightened off a cod washed up onto the shore. I saw there was a litter of no few sticks, even a balk of timber . . . from some ship carrying it that broke up during the night, I suppose. That was a useful find, though as a careful man I would later sacrifice to be sure the owner's ghost wouldn't plague me.

We had fallen to and were dragging the balk toward the shed when Helgi cried out. I ran for my ax as I looked the way he pointed. We had no feuds then, but there are always outlaws.

This one seemed harmless, though. Indeed, as he stumbled nearer across the black sand I thought him quite unarmed and wondered what had happened. He was a big man and strangely clad—he wore coat and breeches and shoes like anyone else, but they were of peculiar cut and he bound his trousers with leggings rather than thongs. Nor had I ever seen a helmet like his: it was almost square, and came down to cover his neck, but it had no noseguard; it was held in place by a leather strap, and I found later that it had no cap beneath it. And this you may not believe, but it was made all in one piece, as if it had been cast, with not a single mark of the hammer!

He broke into a staggering run as he neared, and flapped his arms and croaked something. The tongue was none I had ever heard, and I have heard many; it was like dogs barking. I saw that he was clean-shaven and his black hair cropped short, and thought he might be French. Otherwise he was a young man, and good-looking, with blue eyes and regular features. From his skin I judged that he spent much time indoors, yet he had a fine manly build.

"Could he have been shipwrecked?" asked Helgi.

"His clothes are dry and unstained," I said; "nor has he been wandering long, for there's no stubble on his chin. Yet I've heard of no strangers guesting hereabouts."

We lowered our weapons, and he came up to us and stood gasping. I saw that his coat and the shirt behind were fastened with brazen buttons rather than laces, and were of heavy weave. About his neck he had fastened a strip of cloth tucked into his coat. These garments were all in hues of greenish brown. His shoes were of a sort new to me, very well cobbled. Here and there on his coat were other bits of brass, and he had three broken stripes on each sleeve. On the left arm, too, was a black band with white letters, the same letters being on his helmet. Those were not runes, but Roman letters—thus: MP. He wore a broad belt, with a small club-like thing of metal in a sheath at the hip.

"I think he must be a warlock," muttered my carle Sigurd. "Why else all those tokens?"

"They may only be ornament, or to ward against witch-craft," I soothed him. Then, to the stranger. "I hight Ospak Ulfsson of Hillstead. What is your errand?"

He stood with his chest heaving and a wildness in his eyes. He must have run a long way. Then he moaned and sat down and covered his face.

"If he's sick, best we get him to the house," said Helgi. His eyes gleamed—we see so few new faces here.

"No . . . no . . ." The stranger looked up. "Let me rest a moment—"

He spoke the Norse tongue readily enough, though with a thick accent not easy to follow and with many foreign words I did not understand.

The other carle, Grim, hefted his spear. "Have vikings landed?" he asked.

"When did vikings ever come to Iceland?" I snorted. "It's the other way around."

The newcomer shook his head, as if it had been struck. He got shakily to his feet. "What happened?" he said. "What happened to the city?"

"What city?" I asked reasonably.

"Reykjavik!" he groaned. "Where is it?"

"Five miles south, the way you came—unless you mean the bay itself," I said.

"No! There was only a beach, and a few wretched huts,
and—"

"Best not let Hjalmar Broadnose hear you call his thorp
that," I counseled.

"But there was a city!" he cried. Wildness lay in his eyes.
"I was crossing the street, it was a storm, and there was a
crash and then I stood on the beach and the city was gone!"

"He's mad," said Sigurd, backing away. "Be careful
. . . if he starts to foam at the mouth, it means he's going
berserk."

"Who are you?" babbled the stranger. "What are you
doing in those clothes? Why the spears?"

"Somehow," said Helgi, "he does not sound crazed—
only frightened and bewildered. Something evil has happened to him."

"I'm not staying near a man under a curse!" yelped
Sigurd, and started to run away.

"Come back!" I bawled. "Stand where you are or I'll
cleave your louse-bitten head!"

That stopped him, for he had no kin who would avenge
him; but he would not come closer. Meanwhile the stranger
had calmed down to the point where he could at least talk
evenly.

"Was it the *aitchbomb?*" he asked. "Has the war
started?"

He used that word often, *aitchbomb*, so I know it now,
though unsure of what it means. It seems to be a kind of
Greek fire. As for the war, I knew not which war he meant,
and told him so.

"There was a great thunderstorm last night," I added.
"And you say you were out in one too. Perhaps Thor's
hammer knocked you from your place to here."

"But where is here?" he replied. His voice was more
dulled than otherwise, now that the first terror had lifted.

"I told you. This is Hillstead, which is on Iceland."

"But that's where I was!" he mumbled. "Reykjavik . . .
what happened? Did the *aitchbomb* destroy everything while
I was unconscious?"

"Nothing has been destroyed," I said.

"Perhaps he means the fire at Olafsvik last month," said Helgi.

"No, no, no!" He buried his face in his hands. After a while he looked up and said, "See here. I am Sergeant Gerald Roberts of the United States Army base on Iceland. I was in Reykjavik and got struck by lightning or something. Suddenly I was standing on the beach, and got frightened and ran. That's all. Now, can you tell me how to get back to the base?"

Those were more or less his words, priest. Of course, we did not grasp half of it, and made him repeat it several times and explain the words. Even then we did not understand, except that he was from some country called the United States of America, which he said lies beyond Greenland to the west, and that he and some others were on Iceland to help our folk against their enemies. Now this I did not consider a lie—more a mistake or imagining. Grim would have cut him down for thinking us stupid enough to swallow that tale, but I could see that he meant it.

Trying to explain it to us cooled him off. "Look here," he said, in too reasonable a tone for a feverish man, "perhaps we can get at the truth from your side. Has there been no war you know of? Nothing which—Well, look here. My country's men first came to Iceland to guard it against the Germans . . . now it is the Russians, but then it was the Germans. When was that?"

Helgi shook his head. "That never happened that I know of," he said. "Who are these Russians?" He found out later that Gardariki was meant. "Unless," he said, "the old warlocks—"

"He means the Irish monks," I explained. "There were a few living here when the Norsemen came, but they were driven out. That was, hm, somewhat over a hundred years ago. Did your folk ever help the monks?"

"I never heard of them!" he said. His breath sobbed in his throat. "You . . . didn't you Icelanders come from Norway?"

"Yes, about a hundred years ago," I answered patiently.
"After King Harald Fairhair took all the Norse lands and—"

"A hundred years ago!" he whispered. I saw whiteness
creep up under his skin. "What year is this?"

We gaped at him. "Well, it's the second year after the
great salmon catch," I tried.

"What year after Christ, I mean?"

"Oh, so you are a Christian? Hm, let me think. . . . I
talked with a bishop in England once, we were holding him
for ransom, and he said . . . let me see . . . I think he said
this Christ man lived a thousand years ago, or maybe a little
less."

"A thousand—" He shook his head; and then something
went out of him, he stood with glassy eyes—yes, I have seen
glass, I told you I am a traveled man—he stood thus, and
when we led him toward the garth he went like a small child.

You can see for yourself, priest, that my wife Ragnhild is
still good to look upon even in eld, and Thorgunna took after
her. She was—is tall and slim, with a dragon's hoard of
golden hair. She being a maiden then, it flowed loose over
her shoulders. She had great blue eyes and a small heart-
shaped face and very red lips. Withal she was a merry one,
and kind-hearted, so that all men loved her. Sverri Snorrason
went in viking when she refused him and was slain, but no
one had the wit to see that she was unlucky.

We led this Gerald Samsson—when I asked, he said his
father was named Sam—we led him home, leaving Sigurd
and Grim to finish gathering the driftwood. There was some
who would not have a Christian in their house, for fear of
witchcraft, but I am a broad-minded man and Helgi, of
course, was wild for anything new. Our guest stumbled like a
blind man over the fields, but seemed to wake up as we
entered the yard. His eyes went around the buildings that
enclosed it, from the stables and sheds to the smokehouse,
the brewery, the kitchen, the bath house, the god-shrine, and
thence to the hall. And Thorgunna was standing in the doorway.

Their gazes locked for a moment, and I saw her color but thought little of it then. Our shoes rang on the flagging as we crossed the yard and kicked the dogs aside. My two thralls paused in cleaning out the stables to gawp, until I got them back to work with the remark that a man good for naught else was always a pleasing sacrifice. That's one useful practice you Christians lack; I've never made a human offering myself, but you know not how helpful is the fact that I could do so.

We entered the hall and I told the folk Gerald's name and how we had found him. Ragnhild set her maids hopping, to stoke up the fire in the middle trench and fetch beer, while I led Gerald to the high seat and sat down by him. Thorgunna brought us the filled horns.

Gerald tasted the brew and made a face. I felt somewhat offended, for my beer is reckoned good, and asked him if there was aught wrong. He laughed with a harsh note and said no, but he was used to beer that foamed and was not sour.

"And where might they make such?" I wondered testily.

"Everywhere. Iceland, too—no . . ." He stared emptily before him. "Let's say . . . in Vinland."

"Where is Vinland?" I asked.

"The country to the west whence I came. I thought you knew . . . wait a bit." He shook his head. "Maybe I can find out—Have you heard of a man named Leif Eiriksson?"

"No," I said. Since then it has struck me that this was one proof of his tale, for Leif Eriksson is now a well-known chief; and I also take more seriously those tales of land seen by Bjarni Herjulfsson.

"His father, maybe—Eirik the Red?" asked Gerald.

"Oh, yes," I said. "If you mean the Norseman who came hither because of a manslaughter, and left Iceland in turn for the same reason, and has now settled with other folk in Greenland."

"Then this is . . . a little before Leif's voyage," he muttered. "The late tenth century."

"See here," demanded Helgi, "we've been patient with you, but this is no time for riddles. We save those for feasts and drinking bouts. Can you not say plainly whence you come and how you got here?''

Gerald covered his face, shaking.

"Let the man alone, Helgi," said Thorgunna. "Can you not see he's troubled?''

He raised his head and gave her the look of a hurt dog that someone has patted. It was dim in the hall, enough light coming in by the loft-windows so no candles were lit, but not enough to see well by. Nevertheless, I marked a reddening in both their faces.

Gerald drew a long breath and fumbled about; his clothes were made with pockets. He brought out a small parchment box and from it took a little white stick that he put in his mouth. Then he took out another box, and a wooden stick from it which burst into flame when scratched. With the fire he kindled the stick in his mouth, and sucked in the smoke.

We all stared. "Is that a Christian rite?" asked Helgi.

"No . . . not just so.'' A wry, disappointed smile twisted his lips. "I'd have thought you'd be more surprised, even terrified.''

"It's something new,'' I admitted, "but we're a sober folk on Iceland. Those fire-sticks could be useful. Did you come to trade in them?''

"Hardly.'' He sighed. The smoke he breathed in seemed to steady him, which was odd, because the smoke in the hall had made him cough and water at the eyes. "The truth is . . . something you will not believe. I can scarce believe it myself.''

We waited. Thorgunna stood leaning forward, her lips parted.

"That lightning bolt—'' Gerald nodded wearily. "I was out in the storm, and somehow the lightning must have struck me in just the right way, a way that happens only once in many thousands of times. It threw me back into the past.''

Those were his words, priest. I did not understand, and told him so.

"It's hard to see,'' he agreed. "God give that I'm only dreaming. But if this is a dream, I must endure till I wake up

. . . well, look. I was born one thousand, nine hundred and thirty-two years after Christ, in a land to the west which you have not yet found. In the twenty-third year of my life, I was in Iceland as part of my country's army. The lightning struck me, and now . . . now it is less than one thousand years after Christ, and yet I am here—almost a thousand years before I was born, I am here!''

We sat very still. I signed myself with the Hammer and took a long pull from my horn. One of the maids whimpered, and Ragnhild whispered so fiercely I could hear. "Be still. The poor fellow's out of his head. There's no harm in him.''

I agreed with her, though less sure of the last part of it. The gods can speak through a madman, and the gods are not always to be trusted. Or he could turn berserker, or he could be under a heavy curse that would also touch us.

He sat staring before him, and I caught a few fleas and cracked them while I thought about it. Gerald noticed and asked with some horror if we had many fleas here.

"Why, of course,'' said Thorgunna. "Have you none?''

"No.'' He smiled crookedly. "Not yet.''

"Ah,'' she sighed, "you *must* be sick.''

She was a level-headed girl. I saw her thought, and so did Ragnhild and Helgi. Clearly, a man so sick that he had no fleas could be expected to rave. There was still some worry about whether we might catch the illness, but I deemed it unlikely; his trouble was all in the head, perhaps from a blow he had taken. In any case, the matter was come down to earth now, something we could deal with.

As a godi, a chief who holds sacrifices, it behooved me not to turn a stranger out. Moreover, if he could fetch in many of those little fire-kindling sticks, a profitable trade might be built up. So I said Gerald should go to bed. He protested, but we manhandled him into the shut-bed and there he lay tired and was soon asleep. Thorgunna said she would take care of him.

The next day I decided to sacrifice a horse, both because of the timber we had found and to take away any curse there

might be on Gerald. Furthermore, the beast I had picked was
old and useless, and we were short of fresh meat. Gerald had
spent the day lounging moodily around the garth, but when I
came into supper I found him and my daughter laughing.

"You seem to be on the road to health," I said.

"Oh, yes. It . . . could be worse for me." He sat down at
my side as the carles set up the trestle table and the maids
brought in the food. "I was ever much taken with the age of
the vikings, and I have some skills."

"Well," I said, "if you've no home, we can keep you here
for a while."

"I can work," he said eagerly. "I'll be worth my pay."

Now I knew he was from a far land, because what chief
would work on any land but his own, and for hire at that? Yet
he had the easy manner of the high-born, and had clearly
eaten well all his life. I overlooked that he had made no gifts;
after all, he was shipwrecked.

"Maybe you can get passage back to your United States,"
said Helgi. "We could hire a ship. I'm fain to see that
realm."

"No," said Gerald bleakly. "There is no such place. Not
yet."

"So you still hold to that idea you came from tomorrow?"
grunted Sigurd. "Crazy notion. Pass the pork."

"I do," said Gerald. There was a calm on him now. "And
I can prove it."

"I don't see how you speak our tongue, if you come from
so far away," I said. I would not call a man a liar to his face,
unless we were swapping brags in a friendly way, but . . .

"They speak otherwise in my land and time," he replied,
"but it happens that in Iceland the tongue changed little since
the old days, and I learned it when I came there."

"If you are a Christian," I said, "you must bear with us
while we sacrifice tonight."

"I've naught against that," he said. "I fear I never was a
very good Christian. I'd like to watch. How is it done?"

I told him how I would smite the horse with a hammer

before the god, and cut its throat, and sprinkle the blood about the willow twigs; thereafter we would butcher the carcass and feast. He said hastily:

"There's my chance to prove what I am. I have a weapon that will kill the horse with . . . with a flash of lightning."

"What is it?" I wondered. We all crowded around while he took the metal club out of its sheath and showed it to us. I had my doubts; it looked well enough for hitting a man, perhaps, but had no edge, though a wondrously skillful smith had forged it. "Well, we can try," I said.

He showed us what else he had in his pockets. There were some coins of remarkable roundness and sharpness, a small key, a stick with lead in it for writing, a flat purse holding many bits of marked paper; when he told us solemnly that some of this paper was money, even Thorgunna had to laugh. Best of all was a knife whose blade folded into the handle. When he saw me admiring that, he gave it to me, which was well done for a shipwrecked man. I said I would give him clothes and a good ax, as well as lodging for as long as needful.

No, I don't have the knife now. You shall hear why. It's a pity, for it was a good knife, though rather small.

"What were you ere the war-arrow went out in your land?" asked Helgi. "A merchant?"

"No," said Gerald. "I was an . . . *engineer* . . . that is, I was learning how to be one. That's a man who builds things, bridges and roads and tools . . . more than just an artisan. So I think my knowledge could be of great value here." I saw a fever in his eyes. "Yes, give me time and I'll be a king!"

"We have no king in Iceland," I grunted. "Our forefathers came hither to get away from kings. Now we meet at the Things to try suits and pass new laws, but each man must get his own redress as best he can."

"But suppose the man in the wrong won't yield?" he asked.

"Then there can be a fine feud," said Helgi, and went on

to relate with sparkling eyes some of the killings there had
lately been. Gerald looked unhappy and fingered his *gun*.
That is what he called his fire-spitting club.

"Your clothing is rich," said Thorgunna softly. "Your
folk must own broad acres at home."

"No," he said, "our . . . our king gives every man in the
army clothes like these. As for my family, we owned no land,
we rented our home in a building where many other families
also dwelt."

I am not purse-proud, but it seemed to me he had not been
honest, a landless man sharing my high seat like a chief.
Thorgunna covered my huffiness by saying, "You will gain
a farm later."

After dark we went out to the shrine. The carles had built a
fire before it, and as I opened the door the wooden Odin
appeared to leap forth. Gerald muttered to my daughter that it
was a clumsy bit of carving, and since my father had made it I
was still more angry with him. Some folks have no understanding of the fine arts.

Nevertheless, I let him help me lead the horse forth to the
altar stone. I took the blood-bowl in my hands and said he
could now slay the beast if he would. He drew his gun, put
the end behind the horse's ear, and squeezed. There was a
crack, and the beast quivered and dropped with a hole blown
through its skull, wasting the brains—a clumsy weapon. I
caught a whiff of smell, sharp and bitter like that around a
volcano. We all jumped, one of the women screamed, and
Gerald looked proud. I gathered my wits and finished the rest
of the sacrifice as usual. Gerald did not like having blood
sprinkled over him, but then, of course, he was a Christian.
Nor would he take more than a little of the soup and flesh.

Afterward Helgi questioned him about the gun, and he said
it could kill a man at bowshot distance but there was no
witchcraft in it, only use of some tricks we did not know as
yet. Having heard of the Greek fire, I believed him. A *gun*
could be useful in a fight, as indeed I was to learn, but it did
not seem very practical—iron costing what it does, and
months of forging needed for each one.

I worried more about the man himself.

And the next morning I found him telling Thorgunna a great deal of foolishness about his home, buildings as tall as mountains and wagons that flew or went without horses. He said there were eight or nine thousand thousands of folk in his city, a burgh called New Jorvik or the like. I enjoy a good brag as well as the next man, but this was too much and I told him gruffly to come along and help me get in some strayed cattle.

After a day scrambling around the hills I knew well enough that Gerald could scarce tell a cow's prow from her stern. We almost had the strays once, but he ran stupidly across their path and turned them so the work was all to do again. I asked him with strained courtesy if he could milk, shear, wield scythe or flail, and he said no, he had never lived on a farm.

"That's a pity," I remarked, "for everyone on Iceland does, unless he be outlawed."

He flushed at my tone. "I can do enough else," he answered. "Give me some tools and I'll show you metalwork well done."

That brightened me, for truth to tell, none of our household was a very gifted smith. "That's an honorable trade," I said, "and you can be of great help. I have a broken sword and several bent spearheads to be mended, and it were no bad idea to shoe all the horses." His admission that he did know how to put on a shoe was not very dampening to me then.

We had returned home as we talked, and Thorgunna came angrily forward. "That's no way to treat a guest, Father!" she said. "Making him work like a carle, indeed!"

Gerald smiled. "I'll be glad to work," he said. "I need a . . . a stake . . . something to start me afresh. Also, I want to repay a little of your kindness."

That made me mild toward him, and I said it was not his fault they had different customs in the United States. On the morrow he could begin work in the smithy, and I would pay him, yet he would be treated as an equal since craftsmen are valued. This earned him black looks from the housefolk.

That evening he entertained us well with stories of his home; true or not, they made good listening. However, he had no real polish, being unable to compose even two lines of verse. They must be a raw and backward lot in the United States. He said his task in the army had been to keep order among the troops. Helgi said this was unheard of, and he must be a brave man who would offend so many men, but Gerald said folk obeyed him out of fear of the king. When he added that the term of a levy in the United States was two years, and that men could be called to war even in harvest time, I said he was well out of a country with so ruthless and powerful a king.

"No," he answered wistfully, "we are a free folk, who say what we please."

"But it seems you may not do as you please," said Helgi.

"Well," he said, "we may not murder a man just because he offends us."

"Not even if he has slain your own kin?" asked Helgi.

"No. It is for the . . . the king to take vengeance on behalf of us all."

I chuckled. "Your yarns are good," I said, "but there you've hit a snag. How could the king even keep track of all the murders, let alone avenge them? Why, the man wouldn't even have time to beget an heir!"

He could say no more for all the laughter that followed.

The next day Gerald went to the smithy, with a thrall to pump the bellows for him. I was gone that day and night, down to Reykjavik to dicker with Hjalmar Broadnose about some sheep. I invited him back for an overnight stay, and we rode into the garth with his son Ketill, a red-haired sulky youth of twenty winters who had been refused by Thorgunna.

I found Gerald sitting gloomily on a bench in the hall. He wore the clothes I had given him, his own having been spoiled by ash and sparks—what had he awaited, the fool? He was talking in a low voice with my daughter.

"Well," I said as I entered, "how went it?"

My man Grim snickered. "He has ruined two spearheads, but we put out the fire he started ere the whole smithy burned."

"How's this?" I cried. "I thought you said you were a smith."

Gerald stood up, defiantly. "I worked with other tools, and better ones, at home," he replied. "You do it differently here."

It seemed he had built up the fire too hot; his hammer had struck everywhere but the place it should; he had wrecked the temper of the steel through not knowing when to quench it. Smithcraft takes years to learn, of course, but he should have admitted he was not even an apprentice.

"Well," I snapped, "what can you do, then, to earn your bread?" It irked me to be made a fool of before Hjalmar and Ketill, whom I had told about the stranger.

"Odin alone knows," said Grim. "I took him with me to ride after your goats, and never have I seen a worse horseman. I asked him if he could even spin or weave, and he said no."

"That was no question to ask a man!" flared Thorgunna. "He should have slain you for it!"

"He should indeed," laughed Grim. "But let me carry on the tale. I thought we would also repair your bridge over the foss. Well, he can just barely handle a saw, but he nearly took his own foot off with the adze."

"We don't use those tools, I tell you!" Gerald doubled his fists and looked close to tears.

I motioned my guests to sit down. "I don't suppose you can butcher a hog or smoke it either," I said.

"No." I could scarce hear him.

"Well, then, man . . . what *can* you do?"

"I—" He could get no words out.

"You were a warrior," said Thorgunna.

"Yes—that I was!" he said, his face kindling.

"Small use in Iceland when you have no other skills," I grumbled, "but perhaps, if you can get passage to the east-

lands, some king will take you in his guard.'' Myself I
doubted it, for a guardsman needs manners that will do credit
to his master; but I had not the heart to say so.

Ketill Hjalmarsson had plainly not liked the way Thorgunna stood close to Gerald and spoke for him. Now he
sneered and said: ''I might even doubt your skill in fighting.''

''That I have been trained for,'' said Gerald grimly.

''Will you wrestle with me, then?'' asked Ketill.

''Gladly!'' spat Gerald.

Priest, what is a man to think? As I grow older, I find life to
be less and less the good-and-evil, black-and-white thing you
say it is; we are all of us some hue of gray. This useless
fellow, this spiritless lout who could even be asked if he did
women's work and not lift ax, went out in the yard with Ketill
Hjalmarsson and threw him three times running. There was
some trick he had of grabbing the clothes as Ketill charged.
. . . I called a stop when the youth was nearing murderous
rage, praised them both, and filled the beer-horns. But Ketill
brooded sullenly on the bench all evening.

Gerald said something about making a gun like his own. It
would have to be bigger, a *cannon* he called it, and could sink
ships and scatter armies. He would need the help of smiths,
and also various stuffs. Charcoal was easy, and sulfur could
be found in the volcano country, I suppose, but what is this
saltpeter?

Also, being suspicious by now, I questioned him closely
as to how he would make such a thing. Did he know just how
to mix the powder? No, he admitted. What size would the
gun have to be? When he told me—at least as long as a
man—I laughed and asked him how a piece that size could be
cast or bored, even if we could scrape together that much
iron. This he did not know either.

''You haven't the tools to make the tools to make the
tools,'' he said. I don't know what he meant by that. ''God
help me, I can't run through a thousand years of history all by
myself.''

He took out the last of his little smoke-sticks and lit it. Helgi had tried a puff earlier and gotten sick, though he remained a friend of Gerald's. Now my son proposed to take a boat in the morning and go up to Ice Fjord, where I had some money outstanding I wanted to collect. Hjalmar and Ketill said they would come along for the trip, and Thorgunna pleaded so hard that I let her come along too.

"An ill thing," muttered Sigurd. "All men know the land-trolls like not a woman aboard a ship. It's unlucky."

"How did your fathers ever bring women to this island?" I grinned.

Now I wish I had listened to him. He was not a clever man, but he often knew whereof he spoke.

At this time I owned a half share in a ship that went to Norway, bartering wadmal for timber. It was a profitable business until she ran afoul of vikings during the disorders while Olaf Tryggvason was overthrowing Jarl Haakon there. Some men will do anything to make a living—thieves, cutthroats, they ought to be hanged, the worthless robbers pouncing on honest merchantmen. Had they any courage or honesty they would go to Ireland which is full of plunder.

Well, anyhow, the ship was abroad, but we had three boats and took one of these. Besides myself, Thorgunna, and Helgi, Hjalmar and Ketill went along, with Grim and Gerald. I saw how the stranger winced at the cold water as we launched her, and afterward took off his shoes and stockings to let his feet dry. He had been surprised to learn we had a bath house—did he think us savages?—but still, he was dainty as a woman and soon moved upwind of our feet.

There was a favoring breeze, so we raised mast and sail. Gerald tried to help, but of course did not know one line from another and got them tangled. Grim snarled at him and Ketill laughed nastily. But erelong we were underway, and he came and sat by me where I had the steering oar.

He had plainly lain long awake thinking, and now he ventured timidly: "In my land they have . . . will have a rig and rudder which are better than this. With them, you can criss-cross against the wind.''

"Ah, so now our skilled sailor must give us redes!'' sneered Ketill.

"Be still,'' said Thorgunna sharply. "Let Gerald speak.''

He gave her a shy look of thanks, and I was not unwilling to listen. "This is something which could easily be made,'' he said. "I've used such boats myself, and know them well. First, then, the sail should not be square and hung from a yard-arm, but three-cornered, with the third corner lashed to a yard swiveling from the mast. Then, your steering oar is in the wrong place—there should be a rudder in the middle of the stern, guided by a bar.'' He was eager now, tracing the plan with his fingernail on Thorgunna's cloak. "With these two things, and a deep keel—going down to about the height of a man for a boat this size—a ship can move across the path of the wind . . . so. And another sail can be hung between the mast and the prow.''

Well, priest, I must say the idea had its merits, and were it not for fear of bad luck—for everything of his was unlucky—I might even now play with it. But there are clear drawbacks, which I pointed out to him in a reasonable way.

"First and worst,'' I said, "this rudder and deep keel would make it all but impossible to beach the ship or sail up a shallow river. Perhaps they have many harbors where you hail from, but here a craft must take what landings she can find, and must be speedily launched if there should be an attack. Second, this mast of yours would be hard to unstep when the wind dropped and oars came out. Third, the sail is the wrong shape to stretch as an awning when one must sleep at sea.''

"The ship could lie out, and you could go to land in a small boat,'' he said, "Also, you could build cabins aboard for shelter.''

"The cabins would get in the way of the oars,'' I said, "unless the ship were hopelessly broad-beamed or unless the oarsmen sat below a deck like the galley slaves of Miklagard; and free men would not endure rowing in such foulness.''

"Must you have oars?" he asked like a very child.

Laughter barked along the hull. Even the gulls hovering to starboard, where the shore rose darkly, mewed their scorn. "Do they also have tame winds in the place whence you came?" snorted Hjalmar. "What happens if you're becalmed—for days, maybe, with provisions running out—"

"You could build a ship big enough to carry many weeks' provisions," said Gerald.

"If you had the wealth of a king, you could," said Helgi. "And such a king's ship, lying helpless on a flat sea, would be swarmed by every viking from here to Jomsborg. As for leaving the ship out on the water while you make camp, what would you have for shelter, or for defense, if you should be trapped there?"

Gerald slumped. Thorgunna said to him, gently: "Some folk have no heart to try anything new. I think it's a grand idea."

He smiled at her, a weary smile, and plucked up the will to say something about a means for finding north even in cloudy weather—he said there were stones which always pointed north when hung by a string. I told him kindly that I would be most interested if he could find me some of this stone; or if he knew where it was to be had, I could ask a trader to fetch me a piece. But this he did not know, and fell silent. Ketill opened his mouth, but got such an edged look from Thorgunna that he shut it again; his looks declared plainly enough what a liar he thought Gerald to be.

The wind turned contrary after a while, so we lowered the mast and took to the oars. Gerald was strong and willing, though clumsy; however, his hands were so soft that erelong they bled. I offered to let him rest, but he kept doggedly at the work.

Watching him sway back and forth, under the dreary creak of the tholes, the shaft red and wet where he gripped it, I thought much about him. He had done everything wrong which a man could do—thus I imagined then, not knowing the future—and I did not like the way Thorgunna's eyes

strayed to him and rested there. He was no man for my
daughter, landless and penniless and helpless. Yet I could not
keep from liking him. Whether his tale was true or only a
madness, I felt he was honest about it; and surely there was
something strange about the way he had come. I noticed the
cuts on his chin from my razor; he had said he was not used to
our kind of shaving and would grow a beard. He had tried
hard. I wondered how well I would have done, landing alone
in this witch country of his dreams, with a gap of forever
between me and my home.

Perhaps that same misery was what had turned Thorgunna's heart. Women are a kittle breed, priest, and you who
leave them alone belike understand them as well as I who
have slept with half a hundred in six different lands. I do not
think they even understand themselves. Birth and life and
death, those are the great mysteries, which none will ever
fathom, and a woman is closer to them than a man.

—The ill wind stiffened, the sea grew iron gray and
choppy under low leaden clouds, and our headway was poor.
At sunset we could row no more, but must pull in to a small
unpeopled bay and make camp as well as could be on the
strand.

We had brought firewood along, and tinder. Gerald,
though staggering with weariness, made himself useful, his
little sticks kindling the blaze more easily than flint and steel.
Thorgunna set herself to cook our supper. We were not
warded by the boat from a lean, whining wind; her cloak
fluttered like wings and her hair blew wild above the steaming flames. It was the time of light nights, the sky a dim
dusky blue, the sea a wrinkled metal sheet and the land like
something risen out of dream-mists. We men huddled in our
cloaks, holding numbed hands to the fire and saying little.

I felt some cheer was needed, and ordered a cask of my
best and strongest ale broached. An evil Norn made me do
that, but no man escapes his weird. Our bellies seemed all the
emptier now when our noses drank in the sputter of a spitted
joint, and the ale went swiftly to our heads. I remember

declaiming the deathsong of Ragnar Hairybreeks for no other reason than that I felt like declaiming it.

Thorgunna came to stand over Gerald where he slumped. I saw how her fingers brushed his hair, ever so lightly, and Ketill Hjalmarsson did too. "Have they no verses in your land?" she asked.

"Not like yours," he said, looking up. Neither of them looked away again. "We sing rather than chant. I wish I had my *guitar* here—that's a kind of harp."

"Ah, an Irish bard!" said Hjalmar Broadnose.

I remember strangely well how Gerald smiled, and what he said in his own tongue, though I know not the meaning: *"Only on me mither's side, begorra."* I suppose it was magic.

"Well, sing for us," asked Thorgunna.

"Let me think," he said. "I shall have to put it in Norse words for you." After a little while, staring up at her through the windy night, he began a song. It had a tune I liked, thus:

> *From this valley they tell me you're leaving,*
> *I shall miss your bright eyes and sweet smile.*
> *You will carry the sunshine with you,*
> *That has brightened my life all the while. . . .*

I don't remember the rest, except that it was not quite decent.

When he had finished, Hjalmar and Grim went over to see if the meat was done. I saw a glimmering of tears in my daughter's eyes. "That was a lovely thing," she said.

Ketill sat upright. The flames splashed his face with wild, running hues. There was a rawness in his tone: "Yes, we've found what this fellow can do: sit about and make pretty songs for the girls. Keep him for that, Ospak."

Thorgunna whitened, and Helgi clapped hand to sword. I saw how Gerald's face darkened, and his voice was thick: "That was no way to talk. Take it back."

Ketill stood up. "No," he said, "I'll ask no pardon of an idler living off honest yeomen."

He was raging, but had had sense enough to shift the insult from my family to Gerald alone. Otherwise he and his father would have had the four of us to deal with. As it was, Gerald stood up too, fists knotted at his sides, and said, "Will you step away from here and settle this?"

"Gladly!" Ketill turned and walked a few yards down the beach, taking his shield from the boat. Gerald followed. Thorgunna stood with stricken face, then picked up his ax and ran after him.

"Are you going weaponless?" she shrieked.

Gerald stopped, looking dazed. "I don't want that," he mumbled. "Fists—"

Ketill puffed himself up and drew sword. "No doubt you're used to fighting like thralls in your land," he said. "So if you'll crave my pardon, I'll let this matter rest."

Gerald stood with drooped shoulders. He stared at Thorgunna as if he were blind, as if asking her what to do. She handed him the ax.

"So you want me to kill him?" he whispered.

"Yes," she answered.

Then I knew she loved him, for otherwise why should she have cared if he disgraced himself?

Helgi brought him his helmet. He put it on, took the ax, and went forward.

"Ill is this," said Hjalmar to me. "Do you stand by the stranger, Ospak?"

"No," I said. "He's no kin or oath-brother of mine. This is not my quarrel."

"That's good," said Hjalmar. "I'd not like to fight with you, my friend. You were ever a good neighbor."

We went forth together and staked out the ground. Thorgunna told me to lend Gerald my sword, so he could use a shield too, but the man looked oddly at me and said he would rather have the ax. The squared away before each other, he and Ketill, and began fighting.

This was no holmgang, with rules and a fixed order of blows and first blood meaning victory. There was death between those two. Ketill rushed in with the sword whistling in his hand. Gerald sprang back, wielding the ax awkwardly. It bounced off Ketill's shield. The youth grinned and cut at Gerald's legs. I saw blood well forth and stain the ripped breeches.

It was murder from the beginning. Gerald had never used an ax before. Once he even struck with the flat of it. He would have been hewed down at once had Ketill's sword not been blunted on his helmet and had he not been quick on his feet. As it was, he was soon lurching with a dozen wounds.

"Stop the fight!" Thorgunna cried aloud and ran forth. Helgi caught her arms and forced her back, where she struggled and kicked till Grim must help. I saw grief on my son's face but a malicious grin on the carle's.

Gerald turned to look. Ketill's blade came down and slashed his left hand. He dropped the ax. Ketill snarled and readied to finish him. Gerald drew his gun. It made a flash and a barking noise. Ketill fell, twitched for a moment, and was quiet. His lower jaw was blown off and the back of his head gone.

There came a long stillness, where only the wind and the sea had voice.

Then Hjalmar trod forth, his face working but a cold steadiness over him. He knelt and closed his son's eyes, as token that the right of vengeance was his. Rising, he said, "That was an evil deed. For that you shall be outlawed."

"It wasn't magic," said Gerald in a numb tone. "It was like a . . . a bow. I had no choice. I didn't want to fight with more than my fists."

I trod between them and said the Thing must decide this matter, but that I hoped Hjalmar would take weregild for Ketill.

"But I killed him to save my own life!" protested Gerald.

"Nevertheless, weregild must be paid, if Ketill's kin will take it," I explained. "Because of the weapon, I think it will be doubled, but that is for the Thing to judge."

Hjalmar had many other sons, and it was not as if Gerald

belong to a family at odds with his own, so I felt he would
agree. However, he laughed coldly and asked where a man
lacking wealth would find the silver.

Thorgunna stepped up with a wintry calm and said we
would pay it. I opened my mouth, but when I saw her eyes I
nodded. "Yes, we will," I said, "in order to keep the
peace."

"Then you make this quarrel your own?" asked Hjalmar.

"No," I answered. "This man is no blood of my own. But
if I choose to make him a gift of money to use as he wishes,
what of it?"

Hjalmar smiled. There was sorrow crinkled around his
eyes, but he looked on me with old comradeship.

"Erelong this man may be your son-in-law," he said. "I
know the signs, Ospak. Then indeed he will be of your folk.
Even helping him now in his need will range you on his
side."

"And so?" asked Helgi, most softly.

"And so, while I value your friendship, I have sons who
will take the death of their brother ill. They'll want revenge
on Gerald Samsson, if only for the sake of their good names,
and thus our two houses will be sundered and one manslaying
will lead to another. It has happened often enough erenow."
Hjalmar sighed. "I myself wish peace with you, Ospak, but
if you take this killer's side it must be otherwise."

I thought for a moment, thought of Helgi lying with his
skull cloven, of my other sons on their garths drawn to battle
because of a man they had never seen, I thought of having to
wear byrnies every time we went down for driftwood and
never knowing when we went to bed whether we would wake
to find the house ringed in by spearmen.

"Yes," I said, "you are right, Hjalmar. I withdraw my
offer. Let this be a matter between you and him alone."

We gripped hands on it.

Thorgunna gave a small cry and fled into Gerald's arms.
He held her close. "What does this mean?" he asked slowly.

"I cannot keep you any longer," I said, "but belike some

crofter will give you a roof. Hjalmar is a law-abiding man
and will not harm you until the Thing has outlawed you. That
will not be before midsummer. Perhaps you can get passage
out of Iceland ere then.''

"A useless one like me?" he replied bitterly.

Thorgunna whirled free and blazed that I was a coward and
a perjurer and all else evil. I let her have it out, then laid my
hands on her shoulders.

"It is for the house," I said. "The house and the blood,
which are holy. Men die and women weep, but while the
kindred live our names are remembered. Can you ask a score
of men to die for your own hankerings?"

Long did she stand, and to this day I know not what her
answer would have been. It was Gerald who spoke.

"No," he said. "I suppose you have right, Ospak . . .
the right of your time, which is not mine." He took my hand,
and Helgi's. His lips brushed Thorgunna's cheek. Then he
turned and walked out into the darkness.

I heard, later, that he went to earth with Thorvald
Hallsson, the crofter of Humpback Fell, and did not tell his
host what had happened. He must have hoped to go un-
noticed until he could arrange passage to the eastlands somehow. But of course word spread. I remember his brag that in
the United States men had means to talk from one end of the
land to another. So he must have looked down on us, sitting
on our lonely garths, and not known how fast word could get
around. Thorvald's son Hrolf went to Brand Sealskin-boots
to talk about some matter, and of course mentioned the
stranger, and soon all the western island had the tale.

Now if Gerald had known he must give notice of a manslaying at the first garth he found, he would have been safe at
least till the Thing met, for Hjalmar and his sons are sober
men who would not kill a man still under the protection of the
law. But as it was, his keeping the matter secret made him a
murderer and therefore at once an outlaw. Hjalmar and his
kin rode up to Humpback Fell and haled him forth. He shot

his way past them with the *gun* and fled into the hills. They followed him, having several hurts and one more death to avenge. I wonder if Gerald thought the strangeness of his weapon would unnerve us. He may not have known that every man dies when his time comes, neither sooner nor later, so that fear of death is useless.

At the end, when they had him trapped, his weapon gave out on him. Then he took up a dead man's sword and defended himself so valiantly that Ulf Hjalmarsson has limped ever since. It was well done, as even his foes admitted; they are an eldritch race in the United States, but they do not lack manhood.

When he was slain, his body was brought back. For fear of the ghost, he having perhaps been a warlock, it was burned, and all he had owned was laid in the fire with him. That was where I lost the knife he had given me. The barrow stands out on the moor, north of here, and folk shun it though the ghost has not walked. Now, with so much else happening, he is slowly being forgotten.

And that is the tale, priest, as I saw it and heard it. Most men think Gerald Samsson was crazy, but I myself believe he did come from out of time, and that his doom was that no man may ripen a field before harvest season. Yet I look into the future, a thousand years hence, when they fly through the air and ride in horseless wagons and smash whole cities with one blow. I think of this Iceland then, and of the young United States men there to help defend us in a year when the end of the world hovers close. Perhaps some of them, walking about on the heaths, will see that barrow and wonder what ancient warrior lies buried there, and they may even wish they had lived long ago in his time when men were free.

PATRON OF THE ARTS

Fred Saberhagen

After some hours' work, Herron found himself hungry, and willing to pause for food. Looking over what he had just done, he could easily imagine one of the sycophantic critics praising it: A huge canvas, of discordant and brutal line, aflame with a sense of engulfing menace! And for once, Herron thought, the critic might be praising something good.

Turning away from his view of easel and blank bulkhead, Herron found that his captor had moved up silently to stand only an arm's length behind him, for all the world like some human kibitzer.

He had to chuckle. "I suppose you've some idiotic suggestion to make?"

The roughly man-shaped machine said nothing, though it had what might be a speaker mounted on what might be a face. Herron shrugged and walked around it, going forward in search of the galley. This ship had been only a few hours out from Earth on C-plus drive when the berserker machine had run it down and captured it; and Piers Herron, the only passenger, had not yet had time to learn his way around.

It was more than a galley, he saw when he reached it—it was meant to be a place where arty colonial ladies could sit and twitter over tea when they grew weary of staring at pictures. The *Franz Hals* had been built as a traveling museum; then the war of life against berserker machine had grown hot around Sol, and BuCulture had ineptly decided that Earth's art treasures would be safer if shipped away to Tau Epsilon. The *Franz* was ideally suited for such a mission, and for almost nothing else.

Looking further forward from the entrance to the galley, Herron could see that the door to the crew compartment had been battered down, but he did not go to look inside. Not that it would bother him to look, he told himself; he was as indifferent to horror as he was to almost all other human things. The *Franz's* crew of two were in there, or what was left of them after they had tried to fight off the berserker's boarding machines. Doubtless they had preferred death to capture.

Herron preferred nothing. Now he was probably the only living being—apart from a few bacteria—within half a light-year; and he was pleased to discover that his situation did not terrify him, that his long-growing weariness of life was not just a pose to fool himself.

His metal captor followed him into the galley, watching while he set the kitchen devices to work. "Still no suggestions?" Herron asked it. "Maybe you're smarter than I thought."

"I am what men call a berserker," the man-shaped thing said to him suddenly, in a squeaky, ineffectual-sounding voice. "I have captured your ship, and I will talk with you through this small machine you see. Do you grasp my meaning?"

"I understand as well as I need to." He knew his captor was an utterly alien and inanimate thing, built in some segment of time and space beyond human ken, built to fight in some ancient war between races who had never heard of Earth, and who perhaps were long dead themselves. Now the berserker machines' war was against all the life of the galaxy.

Herron had not yet seen the berserker itself but he knew it would be a sphere the size of a planetoid, now a few miles away, or perhaps a few hundred or a thousand miles, from the ship it had captured. Captain Hanus had tried desperately to escape it, diving the *Franz* into a cloud of dark nebula where no ship or machine could move faster than light, and where the advantage in speed lay with the small hull.

The chase had been at speeds up to a thousand miles a second. Forced to remain in normal space, the berserker could not steer its bulk among the meteoroids and gas-wisps as well as the *Franz's* radar-computer system could maneuver the fleeing ship. But the berserker had sent an armed launch of its own to take up the chase, and the weaponless *Franz* had had no chance.

Now, dishes of food, hot and cold, popped out on a galley table, and Herron bowed to the machine. "Will you join me?"

"I need no organic food."

Herron sat down with a sigh. "In the end," he told the machine, "you'll find that lack of humor is as pointless as laughter. Wait and see if I'm not right." He began to eat, and found himself not so hungry as he had thought. Evidently his body still feared death—this surprised him a little.

"Do you normally function in the operation of this ship?" the machine asked.

"No," he said, making himself chew and swallow. "I'm not much good at pushing buttons." A peculiar thing that had happened was nagging at Herron. When capture was only minutes away, Captain Hanus had come dashing aft from the control room, grabbing Herron and dragging him along in a tearing hurry, aft past all the stored art treasures.

"Herron, listen—if we don't make it, see here?" Tooling open a double hatch in the stern compartment, the captain

had pointed into what looked like a short padded tunnel, the
diameter of a large drain pipe. "The regular lifeboat won't
get away, but this might."

"Are you waiting for the Second Officer, Captain, or
leaving us now?"

"There's room for only one, you fool, and I'm not the one
who's going."

"You mean to save me? Captain, I'm touched!" Herron
laughed, easily and naturally. "But don't put yourself out."

"You idiot. Can I trust you?" Hanus lunged into the boat,
his hands flying over its controls. Then he backed out,
glaring like a madman. "Listen. Look here. This button is
the activator; now I've set things up so the boat should come
out in the main shipping lanes and start sending a distress
signal. Chances are she'll be picked up safely then. Now the
controls are set, only this activator button needs to be pushed
down—"

The berserker's launch had attacked at that moment, with a
roar like mountains falling on the hull of the ship. The lights
and the artificial gravity had failed and then come abruptly
back. Piers Herron had been thrown on his side, his wind
knocked out. He had watched while the captain, regaining
his feet and moving like a man in a daze, had closed the hatch
on the mysterious little boat again and staggered forward
toward his control room.

"Why are you here?" the machine asked Herron.

He dropped the forkful of food he had been staring at. He
didn't have to hesitate before answering the question. "Do
you know what BuCulture is? They're the fools in charge of
Art, on Earth. Some of them, like a lot of other fools, think
I'm a great painter. They worship me. When I said I wanted
to leave Earth on this ship, they made it possible.

"I wanted to leave because almost everything that is
worthwhile in any true sense is being removed from earth. A
good part of it is on this ship. What's left behind on the planet
is only a swarm of animals, breeding and dying, fighting—"
He paused.

"Why did you not try to fight or to hide when my machines boarded this ship?"

"Because it would have done no good."

When the berserker's prize crew had forced their way in through an airlock, Herron had been setting up his easel in what was to have been a small exhibition hall, and he had paused to watch the uninvited visitors file past. One of the man-shaped metal things, the one through which he was being questioned now, had stayed to stare at him through its lenses while the others had moved on forward to the crew compartment.

"Herron!" the intercom had shouted. "Try, Herron, please! You know what to do!" Clanging noises followed, and gunshots and curses.

What to do, Captain? Why, yes. The shock of events and the promise of imminent death had stirred up some kind of life in Piers Herron. He looked with interest at the alien captor, the inhuman cold of deep space frosting over its metal here in the warm cabin. Then he turned away from it and began to paint the berserker, trying to catch not the outward shape he had never seen, but what he felt of its inwardness. He felt the emotionless deadliness of its watching lenses boring into his back. The sensation was faintly pleasurable, like cold spring sunshine.

"What is good?" the machine asked Herron, standing over him in the galley while he tried to eat.

He snorted. "You tell me."

It took him literally. "To serve the cause of what men call death is good. To destroy life is good."

Herron pushed his nearly full plate into a disposal slot and stood up. "You're almost right—but even if you were entirely right, why so enthusiastic? What is there praiseworthy about death?" Now his thoughts surprised him as his lack of appetite had.

"I am entirely right," said the machine.

For long seconds Herron stood still as if thinking, though his mind was almost entirely blank. "No," he said finally, and waited for a bolt to strike him.

"In what do you think I am wrong?" it asked.

"I'll show you." He led it out of the galley, his hands sweating and his mouth dry. Why wouldn't the damned thing kill him and have done?

The paintings were racked row on row and tier on tier; there was no room in the ship for more than a few to be displayed in a conventional way. Herron found the drawer he wanted and pulled it open so the portrait inside swung into full view, lights springing on around it to bring out the rich colors beneath the twentieth-century statglass coating.

"This is where you're wrong," Herron said.

The man-shaped thing's scanner studied the portrait for perhaps fifteen seconds. "Explain what you are showing me," it said.

"I bow to you!" Herron did so. "You admit ignorance! You even ask an intelligible question, if one that is somewhat too broad. Explain, you say. First, tell me what *you* see here."

"I see the image of a life-unit, its third spatial dimension of negligible size as compared to the other two. The image is sealed inside a protective jacket transparent to the wavelengths used by the human eye. The life-unit image is, or was, an adult male apparently in good functional condition, garmented in a manner I have not seen before. What I take to be one garment is held before him—"

"You see a man with a glove," Herron cut in, wearying of his bitter game. "That is the title, *Man With A Glove*. Now what do you say it means?"

There was a pause of twenty seconds. "Is it an attempt to praise life, to say that life is good?"

Looking now at Titian's eight-hundred-year-old more-than-masterpiece, Herron for the moment hardly heard what the machine was saying; he was thinking helplessly and hopelessly of his own most recent work.

"Now you will tell me what it means," said the machine without emphasis.

Herron walked away without answering, leaving the drawer open.

The berserker's mouthpiece walked at his side. "Tell me what it means or you will be punished."

"If you can pause to think, so can I." But Herron's stomach had knotted up at the threat of punishment, seeming to feel that pain mattered even more than death. Herron had great contempt for his stomach.

His feet took him back to his easel. Looking at the discordant and brutal line that a few minutes ago had pleased him, he now found it as disgusting as everything else he had tried to do in the past year.

The berserker asked: "What have you made here?"

Herron picked up a brush he had forgotten to clean, and wiped at it irritably.

"It is my attempt to get at your essence, to capture you with paint and canvas as you have seen those humans captured." He waved at the storage racks. "My attempt has failed, as most do."

There was another pause, which Herron did not try to time.

"An attempt to praise me?"

Herron broke the spoiled brush and threw it down. "Call it what you like."

This time the pause was short, and at its end the machine did not speak, but turned away and walked in the direction of the airlock. Some of its fellows clanked past to join it. From the direction of the airlock there began to come sounds like those of heavy metal being worked and hammered. The interrogation seemed to be over for the time being.

Herron's thoughts wanted to be anywhere but on his work or on his fate, and they returned to what Hanus had shown him, or tried to show him. Not a regular lifeboat, but she might get away, the captain had said. All it needs now is to press the button.

Herron started walking, smiling faintly as he realized that if this berserker was as careless as it seemed, he might possibly escape it.

Escape to what? He couldn't paint anymore, if he ever

could. All that really mattered to him now was here, and on other ships leaving Earth.

Back at the storage rack, Herron swung the *Man With A Glove* out so its case came free from the rack and became a handy cart. He wheeled the portrait aft. There might yet be one worthwhile thing he could do with his life.

The picture was massive in its statglass shielding, but he thought he could fit it into the boat.

As an itch might nag a dying man, the question of what the captain had been intending with the boat nagged Herron. Hanus hadn't seemed worried about Herron's fate, but instead had spoken of trusting Herron. . . .

Nearing the stern, unwatched by the machines, Herron passed a strapped-down stack of crated statuary, and heard a noise, a rapid feeble pounding.

It took several minutes to find and open the proper case. When he lifted the lid with its padded lining, a girl wearing a coverall sat up, her hair all wild as if standing in terror.

"Are they gone?" She had bitten at her fingers and nails until they were bleeding. When he didn't answer at once, she repeated her question again and again, in a rising whine.

"The machines are still here," he said at last.

Literally shaking in her fear, she climbed out of the case. "Where's Gus? Have they taken him?"

"Gus?" But he thought he was beginning to understand.

"Gus Hanus, the captain. He and I are—he was trying to save me, to get me away from Earth."

"I'm quite sure he's dead," said Herron. "He fought the machines."

Her bleeding fingers clutched at her lower face. "They'll kill us, too. Or worse! What can we do?"

"Don't mourn your lover so deeply," he said. But the girl seemed not to hear him; her wild eyes looked this way and that, expecting the machines. "Help me with this picture," he told her calmly. "Hold the door there for me."

She obeyed as if half hypnotized, not questioning what he was doing.

"Gus said there'd be a boat," she muttered to herself. "If he had to smuggle me down to Tau Epsilon he was going to use a special little boat—" She broke off, staring at Herron, afraid that he had heard her and would steal her boat. As indeed he was going to do.

When he had the painting in the stern compartment, he stopped. He looked long at the *Man With A Glove*, but in the end all he could seem to see was that the fingertips of the ungloved hand were not bitten bloody.

Herron took the shivering girl by the arm and pushed her into the tiny boat. She huddled there in her dazed terror; she was not good-looking. He wondered what Hanus had seen in her.

"There's room for only one," he said, and she shrank and bared her teeth as if afraid he meant to drag her out again. "After I close the hatch, push that button there, the activator. Understand?"

That she understood at once. He dogged the double hatch shut, and waited. Only about three seconds passed before there came a soft scraping sound that he supposed meant that the boat had gone.

Nearby was a tiny observation blister, and Herron put his head into it and watched the stars turn beyond the dark blizzard of the nebula. After a while he saw the berserker through the blizzard, turning with the stars, black and rounded and bigger than any mountain. It gave no sign that it had detected the tiny boat slipping away. Its launch was very near the *Franz* but none of the commensal machines were in sight.

Looking the *Man With A Glove* in the eye, Herron pushed him forward again, to a spot near his easel. The discordant lines of Herron's own work were now worse than disgusting, but Herron made himself work on them.

He hadn't time to do much before the man-shaped machine came walking back to him; the uproar of metalworking had ceased. Wiping his brush carefully, Herron put it down, and nodded at his berserker-portrait. "When you destroy all the rest, save this painting. Carry it back to those who built you, they deserve it.''

The machine-voice squeaked back at him: "Why do you think I will destroy paintings? Even if they are attempts to praise life, they are dead things in themselves, and so in themselves they are good.''

Herron was suddenly too frightened and weary to speak. Looking dully into the machine's lenses, he saw there tiny flickerings, keeping time with his own pulse and breathing like the indications of a lie-detector.

''Your mind is divided,'' said the machine. ''But with its much greater part you have praised me. I have repaired your ship, and set its course. I now release you, so other life-units can learn from you to praise what is good.''

Herron could only stand there staring straight ahead of him, while a trampling of metal feet went past, and there was a final scraping on the hull.

After some time he realized he was alive and free.

At first he shrank from the dead men, but after once touching them he soon got them into a freezer. He had no particular reason to think either of them Believers, but he found a book and read Islamic, Ethical, Christian, and Jewish burial services.

Then he found an undamaged handgun on the deck, and went prowling the ship, taken suddenly with the wild notion that a machine might have stayed behind. Pausing only to tear down the abomination from his easel, he went on to the very stern. There he had to stop, facing the direction in which he supposed the berserker now was.

''Damn you, I can change!'' he shouted at the stern bulkhead. His voice broke. ''I can paint again. I'll show you . . . I can change. I am alive.''

TIME PIECE

Joe W. Haldeman

They say you've got a fifty-fifty chance every time you go out. That makes it one chance in eight that you'll live to see your third furlough; the one I'm on now.

Somehow the odds don't keep people from trying to join. Even though not one in a thousand gets through the years of training and examination, there's no shortage of cannon fodder. And that's what we are. The most expensive, best trained cannon fodder in the history of warfare. Human history, anyhow; who can speak for the enemy?

I don't even call them snails anymore. And the thought of them doesn't trigger that instant flash of revulsion, hate, kill-fever—the psyconditioning wore off years ago, and they didn't renew it. They've stopped doing it to new recruits; no percentage in berserkers. I was a wild one the first couple of trips, though.

Strange world I've come back to. Gets stranger every time, of course. Even sitting here in a bogus twenty-first-century bar, where everyone speaks Basic and there's real wood on the walls and peaceful holograms instead of plugins, and music made by men . . .

But it leaks through. I don't pay by card, let alone by coin. The credit register monitors my alpha waves and communicates with the bank every time I order a drink. And, in case I've become addicted to more modern vices, there's a feelie matrix (modified to look like an old-fashioned visiphone booth) where I can have my brain stimulated directly. Thanks but no, thanks—always get this picture of dirty hands inside my skull, kneading, rubbing. Like when you get too close to the enemy and they open a hole in your mind and you go spinning down and down and never reach the bottom till you die. I almost got too close last time.

We were on a three-man reconnaissance patrol, bound for a hellish little planet circling the red giant Antares. Now red giant stars don't form planets in the natural course of things, so we had ignored Antares; we control most of the space around it, so why waste time in idle exploration? But the enemy had detected this little planet—God knows how—and about ten years after they landed there, we monitored their presence (gravity waves from the ships' braking) and my team was assigned the reconnaissance. Three men against many, many of the enemy—but we weren't supposed to fight if we could help it; just take a look around, record what we saw, and leave a message beacon on our way back, about a light-year out from Antares. Theoretically, the troopship following us by a month will pick up the information and use it to put together a battle plan. Actually, three more recon patrols precede the troop ship at one-week intervals; insurance against the high probability that any one patrol will be caught and destroyed. As the first team in, we have a pretty good chance of success, but the ones to follow would be in trouble if we didn't get back out. We'd be past caring, of course: the enemy doesn't take prisoners.

We came out of lightspeed close to Antares, so the bulk of the star would mask our braking disturbance, and inserted the ship in a hyperbolic orbit that would get us to the planet—Anomaly, we were calling it—in about twenty hours.

"Anomaly must be tropical over most of its surface." Fred Sykes, nominally the navigator, was talking to himself and at the two of us while he analyzed the observational data rolling out of the ship's computer. "No axial tilt to speak of. Looks like they've got a big outpost near the equator, lots of electromagnetic noise there. Figures . . . the goddamn snails like it hot. We requisitioned hot-weather gear, didn't we, Pancho?"

Pancho, that's me. "No, Fred, all we got's parkas and snowshoes." My full name is Francisco Jesus Mario Juan-José Hugo de Naranja, and I outrank Fred, so he should at least call me Francisco. But I've never pressed the point. Pancho it is. Fred looked up from his figure and the rookie, Paul Spiegel, almost dropped the pistol he was cleaning.

"But why . . . " Paul was staring. "We knew the planet was probably Earthlike if the enemy wanted it. Are we gonna have to go tromping around in spacesuits?"

"No, Paul, our esteemed leader and supply clerk is being sarcastic again." He turned back to his computer. "Explain, Pancho."

"No, that's all right." Paul reddened a bit and also went back to his job. "I remember you complaining about having to take the standard survival issue."

"Well, I was right then and I'm doubly right now. We've *got* parkas back there, and snowshoes, and a complete terranorm environment recirculator, and everything else we could possibly need to walk around in comfort on every planet known to man—*Dios!* That issue masses over a metric ton, more than a bevawatt laser. A laser we could use, but crampons and pith helmets and elephant guns . . . "

Paul looked up again. "Elephant guns?" He was kind of a freak about weapons.

"Yeah."

"That's a gun that shoots elephants?"

"Right. An elephant gun shoots elephants."

"Is that some new kind of ammunition?"

I sighed, I really sighed. You'd think I'd get used to this after twelve years—or four hundred—in the service. "No, kid, elephants were animals, big gray wrinkled animals with horns. You used an elephant gun to shoot *at* them.

"When I was a kid in Rioplex, back in the twenty-first, we had an elephant in the zoo; used to go down in the summer and feed him synthos through the bars. He had a long nose like a fat tail, he ate with that."

"What planet were they from?'

It went on like that for a while. It was Paul's first trip out, and he hadn't yet gotten used to the idea that most of his compatriots were genuine antiques, preserved by the natural process of relativity. At lightspeed you age imperceptibly, while the universe's calendar adds a year for every light-year you travel. Seems like cheating. But it catches up with you eventually.

We hit the atmosphere of Anomaly at an oblique angle and came in passive, like a natural meteor, until we got to a position where we were reasonably safe from detection (just above the south polar sea), then blasted briefly to slow down and splash. Then we spent a few hours in slow flight at sea level, sneaking up on their settlement.

It appeared to be the only enemy camp on the whole planet, which was typical. Strange for a spacefaring, aggressive race to be so incurious about planetary environments, but they always seemed to settle in one place and simply expand radially. And they do expand; their reproduction rate makes rabbits look sick. Starting from one colony, they can fill a world in two hundred years. After that, they control their population by infantiphage and stellar migration.

We landed about a hundred kilometers from the edge of their colony, around local midnight. While we were outside setting up the espionage monitors, the ship camouflaged itself to match the surrounding jungle optically, thermally, magnetically, etc.—we were careful not to get too far from the ship; it can be a bit hard to find even when you know where to look.

The monitors were to be fed information from flea-sized flying robots, each with a special purpose, and it would take several hours for them to wing into the city. We posted a one-man guard, one-hour shifts; the other two inside the ship until the monitors started clicking. But they never started.

Being senior, I took the first watch. A spooky hour, the jungle making dark little noises all around, but nothing happened. Then Fred stood the next hour, while I put on the deepsleep helmet. Figured I'd need the sleep—once data started coming in, I'd have to be alert for about forty hours. We could all sleep for a week once we got off Anomaly and hit lightspeed.

Getting yanked out of deepsleep is like an ice-water douche to the brain. The black nothing dissolved and there was Fred a foot away from my face, yelling my name over and over. As soon as he saw my eyes open, he ran for the open lock, priming his laser on the way (definitely against regulations, could hole the hull that way; I started to say something but couldn't form the words). Anyhow, what were we doing in free fall? And how could Fred run across the deck like that while we were in free fall?

Then my mind started coming back into focus and I could analyze the sinking, spinning sensation—not free-fall vertigo at all, but what we used to call snail-fever. The enemy was very near. Crackling combat sounds drifted in from outdoors.

I sat up on the cot and tried to sort everything out and get going. After long seconds my arms and legs got the idea, I struggled up and staggered to the weapons cabinet. Both the lasers were gone, and the only heavy weapon left was a grenade launcher. I lifted it from the rack and made my way to the lock.

Had I been thinking straight, I would've just sealed the lock and blasted—the presence in my mind was so strong that I should have known there were too many of the enemy, too close, for us to stand and fight. But no one can think while their brain is being curdled that way. I fought the urge to just

let go and fall down that hole in my mind, and slid along the
wall to the airlock. By the time I got there my teeth were
chattering uncontrollably and my face was wet with tears.

Looking out, I saw a smoldering gray lump that must have
been Paul, and Fred screaming like a madman, fanning the
laser on full over a 180-degree arc. There couldn't have been
anything alive in front of him; the jungle was a lurid curtain
of fire, but a bolt lanced in from behind and Fred dissolved in
a pink spray of blood and flesh.

I saw them then, moving fast for snails, shambling in over
thick brush toward the ship. Through the swirling fog in my
brain I realized that all they could see was the light pouring
through the open lock, and me silhouetted in front. I tried to
raise the launcher but couldn't—there were too many, less
than a hundred meters away, and the inky whirlpool in my
mind just got bigger and bigger and I could feel myself
slipping into it.

The first bolt missed me; hit the ship and it shuddered,
ringing like a huge cathedral bell. The second one didn't
miss, taking off my left hand just above the wrist, roasting
what remained of my left arm. In a spastic lurch I jerked up
the launcher and yanked the trigger, holding it down while
dozens of microton grenades popped out and danced their
blinding way up to and across the enemy's ragged line.
Dazzled blind, I stepped back and stumbled over the med-
robot, which had smelled blood and was eager to do its duty.
On top of the machine was a switch that some clown had
labeled EMERGENCY EXIT; I slapped it, and as the lock clanged
shut the atomic engines muttered—growled—screaming into
life and a ten-gravity hand slid me across the blood-slick deck
and slammed me back against the rear-wall padding. I felt
ribs crack and something in my neck snapped. As the world
squeezed away, I knew I was a dead man but it was better to
die in a bed of pain than to just fall and fall. . . .

I woke up to the less-than-tender ministrations of the
med-robot, who had bound the stump of my left arm and was
wrapping my chest in plastiseal. My body from forehead to

shins ached from radiation burns, earned by facing the grenades' bursts, and the nonexistent hand seemed to writhe in
painful, impossible contortions. But numbing anesthetic
kept the pain at a bearable distance, and there was an empty
space in my mind where the snail-fever had been, and the
gentle hum told me we were at lightspeed; things could have
been one flaming hell of a lot worse. Fred and Paul were gone
but that just moved them from the small roster of live friends
to the long list of dead ones.

A warning light on the control panel was blinking strobo-
scopically. We were getting near the hole—excuse me, "rel-
ativistic discontinuity"—and the computer had to know
where I wanted to go. You go in one hole at lightspeed and
you'll come out of some other hole; *which* hole you pop out
of depends on your angle of approach. Since they say that
only about one per cent of the holes are charted, if you go in at
any old angle you're liable to wind up in Podunk, on the other
side of the galaxy, with no ticket back.

I just let the light blink, though. If it doesn't get any
response from the crew, the ship programs itself automatically to go to Heaven, the hospital world, which was fine
with me. They cure what ails you and then set you loose with
a compatible soldier of the opposite sex, for an extended
vacation on that beautiful world. Someone once told me that
there were over a hundred worlds named Hell, but there's
only one Heaven. Clean and pretty from the tropical seas to
the Northern pine forests. Like Earth used to be, before we
strangled it.

A bell had been ringing all the time I'd been conscious, but
I didn't notice it until it stopped. That meant that the information capsule had been jettisoned, for what little it was worth.
Planetary information, very few espionage-type data; just a
tape of the battle. Be rough for the next recon patrol.

I fell asleep knowing I'd wake up on the other side of the
hole, bound for Heaven.

I pick up my drink—an old-fashioned old-fashioned—
with my new left hand and the glass should feel right, slick

but slightly tacky with the cold-water sweat, fine ridges
molded into the plastic. But there's something missing, hard
to describe, a memory stored in your fingertips that a new
growth has to learn all over again. It's a strange feeling, but
in a way seems to fit with this crazy Earth, where I sit in my
alcoholic time capsule and, if I squint with my mind, can
almost believe I'm back in the twenty-first.

I pay for the nostalgia—wood and natural food, human
bartender and waitress who are also linguists, it all comes
dear—but I can afford it, if anyone can. Compound interest,
of course. Over four centuries have passed on Earth since I
first went off to the war, and my salary's been deposited at
the Chase Manhattan Credit Union ever since. They're glad
to do it; when I die, they keep the interest and the principal
reverts to the government. Heirs? I had one illegitimate son
(conceived on my first furlough) and when I last saw his
gravestone, the words on it had washed away to barely
legible dimples.

But I'm still a young man (at lightspeed you age imperceptibly while the universe winds down outside) and the time
you spend going from hole to hole is almost incalculably
small. I've spent most of the past half millenium at lightspeed, the rest of the time usually convalescing from battle.
My records show that I've logged a trifle under one year in
actual combat. Not bad for 438 years' pay. Since I first lifted
off I've aged twelve years by my biological calendar. Complicated, isn't it—next month I'll be thirty, 456 years after
my date of birth.

But one week before my birthday I've got to decide
whether to try my luck for the fourth trip out or just collect my
money and retire. No choice, really. I've got to go back.

It's something they didn't emphasize when I joined up,
back in 2088—maybe it wasn't so obvious back then, the war
only decades old—but they can't hide it nowadays. Too
many old vets wandering around, like animated museum
pieces.

I could cash in my chips and live in luxury for another

hundred years. But it would get mighty lonely. Can't talk to anybody on Earth but other vets and people who've gone to the trouble to learn Basic.

Everyone in space speaks Basic. You can't lift off until you've become fluent. Otherwise, how could you take orders from a fellow who should have been food for worms centuries before your grandfather was born? Especially since language melted down into one Language.

I'm tone-deaf. Can't speak or understand Language, where one word has ten or fifteen different meanings, depending on pitch. To me it sounds like puppydogs yapping. Same words over and over; no sense.

Of course, when I first lived on Earth there were all sorts of languages, not just one Language. I spoke Spanish (still do when I can find some other old codger who remembers) and learned English—that was before they called it Basic—in military training. Learned it damn well, too. If I weren't tone-deaf I'd crack Language and maybe I'd settle down.

Maybe not. The people are so strange, and it's not just the Language. Mindplugs and homosex and voluntary suicide. Walking around with nothing on but paint and powder. We had Fullerdomes when I was a kid; but you didn't *have* to live under one. Now if you take a walk out in the country for a breath of fresh air, you'll drop over dead before you can exhale.

My mind keeps dragging me back to Heaven. I'd retire in a minute if I could spend my remaining century there. Can't, of course; only soldiers allowed in space. And the only way a soldier gets to Heaven is the hard way.

I've been there three times; once more and I'll set a record. That's motivation of a sort, I suppose. Also, in the unlikely event that I should live another five years, I'll get a commission, and a desk job if I live through my term as a field officer. Doesn't happen too often—but there aren't too many desk jobs that people can handle better than cyborgs.

That's another alternative. If my body gets too garbaged for regeneration, and they can save enough of my brain, I could spend the rest of eternity hooked up to a computer, as a cyborg. The only one I've ever talked to seemed to be happy.

I once had an African partner named N'gai. He taught me how to play O'wari, a game older than Monopoly or even chess. We sat in this very bar (or the identical one that was in its place two hundred years ago) and he tried to impress on my non-Zen-oriented mind just how significant this game was to men in our position.

You start out with forty-eight smooth little pebbles, four in each one of the twelve depressions that make up the game board. Then you take turns, scooping the pebbles out of one hole and distributing them one at a time in holes to the left. If you dropped your last pebble in a hole where your opponent had only one or two, why, you got to take those pebbles off the board. Sounds exciting, doesn't it?

But N'gai sat there in a cloud of bhang-smoke and mumbled about the game and how it was just like the big game we were playing, and everytime he took a pebble off the board, he called it by name. And some of the names I didn't know, but a lot of them were on my long list.

And he talked about how we were like the pieces in this simple game; how some went off the board after the first couple of moves, and some hopped from place to place all through the game and came out unscathed, and some just sat in one place all the time until they got zapped from out of nowhere. . . .

After a while I started hitting the bhang myself, and we abandoned the metaphor in a spirit of mutual intoxication.

And I've been thinking about that night for six years, or two hundred, and I think that N'gai—his soul find Buddha—was wrong. The game isn't all that complex.

Because in O'wari, either person can win.

The snails populate ten planets for every one we destroy.

Solitaire, anyone?

RICOCHET ON MIZA

Gordon R. Dickson

If you decide to go hunting the Warlin, which is an intelligent creature, it is almost necessary to know three things. First, that the female, who has the more valuable hide, will invariably be holed up somewhere while her mate is out hunting. Second, that the male is telepathically sensitive and can be dominated by the human mind. And third, that the Warlin is very good at playing dead.

Bill Raush, of course, knew all of these things, although he had never gone Warlin-hunting before. In various of Carlin City's dives and dens—for Warlin-hunting is strictly illegal—he had listened to other hunters and made due note of the mistakes which might trip up a beginner. He had heard, and believed, that the Warlin loves its mate and will go to any lengths and risks to protect her. He had memorized the countless dodges used by the creature. And he had sworn to himself that, above all, his Warlin would not trick him into losing his mental control by playing dead.

Now he crouched in a jumble of rocks, under the starlit heavens of Miza, and waited. Below him he could see what was the equivalent of a waterhole in an Earthly jungle, although the fluid in it would have poisoned a human in short order. Many creatures had already come down to drink in spite of the fact that the long Mizan night was only some three hours gone and there were another sixteen yet to go before the corrugated red sun poked above the long horizon. Unfortunately none of these had been a Warlin.

Bill shifted uncomfortably upon his rocks and cursed Miza's unfriendly atmosphere that forced him to encase himself in a rubber suit and air helmet. The process of waiting was tedious. He wanted a smoke and his back itched. And nothing could be done about these things.

So obsessed was he, in fact, with his own discomforts that he almost missed the Warlin when it did come. One second, to Bill's eyes, and it was not there. The next, and it was in plain sight, shuffling down the trail to the waterhole and looking like nothing so much as a gigantic anteater with thick, woolly fur.

Bill grinned to himself. It was a big male, half again as heavy as Bill himself, although he weighed close to a hundred kilograms. The animal was physically the match for a half a dozen men. Unfortunately, as has been mentioned, it was susceptible to mental domination. It gave Bill a dark sense of pleasure to think of that mountain of muscle and bone completely at his mercy, obeying whatever commands his whim dictated.

He crouched silently, watching the Warlin approach the side of the pool, forcing his mind to lie blank and quiet like the surface of a pool of quicksand. The Warlin must not sense his presence until it was within the minimum two meters of distance. Otherwise it might be able to fight off his commands and escape.

The Warlin stopped on the edge of the pool, raised its trunk and waved it questioningly about in the darkness. Then, satisfied that the coast was clear—indeed, outside of Bill or some other human, there was little on Miza that could have harmed it—lowered its head to the waterhole.

Bill leaped!

Seizing the boulder in front of him to gain leverage, he suddenly sent his body sailing over the edge of rocks to land feet first beside the Warlin. The shouted intention of his mind had gone before him to warn the male, who whirled. But the space beside the waterhole was too limited and the Warlin found himself within the two-meter minimum distance at which Bill's mind could control him.

For a second he stood there, thick trunk upraised, half reared on his massive hind legs in the instinctive stance of battle. Then his trunk wavered and drooped, his front legs fell to the earth, and he dropped at Bill's feet like a huge, shaggy dog that cringes before its master.

"Down!" Bill was shouting in his air helmet, the better to focus his mind. "Down! Down! Down!"

He could feel the mind of the Warlin recoil beneath the savage pound of his thought, and the sudden realization came to him that, emotionally, the creature could not stand it. If he kept on this way, in his eagerness to dominate, he might easily kill this male and then he would have a battle-scarred and dirt-snaggled hide to take back instead of the smooth, silky female one which would be worth a hundred times its value.

So, exultant but wary, he relaxed and the mind of the Warlin came up under the released pressure, came up like a cork through water.

"I've got you now," said Bill, tightly. "You can't get away. You can't get away. Now, take me to your den, to your den. Do you hear me? Take me to your den."

The mind of the Warlin shifted in sudden panic. For a second Bill caught a flashing impression of a dark and guarded place where there was the warmth of another body and love and peace. Then the impression was gone and only stubbornness remained.

"Take me," Bill was chanting inside the air helmet. "Take me. Take me to your den. Take me there. Take me there. . . ."

The Warlin stood still but Bill could feel its mental opposition weakening beneath the steady forcing of his human mind. Warned by the reaction he had felt when he captured the creature, he did not insist too strongly. A dead male Warlin is of little use to a hunter. Over and over again, lightly but with firm insistence, his thought beat at the male.

"Take me there. Take me there."

Suddenly the Warlin's opposition collapsed. He stood still, trembling, and Bill felt a wave of utter despair. Then the shaggy bulk turned and ambled away from the waterhole.

Bill walked close beside, one gloved hand grasping the thick fur. The night was dark, but the Warlin went surely ahead. There was no doubt that he led the way directly to his den, for his mind was opened like a box to the eyes of the human's mind and there was no deceit there.

Now that they moved in temporary cooperation, Bill was able to sense more of what the Warlin was thinking. There was a hidden level below the surface where the creature might possibly be planning something against him, for it was not Bill's ability that bridged the gap between the two minds, but the Warlin's, an ability the creature could no more negate than he could stop breathing.

The Warlin was not frightened. As one of the largest creatures on Miza, fear was very nearly foreign to it. Nor, at the moment, did it hate Bill. At the moment its mind was filled with a sense of desolation, and an odd emotion that Bill did not at first understand. When he finally did, he chuckled in his air helmet.

The male had realized that Bill was out to kill his mate. He had realized that he could do nothing to stop the Earthman and was crying deep in his alien soul—the crying of a race that had never known tears—tearing at himself with bitter reproach and pain for being the helpless instrument of his mate's imminent capture and death.

Bill chuckled and asked:

"Damn near human, aren't you?"

A flood of black hate welled up suddenly from the other mind. Partially, the Warlin had understood him—well enough, at least, so that the comparison to a human had been comprehended. So savage, so cruel, so devastating was the reaction that it stopped Bill in his tracks and he went cold with fear. It was only sheer paralysis that enabled him to keep his grasp on the Warlin's fur.

"None of that, now!" he growled, recovering. "None of your tricks." And using his mind like a bludgeon he beat the male back into temporary submission.

They went on through the night. Bill had resigned himself to a long walk. Warlins, he knew, hunted and drank far from their dens for the maximum amount of safety. How far they had already gone he had no way of telling but it was reasonable to assume that it was quite a way. In fact it might take all night. It was even reasonable that they might walk like this for days and days.

Bill jerked himself savagely alert.

"Oh, you would, would you!" he snarled, and his fury unleashed itself to the tune of curses upon the Warlin until he felt the male's mind tremble and totter beneath his onslaught. Finally, fearful of either driving the creature insane or of killing it, he let up.

The male shivered beneath his hand and abruptly collapsed. Bill stiffened, ready to apply fresh force, then realized that the creature was exhausted by the beating it had taken and close to unconsciousness.

Bill sat down beside it, keeping his hold on the fur.

"Rest then," he said. "But don't try anything. You aren't getting away from me."

Released, the Warlin's mind dropped like a stone into the mists of sleep.

They sat for an hour by the human's watch while the Warlin slept and Bill fidgeted, jumpy and nervous under the effects of the benzedrine tablet he had taken to ensure his staying alert. At the end of that time he tugged at the handful of fur.

"Come on," he growled. "Get up."

The Warlin's mind was reluctant to abandon the comfortable oblivion of sleep. It came back to awareness slowly, with the somewhat confused impression that it was back in its den and that its mate was nipping playfully at its woolly hide. Then memory returned with a rush and its mind surged in an abrupt, insane effort to throw off the human's control.

Bill beat it down. He was becoming more expert with practice and managed to return it to submission without wearing it out so much. He pulled the male to his feet.

"Let's go," he said.

Despairingly, the Warlin led off into the darkness once more. Now, it seemed, it had truly given up, for its mind was openly, nakedly sorrowing over memories of past happinesses. As if not caring whether the human mind could read it or not, the male's memory evoked pictures of meetings with his mate, of huntings, of homecomings to the den, of past victorious fights with others of his kind and of the tumbling of his young in play between his mighty front paws.

"Cut it out," said Bill derisively, "or I'll bust right out into tears."

But the Warlin ignored him. It thought on until gradually its mind began to dull and slow down like a whirlpool coming to rest. Gradually its thoughts became less and less perceptible, more and more unintelligible and feeble, like the fragmentary mumblings of a dying man. Until they ceased altogether and the Warlin stumbled, fell suddenly, and lay still.

Bill stared down at it.

"Damn it!" he swore. "Did he kick off on me after all?"

He probed the creature's mind with his own. It gave, soggily, without resistance, but with no reaction. He kicked the inert body but there was no response. Chagrined, he was reaching for his skinning knife when remembrance of what he had heard came back to him.

"Oh?" he said with a lopsided grin. "Playing dead, huh?"

His grip tightened on the Warlin's wool, his lips skinned back over his teeth, and he began to talk.

"Get up," he said, and continued to repeat the command monotonously. "Get up. Get up. Get up. Get up."

For a long minute there was no response. Then, with what was the equivalent of a sigh, life returned to the Warlin's mind and the creature stood up.

"To your den," commanded Bill. "Go!"

They went on.

From the number of tricks the male had been playing recently, Bill reasoned, his den must not now be far off. The man exulted in the thought without bothering to hide his exultation from the creature at his side. But the Warlin no longer seemed capable of resentment, or indeed of any feeling. He plodded on mechanically, and it was not far until Bill was able to sense from his mind that the den entrance would shortly be within sight.

They were passing through a particularly rough section of country. All Miza is tumbled with rock for reasons the geologists have not been able to agree on. But this was one of those unusually bad parts where you progressed by scrambling from boulder to boulder and it was necessary to watch closely for fear of slipping into the cracks.

In spite of this the Warlin led the human on, as though in a dream. He did not even look where his massive feet must go but strode surely forward while Bill scrambled beside him. The man cursed the terrain, then reflected that it would naturally be in such inaccessible sections that the Warlins would make their dens. Cheered up by this thought, he continued without complaint. Still, it was precarious going and only his firm grip on the Warlin's wool kept him from falling more than once.

Now, with the den entrance only a short distance away, Bill began to make his plans. The female would not be too much trouble but it was smart to have everything worked out in advance. He had a smoke bomb which would drive her out into the open. It would be a simple matter to stand by the side of the hole until she came out, coughing and blinded, and then shoot her.

Credits. Bill licked his lips, tasting in anticipation the smoky Earth-bottled Scotch, the rich Venusian cigars that would be his portion once he had sold the skins. He would go back to one of the inner systems—he thought of going all the way back to Mars but that would be too expensive—and allow himself a three-month spree before coming back for another hunt. This was the kind of work for a strong man—a short term of discomfort for high rewards. Eventually he would retire when the fascination of the hunt ceased to attract him. But by that time he would be rich.

Danger!

The warning rang suddenly in his mind as he felt a sudden blaze of defiance from the Warlin beside him. His mind, caught off balance, scrambled furiously to reassert itself but as it did so he felt the creature at his side lurch away, leaving only a handful of fur in his grasp.

The Warlin leaped—away from Bill—and head foremost into the pit between two huge boulders. Bill tottered on the edge.

In a second, however, he had righted himself and a furious wave of anger flooded through him.

"You stupid fool!" he yelled at the motionless bulk of the Warlin, crouched on the floor of the pit. "Don't you know you can't get away?"

There was no response from the Warlin mind and for a second Bill thought that it had found some hole down there and escaped, that it was just his imagination seeing it in the shadows of the pit. Then he realized that the pit was all of four meters deep—too far for mental contact to be maintained unless the Warlin wanted it and the Warlin quite evidently didn't.

Bill cursed again, and peered down. Yes, the creature was there, all right. Probably waiting poised to jump him the minute he came down. Probably hoping he wouldn't dare to come down.

Bill grinned sourly. If the Warlin thought it was going to get away that easily it was mistaken. It was a dangerous thing to jump down there and risk getting his skull beaten in before he could seize control of the Warlin's mind. But what were a few risks when a fortune was at stake?

Cautiously he lowered his legs over the edge of the boulder, hung for a moment, and then let go. There was a rush of wind past his ears and he half slid, half fell to the bottom of the pit. Above his head the night sky was now a small, irregular, star-studded patch of lighter black than that which surrounded him.

He landed on his feet, gun in hand, his mind flashing out, ready to overcome the mind that faced him. But there was no response and the dark bulk of the Warlin did not come leaping at him.

Bill laughed out loud.

"Chickened out, huh?" he said. Contemptuously, he ignored the creature and looked up at the little patch of sky above him. What he saw made him swear suddenly.

In his haste to recapture the Warlin he had neglected to think of how he would get back out of the pit. Now he looked up at four meters of precipitous stone walls which were absolutely unclimbable.

For a second fear crept into his mind. Then a sudden thought sent it scurrying with its tail between its legs. He looked over at the Warlin, who still had not moved.

"You outsmarted yourself that time, sonny boy," he said. "You thought I'd be trapped down here with you. But I'm not. I'll just get you to use some of that beef and toss me up to where I can grab a hold of the edge of that boulder."

He reached out to the creature's mind. It gave, soggily, without resistance, but with no reaction. Bill sneered.

"You poor stupe," he said, "lying doggo again. Don't you remember you pulled that trick on me once before and it wouldn't work?"

Striding over to the Warlin, he kicked it viciously.

"Get up," he said, without heat, but with a bitter relentlessness. "Get up. Get up. Get up. Get up."

As has been said, the male Warlin will go to almost any lengths to protect its mate. Also, it is very good at playing dead.

Only, as Bill Raush eventually discovered, this one wasn't playing.

THE SCAVENGERS

James White

The ship was in a hurry. It flashed through the frigid upper reaches of the atmosphere like a great silvery dart. A dart whose needle prow and stabilizers glowed with the furious, angry red of air resistance, and whose flight path was drawn across the dark blueprint of the sky by a thin, perfectly straight white line of vapor condensation. Far below it the planetary surface slid by with deceptive slowness.

In the ship's tiny control room a loud-speaker clicked, hummed, and said, "Flagship to S-Five-Three—" The eyes of the three-man crew flickered briefly towards it, then switched back to their respective instrument panels. A tightness about their mouths and an involuntary jerk of their heads towards the sound betrayed the strain they were under. They relaxed, a little, when it merely stated, "This is the commander. Your ETA over target is nine minutes, fifteen seconds from—now. What have you in mind, captain?"

Spence, the ship's captain, reached out quickly—too

quickly—and fumbled the switch to the "Transmit" position. But his voice was quite steady as he replied.

"The usual thing, sir. Direct, high-level approach to
within fifty miles, dive, level off at five thousand, spray
them, then decelerate and land. Normal procedure from there
on in. It should take about two hours."

There was silence for a long moment, broken only by the
faint, background hum from the speaker. The miles fled by, a
large number of miles. Then the commander spoke again.

"That seems satisfactory, but we are taking too long over
this, captain. Hurry it up, please. Have you looked at a clock
recently? Off."

Beside the captain, the engineer and servomech officer,
Bennett, moved restively. He looked straight at Spence, then
at the now quiescent speaker, and inclined his closecropped,
grayish-blonde head at two dials on the wide panel before
him. The dials showed the hull temperature and the output of
the cooling units. They each bore a conspicuous red mark,
and their indicator needles seemed to be glued to these
marks. Bennett gave a short, interrogatory grunt. It was his
way of saying that if they hurried it up any faster they'd
probably vaporize themselves, but it was for the captain to
decide one way or the other. Bennett was a man of few
words.

Spence shook his head curtly. There would be no increase
in speed. Then he turned abruptly to the third member of the
crew, Harrison, the gunnery officer.

Harrison was muttering angrily, "What did he mean by
that last crack? Have we looked at anything else *but* clocks
recently? Just who does he think he is—?"

"That's enough," said Spence sharply, as a light flashed
urgently on his panel, "I haven't time to listen to you. We
dive in three seconds. Brace yourselves." His hands flickered about, checking, then settled on the twin grips of a
lever that grew solidly from the floor between his feet. He
began to edge it slowly forward.

The great ship curved smoothly downwards into a steep

dive. Straining against the straps, the crew hung forward in
their seats, their faces pop-eyed, dark red masks of mounting
blood pressure. The dive lasted eight seconds, then the pull-
out flattened them back into the padding. That was much
easier to take, thought Spence. The seats were designed to
swing to compensate for any sudden change in direction, but
on a planetary operation like this they had, of course, to be in
a fixed up-down position.

But it wasn't the ill-treatment his body was being subjected to that was worrying him. No, that was the least of his
troubles. It was Harrison.

Harrison was going soft.

Captain Spence couldn't altogether blame him. Harrison
had been under a killing pressure, both physical and mental
these last few days, but this was certainly not the time to
develop a hypersensitive conscience.

Harrison had joined the ship only a week ago, just two
days before the current emergency, as a replacement for
Walters who was still recuperating with a leg graft after that
mess on Torcin Eight. He was a new boy, just out of Basic
Training, and like all the freshly-qualified entrants to the
Force, he'd worn the dedicated, near-exalted look that sometimes took months to wear off. The great motto of the Force,
implying the ultimate in selfless service to humanity, was
practically written in letters of light across his forehead as
well as being traced in gold thread on cap and shoulder
badges. It said, in a language long dead before the motto was
even coined, ''There is nothing more important than a human
life,'' and Harrison was intensely eager to start saving lives.
He was going to save lives if he had to kill himself doing it.
Spence had felt the same way at the start, but that idea had
been soon knocked out of him. There was no future in it;
besides, it was wasteful of highly-trained technicians.

All this did not mean that Harrison had been naive or
unrealistic about things. He'd known that the Force must, by
its very nature, be called on to do an occasional little job that

was just a shade off-color—for the greatest common good, of course. It was a pity, thought Spence, that his first job had been a five-star alarm, a very big one and the grimmest the captain had ever encountered in his twelve years of service. It was one way of finding out whether a man had what it took, but it was a rather drastic way.

Now Harrison was sitting hunched forward in his seat, staring at the screen which showed the surface ahead and below. From five thousand feet the ground was a dull, reddish-brown carpet unrolling monotonously below the furiously speeding ship. Occasionally there would be a stain on the carpet—an ugly black stain five miles across that had been the site of one of the Crawler cities. The ship had been directly responsible for quite a few of those. There was nothing like a medium-sized H-bomb exploded well under-ground to really *reduce* a city. The shock-wave left the resultant rubble looking like fine gravel. The placing and detonation of the bombs was the gunnery officer's depart-ment, so he was sitting there beginning to hate himself.

Good thing, thought Spence, that the Crawler civilization was concentrated in large, widely-separate cities. It was less wasteful of bombs and made the cleanup job a lot simpler. There were no farms or villages to deal with, but there were groups of survivors, who had somehow managed to evade the first sweep, holing up in various places. It was towards one of these groups, one of the few remaining on the planet, that Spence's ship was splitting the air.

A low range of mountains crept gradually over the hori-zon. The aliens were behind them. The ship had chosen this course so that the mountains would shield it from radar until the last possible moment, always supposing the Crawlers *had* radar. There was no sense in taking chances. Spence's voice was harsh as he said sharply, "Five seconds to target. Gunnery Officer stand by!"

And, thought the captain, if he flunks it now that he's gone this far, I shall certainly kick him to a bleeding pulp.

The aliens had not got radar, but from bits and pieces of mining machinery they had somehow fashioned a multi-barreled antiaircraft weapon. It didn't make the slightest difference, they hadn't a chance. A gray blur streaked across the sky. For a split second they were bathed in a wide cone of invisible radiation. The effect was instantaneous. The group of Crawlers around the gun jerked convulsively as their voluntary muscles reacted to the radiation, then they rolled flabbily to the ground.

And when the lagging thunder of the ship's passage across the sky beat down on the Crawler mining settlement, the ship itself was a shrinking dot on the horizon, and nothing on the ground was moving. It was as easy as that.

The ship decelerated furiously to subsonic and circled back. It hung motionless over the settlement. From the projector under its nose the radiation again flared out; this time it was maintained for fully two seconds, then the ship settled slowly towards the ground.

That second dose was unnecessary, Spence thought, as the surface expanded below them. It was merely another added precaution. There was not a race known in the galaxy immune to that radiation. It really was the nearest thing to the Perfect Weapon ever discovered; it did not harm the body at all, but struck directly at the brain in such a way that the mind affected was rendered completely unconscious, all the voluntary muscles were paralyzed, and the metabolic rate was slowed to almost nothing. Its beauty lay in the fact that it was reversible. If you potted a friend by mistake, he could be revived. On the other hand, if it was an enemy, you could come back at leisure and burn him, or blow holes in him—he was helpless. The easy way was just to leave him and he'd starve to death.

The trend of the captain's thoughts was becoming too morbid. He pulled himself out of it to find the ship about to touch down. He started doing rapid, complicated things with the controls before him. When he looked up they were down and he hadn't felt it.

"Locks One to Six open. Holds A and B ready for load-ing," he announced crisply, "Go to it, Mr. Bennett." He sat back tiredly. For the time being he had nothing to do.

Up to this moment the servomech officer had been little more than a passenger, but now he went to work. A stream of robots, functionally specialized, began to walk, roll, or fly out of the opened locks. Some were merely camera pickups, others consisted of a cluster of extensibly grabs of various sizes mounted on caterpillar treads, the rest were simply remote-controlled wheelbarrows. The grabs spread out, each trailed by an attentive trio of barrows. When they came to a limp alien, it would be lifted, dumped into a barrow, which would whisk it back to the ship where other types of special machinery would stow it carefully away where it would be sure to keep. Meanwhile, the grab had moved on to the next alien, and the first barrow, now empty, hurried back to wait for a refill.

At various heights above all this activity hovered the camera pickups, constantly sending pictures and pertinent data back to the semicircle of screens around Bennett's control panel. And Bennett, by glancing at a screen and fiddling with a few knobs, would send several tons of highly-complex machinery where it would do the most good. The robots were almost fully automatic, needing only the minimum of guidance, but keeping his eyes on over fifty of the things was a nerve-racking job.

The captain, watching with approval, thought how effi-cient it was, and how quick. Bennett was good at this. Suddenly he started forward and snapped a reproof.

"Careful there. Take it easy. What do you think you're doing? They're not sacks of flour, you know. Watch it."

One of the grabs in dropping a Crawler into a barrow had misjudged. Its flaccid burden had fouled a sharp-edged pro-jection on its way in. A great, three-foot gash appeared in its side and the treacly goo it used for blood welled out, making a dirty, ever-widening stain on the beautiful, iridescent fur.

"Sorry," Bennett muttered abstractedly, "I was in a hurry." Which was a pretty good excuse, all things considered.

The captain kept quiet. A tricky piece of work had come up and he didn't want to distract the other.

It was one of the Crawler gunners. It had been manning the gun when the projector had caught it, and it was practically tied to its post. The Crawler method of operating their machinery was either to wrap themselves around it or to insinuate themselves right into it, or preferably both, so as to use to the best advantage the five pairs of hands and feet which made them so closely resemble the centipede. This one was so mixed up with the gun that Bennett had brought up another grab to help untangle it. But it wasn't until another specialized servo arrived from the ship and partially dismantled the gun that they were able to draw the alien free. While it was being carted back to the ship the two grabs wheeled about and went hunting again.

But game was becoming scarce. On a large screen in front of the servomech officer a dim gray picture of the mining settlement as seen from the air appeared. Here and there on the picture a hot orange spark burned. Each spark showed the position of one of the Crawlers. It didn't matter if they were out in the open or coiled in some dark corner of their low, dome-shaped shelters. They weren't quite dead, so their brainwaves were detectable and their positions showed plain.

It was another one of the advantages of using the projector—one was able to find the victims without any trouble. When the ship had landed, more than fifty glowing sparks had dotted the screen. Now there were fourteen. Bennett brought thirty of the robots back to the ship, where they automatically sorted and stored themselves away. The job was almost finished and they were only cluttering up the place.

Less than an hour of his estimated two had passed, Spence thought. We've made good time. We should do it comfortably. He began to relax.

Suddenly the wall speaker burst into life again. The harsh
voice of the fleet commander pervaded the room.

"Flagship to Scavenger Five-Three. How is it going,
captain? Report, please."

Spence took a deep breath, then recited briskly, "Everything going according to plan, sir. We found a sort of mining
settlement—the first I've seen here that hadn't a city built
over it—with between fifty and sixty Crawler survivors.
They had a gun of sorts rigged up but didn't get a chance to
use it. We're loading in the last few stiffs now."

He stopped. Bennett was waving at him urgently, trying to
attract his attention. Harrison, white-faced, was bending
over the other's shoulder and staring at the servo panel as if
he didn't believe it. Spence nodded curtly and said into the
mike, "Excuse me, sir. Something has come up." He turned
impatiently to the others.

"Well?"

Bennett didn't say anything. He didn't need to. His finger
indicated five lights burning on the screen before him. A
graduated dial showed the depth of the objects which caused
the lights to be two hundred feet. Another gave the information that the objects were in fairly rapid motion. He let his
hands fall to his lap and looked gloomy.

There were five aliens on the loose.

This was too much to take. Of all the blind, senseless, bad
luck. Spence was too angry to be frightened—yet. He'd
expected to be clear of this stinking planet in another ten
minutes. Now *this*.

The five Crawlers must have been down the mine both
times the ship had passed over. The projector lacked the
power to penetrate two hundred feet of solid, ore-bearing
rock, so the radiation hadn't touched them. They were down
there now, five alien snakes with beautiful, shimmering
pelts, each of whose bodies measured two feet thick and eight
feet wide. Their feelings towards the beings in the ship were
probably indescribable, but they were certainly hostile.
Spence's voice shook a little as he related this latest de-

velopment to the waiting fleet commander. When he finished he was sweating.

It was all right while I was busy, he thought, there was no time to be afraid—not really afraid. But this sitting around while the clock ticked off the seconds—He felt almost like asking if the commander had gone to sleep or something, it was taking him so long to answer. He tapped his foot rapidly, nervously against his seat support. When the voice came again he leaned forward anxiously.

"That is bad, captain. Very bad," it said gravely, "but whatever means you use to deal with it, remember that speed must be the first consideration. I will remain in this orbit for exactly fifty-three minutes. You have until then to clear things up." The commander stopped, but he hadn't quite finished. When he went on his tone was just a little warmer and more human.

He said, "I'd better tell you that, if circumstances warrant it, I'll have to leave before the expiration of the time-limit I've just given you. Also, we can't send you any help as you are now the only ship remaining on the planet. When you're through we can all go home. You are last man in, captain. I'll leave you to it. Luck. Off."

Spence had often wondered how it felt to be last man in from one of these clean-up jobs. Now that he knew, he wished that he didn't. But he had only fifty minutes to get something done. He'd have to think, hard.

But he couldn't think of anything but the fact that far below him crawled the last living things native to this planet, and that his ship was all alone on its whole wide, poisonous surface. He almost felt like blasting off right now, but he had a duty. None of his thoughts showed on his face, they never did unless he wanted them to. His voice was even as he turned to the other two and asked, "Has anyone an idea?"

Harrison shook his head.

Bennett said, "I've already activated a couple of diggers. They're on the way to the mine shaft now. They will be able

to widen the tunnel enough to allow the grabs to get to the
aliens. There aren't any lifts to worry about—the main shaft
is in the form of a descending spiral with branching tunnels
leading off it at different levels. It's very confusing—''

He stopped talking to snap down a few switches on his
panel. On a screen before him a monster of flashing and
rotating blades mounted on caterpillar treads nosed over into
a small hole in the ground. Soil flew skyward. When it had
sunk from sight the hole was much bigger. Other machines
hurried in and came out filled with loose earth, then went
back for more. Two grabs stood aloofly by, waiting for them
to finish.

Bennett went on, a little apologetically, ''This isn't such a
hot idea, it may take too much time. Unless, of course, we
can get them trapped in a dead end, and I don't think they'll
let us do that. But I can't think of any other way of doing the
job. How about you?''

Spence shook his head, then asked, ''How many entrances
are there?'' He wanted the overall picture before he started
making suggestions. Time was too short.

''Just the one,'' Bennett answered, and waited.

There was probably a very simple answer to this problem,
Spence thought, but the terrible urgency of finding that
answer so clouded his brain that he couldn't think at all.
Performance data of the armaments carried by the ship,
together with all the odd items of the Crawler physiology that
they'd been able to pick up, tumbled through his mind like
a pack of spilled cards, but nothing would make sense.
Nothing fitted. And always there was the clock ticking— like
a mouse scratching and nibbling away at their dwindling
store of time.

He put his finger and thumb to the bridge of his nose and
shut his eyes tightly. Steady now, he thought intensely, this
is getting you nowhere. Take it easy. *Think.*

Question. How to catch five aliens hiding underground.
Answer. Send robots to dig them out. That was logical, and
the servomech officer had done the right thing. But any of the

robots capable of taking the aliens were too big to traverse the tunnels. If, however, the tunnels were widened, and if the aliens stayed put until the grabs arrived, and if they were unarmed or incapable of damaging the grabs sent after them, then that solution might work out. Spence shook his head impatiently. There were too many "ifs".

Harrison had been figuring out something on his scratchpad. He straightened up, looked at Bennett, then bent over his calculations again and began to check them carefully.

Finally he said, "This isn't going to work. The farther down we dig the slower we'll go. The way I figure it we won't even be able to reach the level the aliens are occupying before it's too late." He jerked his head upwards slightly. The movement took in their great flagship hovering impatiently out in space as well as the chronometer on the wall. There was something about the way he said the words, Spence thought. As if he'd been thinking about an entirely different matter.

Spence wondered if the other was getting an idea, and kept silent. Dragging it out of him half-formed wouldn't do any good, he'd spit it out himself if it amounted to anything. Meanwhile, how to get at five aliens two hundred-odd feet underground in a tunnel four feet wide?

All over the ship automatic machinery made small furtive, clicking noises, but the clock above his head sounded the loudest.

Harrison broke the silence. Strain made his first few words an almost unintelligible croak.

"We're going about this the wrong way. Robots are no good for this job. We—We—" He hesitated, then blurted, "We'll have to go after them ourselves."

Nobody said anything for a moment. Spence's mind raced ahead. It might work at that. It just might.

The tunnels were wide enough. They had suits, guns, means of detecting their prey, and this way they might even have enough time. But the crew, or any part of it, wasn't supposed to leave the ship during operations, especially if the ship was a Scavenger Fleet cruiser.

The crew on these boats was small, specialized, and interdependent to a high degree. They carried a thousand-odd cubic yards of near-human machinery which was designed to cope with anything that could conceivably turn up in the way of emergencies, so that the crew need never leave the ship at all.

But this particular situation was without precedent, Spence thought angrily, he'd just have to break the rules. He had a brilliant record up to now. He hoped desperately that nothing would go wrong.

But it was the job that mattered, not the individuals taking part in it. The problem now, he thought, was which member or members of the crew was the most dispensable.

Bennett spoke up, low-voiced and unhurried. He mentioned just how irregular was Harrison's suggestion, but seconded it. He also pointed out that when the robots could not be made to function efficiently, the job of servomech officer automatically became superflous, or words to that effect. He ended by confessing to a yen to stretch his legs outside the ship.

Bennett's volunteering for the job beat Harrison's by split seconds. The gunnery officer also gave reasons, good ones—the same ones in fact.

Spence sighed. He'd expected this. He said quietly, "We all volunteer, naturally, but someone will have to stay in the ship. Now," he argued, "two people will stand a better chance out there than one, but we've got to increase that chance as much as possible. The way I see it, Mr. Harrison and myself will attend to the Crawlers, while you, Mr. Bennett, will support us whenever possible with your servos. That way we will all be gainfully employed."

The captain wanted to go, too.

But Bennett had an objection. Supposing something should happen to the captain when he was outside. If he was killed, or injured maybe, what about the ship? The servomech officer couldn't handle it, that he was sure of. The cargo was far too valuable to risk leaving it stranded on the planet in the face of what was coming, or to lose in space because of an untrained pilot. The captain shouldn't go out.

He was right, of course. On a job like this the cargo came first, always. But Spence was annoyed. He showed it by being very sarcastic at first, but the mood left him quickly. This was no time to lose his temper.

"All right, heroes," he said, "get going. You'll need suits. The lightweight type will do here—the pressure is nearly Earth-normal. I'll give you the details while you're climbing in. Hurry it up."

The suits arrived. With rapid, practiced movements Bennett and Harrison dropped onto their backs, wriggled their legs into the lower half, then flipped over and began pushing in their arms. It looked like the donning of long flannel underwear, the hard way. The came the fish bowls. In eighty seconds they were dressed. Pretty good going. Spence kept talking all the time.

"The air contains about thirty percent oxygen. It isn't poisonous, exactly, but you'd strangle or burst your hearts through coughing if you had to breathe it for more than a few seconds, it irritates the breathing passages so much. Gravity is point six five Gee, so be careful—" He broke off and said sharply to Harrison, "Check that seam at your shoulder. Is it tight? Slap some cement on it and make sure. No, give it to me. I'll do it. Get the walkie-talkie strapped on."

Dressed, the two men began stretching and bending vigorously, testing for leaks. The captain continued.

"For weapons, better take gas guns and pistols firing nonexplosive bullets. Use the pistols only as a last resort. The reports will probably bring down the tunnel roof, and we've got to avoid damaging the things if possible. Concentrate on gassing them, we know enough about their body chemistry now to do that. There are a couple of gases in stock that will knock them out like a light. But if something should come up

and you *have* to shoot, aim for the center of the twin flaps of
muscle which cover their retractable eyes. These are at the
top of their heads, which are very heavily boned, almost
armor-plated, so don't miss them, the brain is located just
behind the flaps. If you should come at them from the side,
shoot at their hearts. They have two, located just above the
second pair of gripping limbs and the fifth pair of walking
limbs respectively. To do a good job you'll have to get
both.'' He paused for breath as the weapons arrived via robot
from the armory, then he went on.

''These three spots are their only vital ones. They are
nearly all muscle, and you can make them look like sieves
without slowing them down very much. Gas is best, anyway.

''Now, git, and keep your suit radios on all the time. I'll be
listening and I want to know everything as it happens.''

Harrison and Bennett ducked out of the control room and
made their way through massed piles of machinery to the tiny
personnel lock in the great ship's outer skin. Two knights in
shining plastic armor, thought Spence bitterly. He wondered
if he would ever see them again. It was times like this that
made him have doubts about the Force, and the Force's
purpose, and whether it was all worth it.

The commissioning plaque on the wall said that it was.
The clock beside it said it was twenty-five minutes before
blast-off time, which was more important at the moment.

The captain took the servomech officer's seat. One of the
plates showed a tiny picture of the two men sprinting for the
mine opening. The sound of their breaths, amplified, came
through the speaker. They paused on the brim for a moment
without speaking, then dropped from sight.

Suddenly the commander's voice burst in on the silence.
He sounded harassed, strained.

''Hello, Fifty-Three. What progress?''

The captain jerked nervously. Then began to give his chief
an account of the present state of affairs on the planet. The
commander interrupted only once to ask incredulously, *''The
men are off the ship?''* Then he let him finish.

Spence waited for the other's reaction. He supposed judgment would be deferred until the successful completion of the operation. But if it wasn't successful—He mustn't even think of that.

"You have exceeded your authority, captain. You had no business risking the ship like this, especially with fifty Crawlers aboard," began the commander harshly.

But before he could get warmed up Spence interrupted him with a level-voiced, "My orders were not to leave a live Crawler on the planet."

"I know that, captain. But let's not be greedy." Craig's tone was quiet, almost conversational, but Spence wasn't fooled a bit. The commander was about ready to blow up as he continued, "I've been looking at your record. It's a very good one. Somehow you've always managed to bring home the bacon, if you'll excuse the expression. This time it's different. Don't get overzealous, captain, that's bad. I am leaving shortly. You have another nineteen minutes. This had better work out, captain. Off."

Spence sat up at the mention of the time left to him. The rest of it he could worry about later, if there was a later. Nineteen minutes! What was the matter with Bennett and Harrison, struck dumb or something? Had the aliens sprung a trap, maybe? He was about to call them when Harrison's voice issued angrily from the speaker.

"Stay farther behind, Bennett. You're stabbing me with your suit antenna."

Subdued bumping and scraping noises came from the speaker, and an answering grunt. Very much relieved, Spence joined in with a faintly sarcastic reproof.

"Bennett. Please refrain from stabbing the gunnery officer. And isn't it about time you told me what was going on down there?"

"Nothing much, sir," Bennett's voice was uneven and a trifle breathless. He was wriggling at top speed along a tunnel and trying to talk at the same time. "We are well past the point in the tunnel at which the digger was stopped. It was a

tight squeeze at first, but the tunnel is beginning to widen out
a lot. We are about thirty feet above the alien positions. The
detector shows four, close-grouped points of mind radiation
about one hundred feet to our right and a single point almost
directly below us. I expect it's a guard, but I'm nearly certain
it isn't aware of us. The tunnel is widening out a lot now, we
can stand up. We're going as fast as we can. Harrison is
getting ready to knock over the Crawler.''

Bennett stopped to get his breath back. Then he went on
quickly, ''I'l have to shut up in a minute. We're closing in on
him fast, and I don't know if these things can hear or not. But
seeing as the tunnel is wide enough for robots down here,
wouldn't it be a good idea to start the digger again? With all
of the tunnel as wide as this we could get some of the bigger
'mechs down here and speed things up a bit. Do you know
how to control the digger?''

A little sarcastically, Spence said yes, he'd been able to
pick up a few little things in his twelve years in the Force.
He'd manage to do that all right. He pressed the necessary
number of buttons and asked was there anything else.

Bennett didn't speak for several minutes. The scuffling
noises from the speaker seemed to increase in volume. Then
he said, with exaggerated lightness, ''Yes, when the tunnel is
wide enough you could send down a barrow for this alien. He
looks untidy lying here.''

Spence was in no mood for levity. ''Right, So you got
one. Was there any trouble?''

''No, but the vibration from the digger is shaking down a
lot of dust. The other Crawlers must know we're here by
now. They'll be waiting for us.''

''Can't be helped, I'm afraid, but it will be over any time
now. The digger is almost through,'' said the captain. He
was about to ask how they were standing conditions down
there generally when Harrison's voice cut in. It sounded,
thought Spence, decidedly uneasy.

''This looks bad, sir. I'm looking down the tunnel which
the alien was guarding. It is perfectly straight, fairly roomy,

and it widens to form a sort of room at the other end. The room is artificially lit and there are aliens in it. I can only see two, but the detector says they are all there. They are working at some kind of machine. I don't like the look of it,'' he ended and waited for the captain to speak.

Machines, thought Spence, it did look bad. He asked, ''Can you tell if the thing is completed or still a-building, or guess at what it's for?''

''No, they're crowding around it. I can't even tell what it looks like. Only parts of it show.''

A small pickup drifted into the tunnel beside Harrison and stared glassily over his shoulder. Back in the control room Spence saw the Crawler machine, too. It seemed to be a lot of queerly twisted plates built on four wheels. Baffled, he shook his head. He was beginning to wonder if it wouldn't be better to just pull out and forget the last handful of aliens when Bennett's voice came again.

''The digger's through. I turned it into a side passage and shut it off. And I hear the barrow coming for the stiff. You'd better send a few more down, we might need them in a hurry. Time is getting short, so we're just going to walk down this passage abreast until their room is in range of our gas guns. There's nothing else to do. Judging by the intensity of the lighting they use we might be able to get close enough without them seeing us. I hope so, anyway. Here we go.''

The voice stopped. Over the speaker came the measured tread of two pairs of feet, slightly out of step.

Twelve minutes to go, thought Spence. The barrow carrying the Crawler guard rolled out of the mine opening and headed for the ship. He sent two others down to replace it. After that he never took his eyes off the scene being relayed from the tunnel. But there wasn't much to see, just two shadowy figures outlined by the light at the other end. The image wavered a little as the pickup moved to keep pace behind them.

Despite the intensity of his concentration, the screen

couldn't fully occupy his mind. Not enough was happening
on it. He kept thinking back. Back an hour, back two days,
back a week. But, Spence realized with a start, a week ago he
hadn't even heard of this planet. Nobody but a few obscure
astronomers had even an inkling of its existence. Then
everybody knew. In the same way as some quiet, unassum-
ing neighborhood is brought suddenly into the limelight by a
couple of juicy ax murders.

Five days ago the alarm had been given. Every unit of the
Force in this sector had lifted itself from its base and made the
twist into subspace. When it returned to the normal con-
tinuum it was eighty million miles from the Crawler planet
and it was part of a fleet of two thousand.

It had been smooth. Not a single hitch anywhere, Spence
knew. First had come the heavies. Twelve hundred fat silver
cigars, each half a mile long, had hit the planet in a wave and
washed around it twice. The first time they passed, not a
single thing moved in the great Crawler cities. The second
time took longer—but when they swept by, the cities were
empty. Then, their holds crammed with the dominant life of
the planet, they had disappeared en masse into subspace.

Then had come the clean-up squad, the Scavenger Fleet.
The ships landed in cities which had been cleared of alien life
by the heavies. When they took off again the cities blew
themselves to pieces in their wake. It was a bit wasteful,
Spence thought, using bombs on empty cities, but they had to
keep the Crawler survivors from returning to shelter in them.
There wouldn't be time to search them twice, because a
common enemy would be along very shortly which would
lap up Crawlers and humans alike with the finest imparti-
ality.

With the cities out of the way, the Scavenger ships had
scattered to route out the stragglers. It wasn't a very difficult
job, but they had to hurry it a lot. There was no trouble in
finding them. Any Crawler whose mind was working, even if
he was asleep, registered on the detectors carried by the
ships. Whether they cowered singly in caves or stood defen-

sively at bay a hundred strong in some fortified position, it
was just the same. A ship would flash over. Its projector
would flicker invisibly down, then it would land and load the
aliens aboard. Dead easy, thought Spence. Nothing to it.
Routine.

Up to now, that is, the captain thought bitterly.

He was dragged out of his deepening mood of self-pity by
the sight of Bennett and Harrison throwing themselves flat on
the ground. Simultaneously the pickup showed the Crawlers
moving their machine into the tunnel mouth. Muffled *plops*
came from the speaker. The range was still too great, but the
men were using their gas guns. A dirty brown fog grew in the
tunnel as the gas combined with the alien atmosphere, blurring the view, but not before Spence saw that the enigmatic
machine had started working.

Strangely enough, nothing much seemed to be happening.
The machine was being pushed slowly down the passage
towards the crouching men, with the aliens sheltering behind
it as it crept along. The gas still obscured everything.

Suddenly Harrison's voice crashed out from the wall
speaker as he shouted, "It's a fan. We're sunk. They're
blowing our gas back at us."

"Stop shouting, Mr. Harrison," Spence said sharply, "I
can hear you." The suit mikes were capable of picking up the
lowest whisper. When Harrison had raised his voice it had
been like sounding the heart of a volcano with a stethescope.
So now the aliens had a fan. That meant his men were
powerless to use gas, and using anything else would be too
risky, now that they knew of the shaky construction of the
tunnel roof.

He'd had about enough of this, Spence decided, it was
time to get out.

"Pull out, you two. Back to the ship."

"Captain, I've got an idea." It was Bennett's voice. Low,
unhurried, completely sure of himself he went on, "We can
still pull it off. If we wait until they're real close and aim for

the rotors, we could disable the fans and—''

"No shooting," the captain interrupted harshly, "You'd bring the roof down. And that's an order—''

A loud, vicious, *crack* came from the speaker. The sound was unmistakable. Spence gripped the edge of the panel before him and paled as he saw a few tiny rocks drop from the tunnel roof beside the two men. In a voice that shook with fury he exploded, "Mr. Harrison, I told you not to use your gun down there. If you've—''

"It wasn't us," Bennett cut in. "One of the Crawlers has a sort of gun. It's sniping at us. And the fan is speeding up, there's a small gale blowing in here now. I think they mean to rush us."

Bennett's tone wasn't quite so unruffled now. Talking rapidly, Harrison took up the troubled tale.

"The way I see it they mean to kill us and get out before the roof comes down completely from the gunfire. It's their mine so I suppose they know better than we do what the tunnel will stand. They're going to risk the shooting and—Down!''

There was another sharp report and simultaneously the screen blanked out. A direct hit on the camera pickup, thought Spence wildly, what a time to go blind. But that wasn't all. There was a close-spaced series of dull crashes from the speaker and the horrible gasping, choking sound of somebody strangling.

"Bennett. Bennett.'' Harrison was shouting again. A continuous, racking cough, unbearably amplified, drowned out his words.

Spence was reaching hurriedly to turn down the volume when the noise shut off and the gunnery officer's voice returned, low and urgent.

"Bennett's helmet cracked—a rock, I think. I've shut off his transmitter and slapped cement on the break. He's partly buried in the fall. I'm trying to get him free now, but the Crawlers are coming up fast.'' Harrison stopped as another explosion shook the tunnel. "Will you send a barrow here so's I can load him aboard? His suit is switched to pure oxygen now, but he looks bad. He's coughing a lot. And can I use my pistol? That Crawler is getting ready to pick me off.''

"I can't see down there now. Do what you think is best. You're on your own.'' Spence answered.

He was beginning to kick himself for sending the men down there in the first place. It looked as if he was going to lose both of them. He thought briefly of cutting his losses and ordering Harrison back immediately, but he knew it would be no use. Harrison was the altruistic type. Besides, he wasn't so sure he could bring himself to abandon Bennett like that anyway. Maybe he was going soft, too.

Two more reports boomed from the speaker in rapid succession. Harrison's voice came again.

"That Crawler's finished. So is the fan, he fell into it when I shot him. It's . . . it's made an awful mess. I'm gassing the others now. There wasn't much of a fall this time, though our guns make a bigger racket than theirs.'' He paused, his breath coming loud over the speaker. Then he said, "I can hear the barrow coming for Bennett. Send the other one in here while I get him onto this one. Maybe we can get a few Crawlers out after all.''

The captain began talking rapidly. He told the gunnery officer not to be a dope. He used even stronger language. Harrison was to forget about the Crawlers. When the barrow arrived he was to pile in with Bennett and come up at once and not be a complete fool. Spence was beginning to repeat himself when a low, ominous rumble sounded, and the floor beneath him quivered slightly. Only then did he realize that Harrison had his transmitter turned off, and possibly his receiver, too.

"I'll break every bone in his body for this,'' Spence fumed helplessly. "What a stupid trick to pull.'' What if he had been calling the other names, it was for his own good. Spence was very worried about Harrison. He was new, he might do something very foolish, his voice had sounded funny just then, come to think of it.

When Harrison switched on his set and spoke, the captain

knew that he hadn't been worrying for nothing.

"Bennett is on the way up. I want to stay here for a bit. There's been another fall, a bad one. The Crawlers are all mashed up. It would take a bucket to load them onto anything, they're all over the place." For a moment Harrison sounded as if he was going to be sick. Then he recovered and went on, "But the detector shows one of them to be still alive, and I'm going to get it if I have to drag it out myself. You see, these last few days have gotten me down, captain. I'm sick of this job. I keep remembering things. All those cities we bombed, and that time the Crawlers came out of that cave and tried to contact us by drawing math symbols on the ground, and the way we gassed them without even acknowledging their signals."

"But we hadn't time," Spence argued. "You know that. And the only telepaths good enough to mesh with them were halfway across the galaxy, and couldn't have reached here in time to do any good. We had to make it a surprise attack or nothing."

"I know, I know. But we didn't even—" Harrison couldn't put it into words. He knew he was right, but the captain was right, too. He changed the subject. "How are we for time, sir?"

"Six and a half minutes," replied Spence, and thought incredulously, *six and a half minutes!*

Just then Bennett came into the control room, still wheezing and smothering an occasional cough. He wasn't much the worse for his near strangulation. Spence nodded at him without turning, and thought angrily that this was mutiny. All he said was, "Harrison. Bennett's here. Come back at once."

Harrison apparently didn't hear him. He said, "That's good." Whether he meant the time or Bennett was an open question. Then he went on in a low, conversational tone, "More stuff is coming down, mostly in the side tunnels which aren't very strongly built. I'm standing beside the alien which the detector says is alive. Funny thing. I tried to drag it out just now and it came to pieces in my hands. I don't get it. The detector says it is alive, but which piece of it is alive? I'm going to have a closer look—"

Harrison was beginning to talk to himself, thought Spence. That was bad. Next thing he'd begin to scream or laugh, and then he'd want to take off his helmet for a smoke. Quietly, coaxingly, the captain began repeating over and over the command to return to the ship, trying desperately to get hypnotic control over the mind that was so far gone that an appeal to reason was useless.

Suddenly Harrison said in a pleased voice, "Well, what d'you know," and burst out laughing.

The captain's eyes looked bleak. He signaled for Bennett to warm up the drive elements. He would try just once more.

But he didn't get the chance. The fleet commander's harsh voice burst in on them, wavering and fading in the way peculiar to a signal that is being transmitted from a ship in subspace.

"Flagship to Scavenger Five-Three. Report please—" The voice broke off as the commander gasped in disbelief, then he shouted urgently, "You're still on the planet, captain. Get off! Get off at once!"

The captain jumped to obey, but his hand froze on the firing key as Harrison's voice came again. It said simply, "I'm coming now, sir."

For seconds that seemed like an eternity the captain fought to reach a decision. Voices were shouting in his head about Service discipline, common sense, safety. Urging him to take off. Other voices were telling him to be a human being for once, instead of a soulless machine. He looked appealingly at Bennett, but the servomech officer wouldn't meet his eyes.

Bennett pointed suddenly at one of the screens. It showed the tiny figure of Harrison emerging from the mine shaft and sprinting for the ship. On one arm, from wrist to elbow, Harrison wore a beautiful, iridescent fur muff.

When Harrison burst into the control room the great ship was already climbing. He had time to get to his couch and settle his burden gently on his stomach before the acceleration started building up, then he couldn't move.

"Seventy-five seconds," Spence whispered, "Oh, come one, *Come on.*" It sounded almost like a prayer.

Slowly the air around the ship thinned. The huge, pock-marked sun, its corona clearly visible, glared in at them through the starboard screen. The sky was black. They were in space, the warp drive could take over.

Twelve seconds after they had twisted themselves into the safety of subspace, the furiously expanding sphere of annihilation brought about by the detonation of the system's sun vaporized the Crawler planet.

Harrison lifted the furry bundle and shook it in the air. "I found it underneath one of the dead Crawlers. It's a youngster. Cute, isn't he?"

"Cute, he says," said Bennett in disgusted tones. He choked, and a fit of coughing took him.

Spence said, "Better put it in suspended animation with the others. This air of ours is bad for it."

He was pleased with Harrison. The gunnery officer was going to turn out all right. Unavoidably, they'd had to kill a few aliens, but Harrison had been able, personally, to rescue one of their young, so that more than made up for it. He had no intention of resigning now, Spence knew; he probably felt quite a knight in shining armor.

The captain had felt that way when he was a new boy, he remembered. Somehow, the feeling never quite wore off. It came of belonging to an organization dedicated to the job of protecting, assisting, and keeping the noses clean generally of every race in the galaxy that walked, wriggled, or flew and had intelligence. We're just a flock of space-going guardian angels, he thought a little cynically, all we need are halos.

He came down out of the clouds with a start to hear Bennett saying, "You know, I'd hate to have the job of explaining all this to the Crawlers when they wake up on their new planet. I wouldn't be a telepath for anything, too dangerous, for one thing—"

If a planet of the pre-nova stage sun is found to contain intelligent life, the Force will assemble an adequate number of transport units to evacuate the planet in question, having first informed the natives of their danger through operatives of the Department of E-T Communications.

Should no ETCOM telepaths be available at the time, the natives must be evacuated forcefully and taken to the planet assigned them by the Department of Colonization, where the situation will be explained to them when they are revived.

From the "Force Handbook," section on Special Duties.

NO WAR, OR BATTLE'S SOUND

Harry Harrison

"Combatman Dom Priego, I shall kill you." Sergeant Toth shouted the words the length of the barracks compartment.

Dom, stretched out on his bunk and reading a book, raised startled eyes just as the sergeant snapped his arm down, hurling a gleaming combat knife. Trained reflexes raised the book and the knife thudded into it, penetrating the pages so that the point stopped a scant few inches from Dom's face.

"You stupid Hungarian ape!" he shouted. "Do you know what this book cost me? Do you know how old it is?"

"Do you know that you are still alive?" the sergeant answered, a trace of a cold smile wrinkling the corners of his cat's eyes. He stalked down the gangway, like a predatory animal, and reached for the handle of the knife.

"No you don't," Dom said, snatching the book away. "You've done enough damage already." He put the book flat on the bunk and worked the knife carefully out of it—then threw it suddenly at the sergeant's foot.

Sergeant Toth shifted his leg just enough so that the knife missed him and struck the plastic deck covering instead. "Temper, Combatman," he said. "You should never lose your temper. That way you make mistakes, get killed." He bent and plucked out the shining blade and held it balanced in his fingertips. As he straightened up there was a rustle as the other men in the barracks compartment shifted weight, ready to move, all eyes on him. He laughed.

"Now you're expecting it, so it's too easy for you." He slid the knife back into his boot sheath.

"You're a sadistic bowb," Dom said, smoothing down the cut in the book's cover. "Getting a great pleasure out of frightening other people."

"Maybe," Sergeant Toth said, undisturbed. He sat on the bunk across the aisle. "And maybe that's what they call the right man in the right job. And it doesn't matter, anyway. I train you, keep you alert, on the jump. This keeps you alive. You should thank me for being such a good sadist."

"You can't sell me with that argument, Sergeant. You're the sort of individual this man wrote about, right here in this book that you did your best to destroy—"

"Not me. You put it in front of the knife. Just like I keep telling you pinkies. Save yourself. That's what counts. Use any trick. You only got one life, make it a long one."

"Right in here—"

"Pictures of girls?"

"No, Sergeant, words. Great words by a man you never heard of, by the name of Wilde."

"Sure. Plugger Wyld, fleet heavyweight champion."

"No, Oscar Fingal O'Flahertie Wills Wilde. No relation to your pug—I hope. He writes, 'As long as war is regarded as wicked, it will always have its fascination. When it is looked upon as vulgar, it will cease to be popular.'"

Sergeant Toth's eyes narrowed in thought. "He makes it sound simple. But it's not that way at all. There are other reasons for war."

"Such as what?"

The sergeant opened his mouth to answer but his voice was

drowned in the wave of sound from the scramble alert. The high-pitched hooting blared in every compartment of the spacer and had its instant response. Men moved. Fast.

The ship's crew raced to their action stations; the men who had been asleep just an instant before were still blinking awake as they ran. They ran and stood, and before the alarm was through sounding the great spaceship was ready.

Not so the combatmen. Until ordered and dispatched they were just cargo. They stood at the ready, a double row of silver-gray uniforms, down the center of the barracks compartment. Sergeant Toth was at the wall, his headset plugged into a phone extension there and listening attentively, nodding at an unheard voice. Every man's eyes were upon him as he spoke agreement, disconnected, and turned slowly to face them. He savored the silent moment, then broke into the widest grin that any of them had ever seen on his normally expressionless face.

"This is it," the sergeant said, and actually rubbed his hands together. "I can tell you now that the Edinburgers were expected, and that our whole fleet is up in force. The scouts have detected them breaking out of jump space and they should be here in about two hours. We're going out to meet them. This, you pinkie combat virgins, is it." A sound, like a low growl, rose from the assembled men, and the sergeant's grin widened.

"That's the right spirit. Show some of it to the enemy." The grin vanished as quickly as it had come and, cold-faced as always, he called the ranks to attention.

"Corporal Steres is in sick bay with the fever so we're one NCO short. When that alert sounded we went into combat condition. I may now make temporary field appointments. I do so. Combatman Preigo, one pace forward." Dom snapped to attention and stepped out of the rank.

"You're now in charge of the bomb squad. Do the right job and the CO will make it permanent. Corporal Priego, one step back and wait here. The rest of you to the ready room, double time—*march*."

Sergeant Toth stepped aside as the combatmen hurried

from the compartment. When the last one had gone he
pointed his finger at Dom.

"Just one word. You're as good as any man here. Better
than most. You're smart. But you think too much about
things that don't matter. Stop thinking and start fighting. Or
you'll never get back to that university. Bowb up and if the
Edinburgers don't get you I will. You come back as a corporal or you don't come back at all. Understood?"

"Understood." Dom's face was as coldly expressionless
as the sergeant's. "I'm as good a combatman as you are,
Sergeant. I'll do my job."

"Then do it—now *jump*."

Because of the delay Dom was the last man to be suited up.
The others were already doing their pressure checks with the
armorers while he was still closing his seals. He did not let it
disturb him or make him try to move faster. With slow
deliberation he counted off the check list as he sealed and
locked.

Once all the pressure checks were in the green, Dom gave
the armorers the thumbs-up okay and walked to the airlock.
While the door closed behind him and the lock was pumped
out he checked all the telltales in his helmet. Oxygen, full.
Power pack, full charge. Radio, one and one. Then the last of
the air was gone and the inner door opened soundlessly in the
vacuum. He entered the armory.

The lights here were dimmer—and soon they would be
turned off completely. Dom went to the rack with his equipment and began to buckle on the smaller items. Like all of the
others on the bomb squad, his suit was lightly armored and he
carried only the most essential weapons. The drillger went on
his left thigh, just below his fingers, and the gropener in its
holster on the outside of his right leg; this was his favorite
weapon. The intelligence reports had stated that some of the
Edinburgers still used fabric pressure suits, so lightning
prods—usually considered obsolete—had been issued. He
slung his well to the rear since the chance that he might need
it was very slim. All of these murderous devices had been

stored in the evacuated and insulated compartment for months so that their temperature approached absolute zero. They were lubrication-free and had been designed to operate at this temperature.

A helmet clicked against Dom's, and Wing spoke, his voice carried by the conducting transparent ceramic.

"I'm ready for my bomb, Dom—do you want to sling it? And congratulations. Do I have to call you Corporal now?"

"Wait until we get back and it's official. I take Toth's word for absolutely nothing."

He slipped the first atomic bomb from the shelf, checked the telltales to see that they were all in the green, then slid it into the rack that was an integral part of Wing's suit. "All set, now we can sling mine."

They had just finished when a large man in bulky combat armor came up. Dom would have known him by his size even if he he had not read HELMUTZ stenciled on the front of his suit.

"What is it, Helm?" he asked when their helmets touched.

"The sergeant. He said I should report to you, that I'm lifting a bomb on this mission." There was an angry tone behind his words.

"Right. We'll fix you up with a back sling." The big man did not look happy and Dom thought he knew why. "And don't worry about missing any of the fighting. There'll be enough for everyone."

"I'm a combatman—"

"We're all combatmen. All working for one thing—to deliver the bombs. That's your job now."

Helmutz did not act convinced and stood with stolid immobility while they rigged the harness and bomb onto the back of his suit. Before they were finished their headphones crackled and a stir went through the company of suited men as a message came over the command frequency.

"Are you suited and armed? Are you ready for illumination adjustment?"

"Combatmen suited and armed." That was Sergeant Toth's voice.

"Bomb squad not ready," Dom said, and they hurried to make the last fastenings, aware that the rest were waiting for them.

"Bomb squad suited and armed."

"Lights."

As the command rang out the bulkhead lights faded out until the darkness was broken only by the dim red lights in the ceiling above. Until their eyes became adjusted it was almost impossible to see. Dom groped his way to one of the benches, found the oxygen hose with his fingers, and plugged it into the side of his helmet; this would conserve his tank oxygen during the wait. Brisk music was being played over the command circuit now as part of morale-sustaining. Here in the semidarkness, suited and armed, the waiting could soon become nerve-racking. Everything was done to alleviate the pressure. The music faded and a voice replaced it.

"This is the executive officer speaking. I'm going to try and keep you in the picture as to what is happening up here. The Edinburgers are attacking in fleet strength and, soon after they were sighted, their ambassador declared that a state of war exists. He asks that Earth surrender at once or risk the consequences. Well, you all know what the answer to that was. The Edinburgers have invaded and conquered twelve settled planets already and incorporated them into their Greater Celtic Coprosperity Sphere. Now they're getting greedy and going for the big one. Earth itself, the planet their ancestors left a hundred generations ago. In doing this . . . just a moment, I have a battle report here . . . first contact with our scouts."

The officer stopped for a moment, then his voice picked up again.

"Fleet strength, but no larger than we expected and we will be able to handle them. But there is one difference in their tactics and the combat computer is analyzing this now. They were the ones who originated the MT invasion technique, landing a number of cargo craft on a planet, all of them loaded with matter-transmitter screens. As you know, the invading forces attack through these screens direct from their planet to the one that is to be conquered. Well, they've changed their technique now. This entire fleet is protecting a *single* ship, a Kriger class scout carrier. What this means . . . hold on, here is the readout from the combat computer. 'Only possibility single ship landing area increase MT screen breakthrough,' that's what it says. Which means that there is a good chance that this ship may be packing a *single* MT screen, bigger than anything every built before. If this is so—and they get the thing down to the surface—they can fly heavy bombers right through it, fire pre-aimed ICBM's, send through troop carriers, anything. If this happens the invasion will be successful.''

Around him, in the red-lit darkness, Dom was aware of the other suited figures who stirred silently as they heard the words.

"*If* this happens." There was a ring of authority now in the executive officer's voice. "The Edinburgers have developed the only way to launch an interplanetary invasion. We have found the way to stop it. You combatmen are the answer. They have now put all their eggs in one basket—and you are going to take that basket to pieces. You can get through where the attack ships or missiles could not. We're closing fast now and you will be called to combat stations soon. So—go out there and do your job. The fate of Earth rides with you.''

Melodramatic words, Dom thought, yet they were true. Everything, the ships, the concentration of firepower, it all depended on them. The alert alarm cut through his thoughts and he snapped to attention.

"Disconnect oxygen. Fall out when your name is called and proceed to the firing room in the order called. Toth. . . .''

The names were spoken quickly and the combatmen moved out. At the entrance to the firing room a suited man

with a red globed light checked the names on their chests
against his roster to make sure they were in the correct order.
Everything moved smoothly, easily, just like a drill. Because
the endless drills had been designed to train them for just this
moment. The firing room was familiar, though they had
never been there before, because their trainer had been an
exact duplicate of it. The combatman ahead of Dom went to
port so he moved to starboard. The man preceding him was
just climbing into a capsule and Dom waited while the
armorer helped him down into it and adjusted the armpit
supports. Then it was his turn and Dom slipped into the
transparent plastic shell and settled against the seat as he
seized the handgrips. The armorer pulled the supports hard
up into his armpits and he nodded when they seated right. A
moment later the man was gone and he was alone in the
semidarkness with the dim red glow shining on the top ring of
the capsule that was just above his head. There was a sudden
shudder and he gripped hard just as the capsule started
forward. As it moved it tilted backward until he was lying on
his back looking up through the metal rings that banded his
plastic shell. His capsule was moved sideways, jerked to a
stop, then moved again. Now the gun was visible, a half-
dozen capsules ahead of his, and he thought, as he always did
during training, how like an ancient quick-firing cannon the
gun was—a cannon that fired human beings. Every two
seconds the charging mechanism seized a capsule from one
of the alternate feed belts, whipped it to the rear of the gun
where it instantly vanished into the breech. Then another and
another. The one ahead of Dom disappeared and he braced
himself—and the mechanism halted.

There was a flicker of fear that something had gone wrong
with the complex gun, before he realized that all of the first
combatmen had been launched and that the computer was
waiting a determined period of time for them to prepare the
way for the bomb squad. His squad now, the men he would
lead.

Waiting was harder than moving as he looked at the black

mouth of the breech. The computer would be ticking away the seconds now, while at the same time tracking the target and keeping the ship aimed to the correct trajectory. Once he was in the gun the magnetic field would seize the rings that banded his capsule and the linear accelerator of the gun would draw him up the evacuated tube that penetrated the entire length of the great ship from stern to bow. Faster and faster the magnetic fields would pull him until he left the mouth of the gun at the correct speed and on the correct trajectory to intercept. . . .

His capsule was whipped up in a tight arc and shoved into the darkness. Even as he gripped tight on the handholds the pressure pads came up and hit him. He could not measure the time—he could not see and he could not breathe as the brutal acceleration pressed down on him. Hard, harder than anything he had ever experienced in training: he had that one thought and then he was out of the gun.

In a single instant he went from acceleration to weightlessness, and he gripped hard so he would not float away from the capsule. There was a puff of vapor from the unheard explosions, he felt them through his feet, and the metal rings were blown in half and the upper portion of the capsule shattered and hurled away. Now he was alone, weightless, holding to the grips that were fastened to the rocket unit beneath his feet. He looked about for the space battle that he knew was in progress, and felt a slight disappointment that there was so little to see.

Something burned far off to his right and there was a wavering in the brilliant points of the stars as some dark object occulted them and passed on. This was a battle of computers and instruments at great distances. There was very little for the unaided eye to see. The spaceships were black and swift and—for the most part—thousands of miles away. They were firing homing rockets and proximity shells, also just as swift and invisible. He knew that space around him was filled with signal jammers and false signal generators, but none of this was visible. Even the target

vessel toward which he was rushing was invisible. For all
that his limited senses could tell he was alone in space,
motionless, forgotten.

Something shuddered against the soles of his boots and a
jet of vapor shot out and vanished from the rocket unit. No,
he was neither motionless nor forgotten. The combat computer was still tracking the target ship and had detected some
minute variation from its predicted path. At the same time the
computer was following the progress of his trajectory and it
made the slight correction for this new data. Corrections
must be going out at the same time to all the other combatmen
in space, before and behind him. They were small and
invisible—doubly invisible now that the metal rings had been
shed. There was no more than an eighth of a pound of metal
dispersed through the plastics and ceramics of a combatman's equipment. Radar could never pick them out from
among all the interference. They should get through.

Jets blasted again and Dom saw that the stars were turning
above his head. Touchdown soon; the tiny radar in his rocket
unit had detected a mass ahead and had directed that he be
turned end for end. Once this was done he knew that the
combat computer would cut free and turn control over to the
tiny set-down computer that was part of his radar. His rockets
blasted, strong now, punching the supports up against him,
and he looked down past his feet at the growing dark shape
that occulted the stars.

With a roar, loud in the silence, his headphones burst into
life.

"Went, went—gone hungry. Went, went—gone hungry."

The silence grew again but, in it, Dom no longer felt alone.
The brief message had told him a lot. Firstly, it was Sergeant
Toth's voice, there was no mistaking that. Secondly, the
mere act of breaking radio silence showed that they had
engaged the enemy and that their presence was known. The
code was a simple one that would be meaningless to anyone
outside their company. Translated it said that fighting was

still going on but the advance squads were holding their own. They had captured the center section of the hull—always the best place to rendezvous since it was impossible to tell bow from stern in the darkness—and were holding it awaiting the arrival of the bomb squad. The retrorockets flared hard and long and the rocket unit crashed hard into the black hull. Dom jumped free and rolled.

As he came out of the roll he saw a suited figure looming above him, clearly outlined by the disc of the sun despite his black nonreflective armor. The top of the helmet was smooth. Even as he realized this Dom was pulling the gropener from its holster.

A cloud of vapor sprang out and the man vanished behind it. Dom was surprised, but he did not hesitate. Handguns, even recoilless ones like this that sent the burnt gas out to the sides, were a hazard in no-G space combat. They were not only difficult to aim but had a recoil that would throw the user back out of position. Or, if the gas was vented sideways, they would blind him for vital moments. And a fraction of a second was all a trained combatman needed.

As the gropener swung free Dom thumbed the jet button lightly. The device was shaped like a short sword, but it had a vibrating saw blade where one sharpened edge should be, with small jets mounted opposite it in place of the opposite edge. The jets drove the device forward, pulling him after it. As soon as it touched the other man's leg he pushed the jets full on. As the vibrating ceramic blade speeded up the force of the jets pressed it into the thin armor. In less than a second it cut its way through and on into the flesh of the leg inside. Dom pressed the reverse jet to pull away as vapor gushed out, condensing to ice particles instantly, and his opponent writhed, clutched at his thigh—then went suddenly limp.

Dom's feet touched the hull and the soles adhered. He realized that the entire action had taken place in the time it took him to straighten out from his roll and stand up. . . .

Don't think, act. Training. As soon as his feet adhered he crouched and turned looking about him. A heavy power ax sliced by just above his head, towing its wielder after it.

Act, don't think. His new opponent was on his left side, away from the gropener, and was already reversing the direction of his ax. A man has two hands. The drillger on his left thigh. Even as he remembered it he had it in his hand, drill on and hilt-jet flaring. The foot-long, diamond-hard drill spun fiercely—its rotation cancelled by the counterrevolving weight in the hilt—while the jet drove it forward.

Into the Edinburger's midriff, scarcely slowing as it tore a hole in the armor and plunged inside. As his opponent folded Dom thumbed the reverse jet to push the drillger out. The power ax, still with momentum from the last blast of its jet, tore free of the dying man's hand and vanished into space.

There were no other enemies in sight. Dom tilted forward on one toe so that the surface film on the boot sole was switched from adhesive to neutral, then he stepped forward slowly. Walking like this took practice, but he had had that. Ahead were a group of dark figures lying prone on the hull and he took the precaution of raising his hand to touch the horn on the top of his helmet so there would be no mistakes. This identification had been agreed upon just a few days ago and the plastic spikes glued on. The Edinburgers all had smooth-topped helmets.

Dom dived forward between the scattered forms and slid, face down. Before his body could rebound from the hull he switched on his belly-sticker and the surface film there held him flat. Secure for the moment among his own men, he thumbed the side of his helmet to change frequencies. There was now a jumble of noise through most of the frequencies, messages—both theirs and the enemy's—jamming, and false messages being broadcast by recorder units to cover the real exchange of information. There was scarcely any traffic on the bomb squad frequency and he waited for a clear spot. His men would have heard Toth's message so they knew where to gather. Now he could bring them to him.

"Quasar, quasar, quasar," he called, then counted carefully for ten seconds before he switched on the blue bulb on his shoulder. He stood as he did this, let it burn for a single second, then dropped back to the hull before he could draw any fire. His men would be looking for the light and would assemble on it. One by one they began to crawl out of the darkness. He counted them as they appeared. A combatman, without the bulge of a bomb on his back, ran up and dived and slid, so that his helmet touched Dom's.

"How many, Corporal?" Toth's voice asked.

"One still missing but—"

"Not buts. We move now. Set your charge and blow as soon as you have cover."

He was gone before Dom could answer. But he was right. They could not afford to wait for one man and risk the entire operation. Unless they moved soon they would be trapped and killed up here. Individual combats were still going on about the hull, but it would not be long before the Edinburgers realized these were just holding actions and that the main force of attackers was gathered in strength. The bomb squad went swiftly and skillfully to work laying the ring of shaped charges.

The rear guards must have been called in because the heavy weapons opened fire suddenly on all sides. These were .30 caliber high-velocity recoilless machine guns. Before firing the gunners had traversed the hull, aiming for a grazing fire that was as close to the surface as possible. The gun computer remembered this and now fired along the selected pattern, aiming automatically. This was needed because as soon as the firing began clouds of gas jetted out obscuring everything. Sergeant Toth appeared out of the smoke and shouted as his helmet touched Dom's.

"Haven't you blown it yet?"

"Ready now, get back."

"Make it fast. They're all down or dead now out there. But they'll throw something heavy into this smoke soon. Now that they have us pinpointed."

The bomb squad drew back, fell flat, and Dom pressed the igniter. Flames and gas exploded high while the hull ham-

mered up at them. Through the smoke rushed up a solid
column of air, clouding and freezing into tiny crystals as it hit
the vacuum. The ship was breeched now and they would
keep it that way, blowing open the sealed compartments and
bulkheads to let out the atmosphere. Dom and the sergeant
wriggled through the smoke together, to the edge of the wide,
gaping hole that had been blasted in the ship's skin.

"Hotside, hotside!" the sergeant shouted, and dived
through the opening.

Dom pushed away through the rush of men who were
following the sergeant and assembled his squad. He was still
one man short. A weapons man with his machine gun on his
back hurried by and leaped into the hole, with his ammunition carriers right behind him. The smoke cloud was growing
because some of the guns were still firing, acting as a rear
guard. It was getting hard to see the opening now. When
Dom had estimated that half the men had gone through he led
his own squad forward.

They pushed down into a darkened compartment, a
storeroom of some kind, and saw a combatman at a hole that
had been blown in one wall, acting as a guide.

"Down to the right, hole about one hundred yards from
here," he said as soon as Dom's helmet touched his. "We
tried to the right first but there's too much resistance. Just
holding them there."

Dom led his men in a floating run, the fastest movement
possible in a null-G situation. The corridor was empty for the
moment, dimly lit by the emergency bulbs. Holes had been
blasted in the walls at regular intervals to open the sealed
compartments and empty them of air, as well as to destroy
wiring and piping. As they passed one of the ragged-edged
openings, space-suited men erupted from it.

Dom dived under the thrust of a drillger, swinging his
gropener out at the same time. It caught his attacker in the
midriff just as the man's other hand came up. The Edinburger folded and died and a sharp pain lanced through
Dom's leg. He looked down at the nipoff that was fastened to
his calf and was slowly severing it.

Nipoff, an outmoded design for use against unarmored suits. It was killing him. The two curved blades were locked around his leg and the tiny, geared-down motor was slowly closing them. Once started the device could not be stopped.

It could be destroyed. Even as he realized this he swung down his gropener and jammed it against the nipoff's handle. The pain intensified at the sideways pressure and he almost blacked out; he attempted to ignore it. Vapor puffed out around the blades and he triggered the compression ring on his thigh that sealed the leg from the rest of his suit. Then the gropener cut through the casing. There was a burst of sparks and the motion of the closing blades stopped.

When Dom looked up the brief battle was over and the counterattackers were dead. The rear guard had caught up and pushed over them. Helmutz must have accounted for more than one of them himself. He held his power ax high, fingers just touching the buttons in the haft so that the jets above the blade spurted alternately to swing the ax to and fro. There was blood on both blades.

Dom switched on his radio; it was silent on all bands. The interior communication circuits of the ship were knocked out here and the metal walls damped all radio signals.

"Report," he said. "How many did we lose?"

"You're hurt," Wing said, bending over him. "Want me to pull that thing off?"

"Leave it. The tips of the blades are almost touching and you'd tear half my leg off. It's frozen in with the blood and I can still get around. Lift me up."

The leg was getting numb now, with blood supply cut off and the air replaced by vacuum. Which was all for the best. He took the roll count.

"We've lost two men but we still have more than enough bombs for this job. Now let's move."

Sergeant Toth himself was waiting at the next corridor, where another hole had been blasted in the deck. He looked at Dom's leg but said nothing.

"How's it going?" Dom asked.

"Fair. We took some losses. We gave them more. En-

gineer says we're over the main hold now so we're going
straight down. Pushing out men on each level to hold. Get
going.''

"And you?"

"I'll bring down the rear guard and pull the men from each
level as we pass. You see that you have a way out for us when
we all get down to you."

"You can count on that."

Dom floated over the hole, then gave a strong kick with his
good leg against the ceiling when he was lined up. He went
down smoothly and his squad followed. They passed one
deck, two, then three. The openings had been nicely aligned
for a straight drop. There was a flare of light and a burst of
smoke ahead as another deck was blown through. Helmutz
passed Dom, going faster, having pushed off harder with
both legs. He was a full deck ahead when he plunged through
the next opening, and the burst of high-velocity machine-gun
fire almost cut him in two. He folded in the middle, dead in
the instant, the impact of the bullets driving him sideways
and out of sight in the deck below.

Dom thumbed the jets on his gropener and it pulled him
aside before he followed the big combatman.

"Bomb squad, disperse," he ordered. "Troops coming
through." He switched to the combat frequency and looked
up at the ragged column of men dropping down toward him.

"The deck below has been retaken. I am at the last oc-
cupied deck."

He waved his hand to indicate who was talking and the
stream of men began to jet their weapons and move on by
him. "They're below me. The bullets came from this side."
The combatmen pushed on without a word.

The metal flooring shook as another opening was blasted
somewhere behind him. The continuous string of men moved
by. A few seconds later a helmeted figure—with a horned
helmet—appeared below and waved the all-clear. The drop
continued.

On the bottom deck the men were jammed almost shoulder
to shoulder and more were arriving all the time.

"Bomb squad here, give me a report," Dom radioed. A combatman with a mapboard slung at his waist pushed back out of the crowd.

"We reached the cargo hold—it's immense—but we're being pushed back. Just by weight of numbers. The Edinburgers are desperate. They are putting men through the MT screen in light pressure suits. Unarmored, almost unarmed. We kill them easily enough but they have pushed us out bodily. They're coming right from the invasion planet. Even when we kill them the bodies block the way. . . ."

"You the engineer?"

"Yes."

"Whereabouts in the hold is the MT screen?"

"It runs the length of the hold and is back against the far wall."

"Controls?"

"On the left side."

"Can you lead us over or around the hold so we can break in near the screen?"

The engineer took a single long look at charts.

"Yes, around. Through the engine room. We can blast through close to the controls."

"Let's go, then." Dom switched to combat frequency and waved his arm over his head. "All combatmen who can see me—this way. We're going to make a flank attack."

They moved down the long corridor as fast as they could, with the combatmen ranging out ahead of the bomb squad. There were sealed pressure doors at regular intervals, but these were bypassed by blasting through the bulkheads at the side. There was resistance and there were more dead as they advanced. Then a group of men gathered ahead and Dom floated up to the greatly depleted force of combatmen who had forced their way this far. A corporal touched his helmet to Dom's , pointing to a great sealed door at the corridor's end.

"The engine room is behind there. These walls are thick. Everyone off to one side because we are going to use an octupled charge."

They dispersed and the bulkheads heaved and buckled when the charge was exploded. Dom, looking toward the corridor, saw a sheet of flame sear by, followed by a column of air that turned instantly to sparkling granules of ice. The engine room had still been pressurized.

There had been no warning and most of the crewmen had not had their helmets sealed. They were violently and suddenly dead. The few survivors were killed quickly when they offered resistance with improvised weapons. Dom scarcely noticed this as he led his bomb squad after the engineer.

"That doorway is not on my charts," the engineer said angrily, as though the spy who had stolen the information were at fault. "It must have been added after construction."

"Where does it go to?" Dom asked.

"The MT hold, no other place is possible."

Dom thought quickly. "I'm going to try and get to the MT controls without fighting. I need a volunteer to go with me. If we remove identification and wear Edinburger equipment we should be able to do it."

"I'll join you," the engineer said.

"No, you have a different job. I want a good combat-man."

"Me," a man said, pushing through the others. "Pimenov, best in my squad. Ask anybody."

"Let's make this fast."

The disguise was simple. With the identifying spikes knocked off their helmets and enemy equipment slung about them they would pass any casual examination. A handful of grease obscured the names on their chests.

"Stay close behind and come fast when I knock the screen out," Dom told the others, then led the combatman through the door.

There was a narrow passageway between large tanks and another door at the far end. It was made of light metal and not locked, but it would not budge when Dom pushed on it. Pimenov joined him and between them they forced it open a few inches. Through the opening they saw that it was blocked by a press of human bodies, spacesuited men who stirred and struggled but scarcely moved. The two combatmen pushed harder and a sudden movement of the mob released the pressure and Dom fell forward, his helmet banging into that of the nearest man.

"What the devil you about?" the man said, twisting his head to look at Dom.

"More of them down there," Dom said, trying to roll his r's the way the Edinburgers did.

"You're no one of us!" the man said and struggled to bring his weapon up.

Dom could not risk a fight here—yet the man had to be silenced. He could just reach the lightning prod and he jerked it from its clip and jammed it against the Edinburger's side. The pair of needle-sharp spikes pierced suit and clothes and bit into his flesh, and when the hilt slammed against his body the circuit was closed. The handle of the lightning prod was filled with powerful capacitors that released their stored electricity in a single immense charge through the needles. The Edinburger writhed and died instantly.

They used his body to push a way into the crowd.

Dom had just enough sensation left in his injured leg to be aware when the clamped-on nipoff was twisted in his flesh by the men about them; he kept his thoughts from what it was doing to his leg.

Once the Edinburger soldiers were aware of the open door they pulled in wide and fought their way through it. The combatmen would be waiting for them in the engine room. The sudden exodus relieved the pressure of the bodies for a moment and Dom, with Pimenov struggling after him, pushed and worked his way toward the MT controls.

It was like trying to move in a dream. The dark bulk of the MT screen was no more than ten yards away, yet they couldn't seem to reach it. Soldiers sprang from the screen, pushing and crowding in, more and more, preventing any motion in that direction. Two technicians stood at the controls, their helmet phones plugged into the board before them. Without gravity to push against, jammed into the crowd that floated at all levels in a fierce tangle of arms and legs, movement was almost impossible. Pimenov touched his helmet to Dom's.

"I'm going ahead to cut a path. Stay close behind me."

He broke contact before Dom could answer him, then let his power ax pull him forward into the press. Then he began to chop it back and forth in a short arc, almost hacking his way through the packed bodies. Men turned on him but he did not stop, lashing out with his gropener as they tried to fight. Dom followed.

They were close to the MT controls before the combatman was buried under a crowd of stabbing, cursing Edinburgers. He had done his job and he died doing it. Dom jetted his gropener and let it drag him forward until he slammed into the thick steel frame of the MT screen above the operators' heads. He slid the weapon back into its sheath and used both hands to pull down along the frame, dragging himself head first through the press of suited bodies. There was a relatively clear space near the controls. He drifted down into it and let his drillger slide into the operator's back. The man writhed and died quickly. The other operator turned and took the weapon in his stomach. His face was just before Dom as his eyes widened and he screamed soundlessly with pain and fear. Nor could Dom escape the dead, horrified features as he struggled to drop the atomic bomb from his carrier. The murdered man stayed, pressed close against him all the time.

Now.

He cradled the bomb against his chest and, in a single swift motion, pulled out the arming pin, twisted the fuse to five seconds, and slammed down hard on the actuator. Then he reached up and switched the MT from *receive* to *send*.

The last soldiers erupted from the screen and there was a growing gap behind them. Into this space and through the screen he threw the bomb.

After that he kept the switch down and tried not to think about what was happening among the men of the invasion army who were waiting before the MT screen on that distant planet.

Then he had to hold this position until the combatmen arrived. He sheltered behind the operator's corpse and used his drillger against the few Edinburgers who were close enough to realize that something had gone wrong. This was easy enough to do because, although they were soldiers, they were men from the invasion army and knew nothing about null-G combat. Very soon after this there was a great stir and the closest ones were thrust aside. An angry combatman blasted through, sweeping his power ax toward Dom's neck. Dom dodged the blow and switched his radio to combat frequency.

"Hold that! I'm Corporal Priego, bomb squad. Get in front of me and keep anyone from making the same mistake."

The man was one of those who had taken the engine room. He recognized Dom now and nodded, turning his back to him and pressing against him. More combatmen stormed up to form an iron shield around the controls. The engineer pushed through between them and Dom helped him reset the frequency on the MT screen.

After this the battle became a slaughter and soon ended.

"Sendout!" Dom radioed as soon as the setting was made, then turned the screen to transmit. He heard the words repeated over and over as the combatmen repeated the withdrawal signal so that everyone could hear it. Safety lay on the other side of the screen, now that it was tuned to Tycho Barracks on the moon.

It was the Edinburgers, living, dead, and wounded, who were sent through first. They were pushed back against the screen to make room for the combatmen who were streaming into the hold. The ones at the ends of the screen simply bounced against the hard surface and recoiled; the receiving screen at Tycho was far smaller than this great invasion screen. They were pushed along until they fell through and combatmen took up positions to mark the limits of operating screen.

Dom was aware of someone in front of him and he had to

blink away the red film that was trying to cover his eyes.

"Wing," he said, finally recognizing the man. "How many others of the bomb squad made it?"

"None I know of, Dom. Just me."

No, don't think about the dead. Only the living counted now.

"All right. Leave your bomb here and get on through. One is all we really need." He tripped the release and pulled the bomb from Wing's rack before giving him a push toward the screen.

Dom had the bomb clamped to the controls when Sergeant Toth slammed up beside him and touched helmets.

"Almost done."

"Done now," Dom, said, setting the fuse and pulling out the arming pin.

"Then get moving. I'll take it from here."

"No you don't. My job." He had to shake his head to make the haze go away but it still remained at the corners of his vision.

Toth didn't argue. "What's the setting?" he asked.

"Five and six. Five seconds after actuation the chemical bomb blows and knocks out the controls. One second later the atom bomb goes off."

"I'll stay to watch the fun."

Time was acting strangely for Dom, speeding up and slowing down. Men were hurrying by, into the screen, first in a rush, then fewer and fewer. Toth was talking on the combat frequency but Dom had switched the radio because it hurt his head. The great chamber was empty now of all but the dead, with the automatic machine guns left firing at the entrances. One of them blew up as Toth touched helmets.

"They're all through. Let's go."

Dom had difficulty talking so he nodded instead and hammered his fist down onto the actuator.

Men were coming toward them but Toth had his arm around him, and full jets on his power ax were sliding them along the surface of the screen. And through.

When the brilliant lights of Tycho Barracks hit his eyes Dom closed them, and this time the red haze came up, over him, all the way.

"How's the new leg?" Sergeant Toth asked. He slumped lazily in the chair beside the hospital bed.

"I can't feel a thing. Nerve channels blocked until it grows tight to the stump." Dom put aside the book he had been reading and wondered what Toth was doing here.

"I came around to see the wounded," the sergeant said, answering the unasked question. "Two more besides you. Captain told me to."

"The captain is as big a sadist as you are. Aren't we sick enough already?"

"Good joke." His expression did not change. "I'll tell the captain. He'll like it. You going to buy out now?"

"Why not?" Dom wondered why the question made him angry. "I've had a combat mission, the medals, a good wound. More than enough points to get my discharge."

"Stay in. You're a good combatman when you stop thinking about it. There's not many of them. Make it a career."

"Like you, Sergeant? Make killing my life's work? Thank you, no. I intend to do something different, a little more constructive. Unlike you, I don't relish this whole dirty business, the killing, the outright plain murder. You like it." This sudden thought sent him sitting upright in the bed. "Maybe that's it. Wars, fighting, everything. It has nothing to do anymore with territory rights or aggression or masculinity. I think that you people make wars because of the excitement of it, the thrill that nothing else can equal. You *like war.*"

Toth rose, stretched easily, and turned to leave. He stopped at the door, frowning in thought.

"Maybe you're right, Corporal. I don't think about it much. Maybe I do like it." His face lifted in a cold tight smile. "But don't forget—you like it, too."

Dom went back to his book, resentful of the intrusion. His literature professor had sent it, with a flattering note. He had heard about Dom on the broadcasts and the entire school was proud, etc. A book of poems, Milton, really good stuff.

> No war, or battle's sound
> Was heard the world around.

Yes, great stuff. But it hadn't been true in Milton's day and it still wasn't true. Did mankind really like war? They *must* like it or it wouldn't have lasted so long. This was an awful, criminal thought.

He, too? Nonsense. He fought well, but he had trained himself. It could not be true that he actually liked all of that.

He tried to read again but the page kept blurring before his eyes.

THE HORARS OF WAR

Gene Wolfe

The three friends in the trench looked very much alike as they labored in the rain. Their hairless skulls were slickly naked to it, their torsos hairless too, and supple with smooth muscles that ran like oil under the wet gleam.

The two, who really were 2909 and 2911, did not mind the jungle around them although they detested the rain that rusted their weapons, and the snakes and insects, and hated the Enemy. But the one called 2910, the real as well as the official leader of the three, did; and that was because 2909 and 2911 had stainless-steel bones; but there was no 2910 and there had never been.

The camp they held was a triangle. In the center, the CP-Aid Station where Lieutenant Kyle and Mr. Brenner slept: a hut of ammo cases packed with dirt whose lower half was dug into the soggy earth. Around it were the mortar pit(NE), the recoilless rifle pit (NW), and Pinocchio's pit (S); and beyond these were the straight lines of the trenches: First

Platoon, Second Platoon, Third Platoon (the platoon of the three). Outside of which were the primary wire and an antipersonnel mine field.

And outside that was the jungle. But not completely outside. The jungle set up outposts of its own of swift-sprouting bamboo and elephant grass, and its crawling creatures carried out untiring patrols of the trenches. The jungle sheltered the Enemy, taking him to its great fetid breast to be fed while it sopped up the rain and of it bred its stinging gnats and centipedes.

An ogre beside him, 2911 drove his shovel into the ooze filling the trench, lifted it to shoulder height, dumped it; 2910 did the same thing in his turn, then watched the rain work on the scoop of mud until it was slowly running back into the trench again. Following his eyes 2911 looked at him and grinned. The HORAR's face was broad, hairless, flat-nosed and high-cheeked; his teeth were pointed and white like a big dog's. And he, 2910, knew that that face was his own. Exactly his own. He told himself it was a dream, but he was very tired and could not get out.

Somewhere down the trench the bull voice of 2900 announced the evening meal and the others threw down their tools and jostled past toward the bowls of steaming mash, but the thought of food nauseated 2910 in his fatigue, and he stumbled into the bunker he shared with 2909 and 2911. Flat on his air mattress he could leave the nightmare for a time; return to the sane world of houses and sidewalks, or merely sink into the blessed nothingness that was far better. . . .

Suddenly he was bolt upright on the cot, blackness still in his eyes even while his fingers groped with their own thought for his helmet and weapon. Bugles were blowing from the edge of the jungle, but he had time to run his hand under the inflated pad of the mattress and reassure himself that his hidden notes were safe before 2900 in the trench outside yelled, "Attack! Fall out! Man your firing points!"

It was one of the stock jokes, one of the jokes so stock, in

fact, that it had ceased to be anything anyone laughed at, to
say "Horar" your firing point (or whatever it was that
according to the book should be "manned"). The HORARS
in the squad he led used the expression to 2910 just as he used
it with them, and when 2900 never employed it the omission
had at first unsettled him. But 2900 did not really suspect.
2900 just took his rank seriously.

He got into position just as the mortars put up a parachute
flare that hung over the camp like a white rose of fire.
Whether because of his brief sleep or the excitement of the
impending fight his fatigue had evaporated, leaving him
nervously alert but unsteady. From the jungle a bugle sang.
"Ta-taa . . . taa-taa . . . " and off to the platoon's left rear
the First opened up with their heavy weapons on a suicide
squad they apparently thought they saw on the path leading to
the northeast gate. He watched, and after half a minute
something stood up on the path and grabbed for its midsection before it fell, so there *was* a suicide squad.

Some one, he told himself. *Someone*. Not *something*.
Someone grabbed for *his* midsection. They were all human
out there.

The First began letting go with personal weapons as well,
each deep cough representing a half dozen dartlike fletchettes
flying in an inescapable pattern three feet broad. "Eyes
front, 2910!" barked 2900.

There was nothing to be seen out there but a few clumps of
elephant grass. Then the white flare burned out. "They ought
to put up another one," 2911 on his right said worriedly.

"A star in the east for men not born of women," said 2910
half to himself, and regretted the blasphemy immediately.

"That's where they need it," 2911 agreed, "The First is
having it pretty hot over there. But we could use some light
here too."

He was not listening. At home in Chicago, during that
inexpressibly remote time which ran from a dim memory of
playing on a lawn under the supervision of a smiling giantess
to that moment two years ago when he had submitted to

surgery to lose every body and facial hair he possessed and undergo certain other minor alterations, he had been unconsciously preparing himself for this. Lifting weights and playing football to develop his body while he whetted his mind on a thousand books; all so that he might tell, making others feel at a remove . . .

Another flare went up and there were three dark silhouettes sliding from the next-nearest clump of elephant grass to the nearest. He fired his M-19 at them, then heard the HORARS on either side of him fire too. From the sharp corner where their own platoon met the Second a machine gun opened up with tracer. The nearest grass clump sprang into the air and somersaulted amid spurts of earth.

There was a moment of quiet, then five rounds of high explosive came in right behind them as though aimed for Pinocchio's pit. *Crump. Crump. Crump . . . Crump. Crump.* (2900 would be running to ask Pinocchio if he were hurt.)

Someone else had been moving down the trench toward them, and he could hear the mumble of the new voice become a gasp when the H.E. rounds came in. Then it resumed, a little louder and consequently a bit more easily understood. "How are you? You feel all right? Hit?"

And most of the HORARS answering, "I'm fine, sir," or "We're okay, sir," but because HORARS did have a sense of humor some of them said things like, "How do we transfer to the Marines, sir?" or, "My pulse just registered nine thou', sir. 3000 took it with the mortar sight."

We often think of strength as associated with humorlessness, he had written in the news magazine which had, with the Army's cooperation, planted him by subterfuge of surgery among these *H*omolog *OR*ganisms (*A*rmy *R*eplacement *S*imulations). *But,* he had continued, *this is not actually the case. Humor is a prime defense of the mind, and knowing that to strip the mind of it is to leave it shieldless, the Army and the Synthetic Biology Service have wisely included a charming dash in the makeup of these synthesized replacements for human infantry.*

That had been before he discovered that the Army and the SBS had tried mightily to weed that sense of the ridiculous out, but found that if the HORARS were to maintain the desired intelligence level they could not.

Brenner was behind him now, touching his shoulder. "How are you? Feel all right?"

He wanted to say, "I'm half as scared as you are, you dumb Dutchman," but he knew that if he did the fear would sound in his voice; besides, the disrespect would be unthinkable to a HORAR.

He also wanted to say simply, "A-okay, sir," because if he did Brenner would pass on to 2911 and he would be safe. But he had a reputation for originality to keep up, and he needed that reputation to cover him when he slipped, as he often did, sidewise of HORAR standards. He answered: "You ought to look in on Pinocchio, sir. I think he's cracking up." From the other end of the squad, 2909's quiet chuckle rewarded him, and Brenner, the man most dangerous to his disguise, continued down the trench. . . .

Fear was necessary because the will to survive was *very* necessary. And a humanoid form was needed if the HORARS were to utilize the mass of human equipment already on hand. Besides, a human-shaped (*homolog?* no, that merely meant *similar, homological*) HORAR had outscored all the fantastic forms SBS had been able to dream up in a super-realistic (public opinion would never have permitted it with human soldiers) test carried out in the Everglades.

(Were they merely duplicating? Had all this been worked out before with some greater war in mind? And had He Himself, the Scientist Himself, come to take the form of His creations to show that he too could bear the unendurable?)

2909 was at his elbow, whispering. "Do you see something, Squad Leader? Over there?" Dawn had come without his noticing.

With fingers clumsy from fatigue he switched the control of his M-19 to the lower, 40mm grenade-launching barrel. The grenade made a brief flash at the spot 2909 had indicated. "No," he said, "I don't see anything now." The fine, soft rain which had been falling all night was getting stronger. The dark clouds seemed to roof the world. (Was he fated to reenact what had been done for mankind? It could happen. The Enemy took humans captive, but there was nothing they would not do to HORAR prisoners. Occasionally patrols found the bodies spread-eagled, with bamboo stakes driven through their limbs; and he could only be taken for a HORAR. He thought of a watercolor of the crucifixion he had seen once. Would the color of his own blood be crimson lake?)

From the CP the observation ornithocopter rose on flapping wings.

"I haven't heard one of the mines go for quite a while," 2909 said. Then there came the phony-sounding bang that so often during the past few weeks had closed similar probing attacks. Squares of paper were suddenly fluttering all over the camp.

"Propaganda shell," 2909 said unnecessarily, and 2911 climbed casually out of the trench to get a leaflet, then jumped back to his position. "Same as last week," he said, smoothing out the damp rice paper.

Looking over his shoulder, 2910 saw that he was correct. For some reason the Enemy never directed his propaganda at the HORARS, although it was no secret that reading skills were implanted in HORAR minds with the rest of their instinctive training. Instead it was always aimed at the humans in the camp, and played heavily on the distaste they were supposed to feel at being "confined with half-living flesh still stinking of chemicals." Privately, 2910 thought they might have done better, at least with Lieutenant Kyle, to have dropped that approach and played up sex. He also got the impression from the propaganda that the Enemy thought there were far more humans in the camp than there actually were.

Well, the Army—with far better opportunities to know—was wrong as well. With a few key generals excepted, the Army thought there were only two. . . .

He had made the All-American. How long ago it seemed. No coach, no sportswriter had ever compared his stocky, muscular physique with a HORAR's. And he had majored in journalism, had been ambitious. How many men, with a little surgical help, could have passed here?

"Think it sees anything?" he heard 2911 ask 2909. They were looking upward at the "bird" sailing overhead.

The ornithocopter could do everything a real bird could except lay eggs. It could literally land on a strand of wire. It could ride thermals like a vulture, and dive like a hawk. And the bird-motion of its wings was wonderfully efficient, saving power-plant weight that could be used for zoom-lenses and telecameras. He wished he were in the CP watching the monitor screen with Lieutenant Kyle instead of standing with his face a scant foot above the mud (they had tried stalked eyes like a crab's in the Everglades, he remembered, but the stalks had become infected by a fungus . . .)

As though in answer to his wish, 2900 called, "Show some snap for once, 2910. He says He wants us in the CP."

When he himself thought *He, He* meant God; but 2900 meant Lieutenant Kyle. That was why 2900 was a platoon leader, no doubt; that and the irrational prestige of a round number. He climbed out of the trench and followed him to the CP. They needed a communicating trench, but that was something there hadn't been time for yet.

Brenner had someone (2788? looked like him, but he couldn't be certain) down on his table. Shrapnel, probably from a grenade. Brenner did not look up as they came in, but 2910 could see his face was still white with fear although the attack had been over for a full quarter of an hour. He and 2900 ignored the SBS man and saluted Lieutenant Kyle.

The company commander smiled. "Stand at ease, HORARS. Have any trouble in your sector?"

2900 said, "No, sir. The light machine gun got one group of three and 2910 here knocked off a group of two. Not much of an attack on our front, sir."

Lieutenant Kyle nodded. "I thought your platoon had the

easiest time of it, 2900, and that's why I've picked you to run
a patrol for me this morning.''

"That's fine with us, sir.''

"You'll have Pinocchio, and I thought you'd want to go
yourself and take 2910's gang.''

He glanced at 2910. "Your squad still at full strength?''

2910 said, "Yes, sir,'' making an effort to keep his face
impassive. He wanted to say: I shouldn't have to go on
patrol. I'm human as you are, Kyle, and patrolling is for
things grown in tubes, things fleshed out around metal skele-
tons, things with no family and no childhood behind them.

Things like my friends.

He added, "We've been the luckiest squad in the company, sir.''

"Fine. Let's hope your luck holds, 2910.'' Kyle's attention switched back to 2900. "I've gotten under the leaf
canopy with the ornithocopter and done everything except
make it walk around like a chicken. I can't find a thing and
it's drawn no fire, so you ought to be okay. You'll make a
complete circuit of the camp without getting out of range of
mortar support. Understand?''

2900 and 2910 saluted, about-faced, and marched out.
2910 could feel the pulse in his neck; he flexed and unflexed
his hands unobtrusively as he walked. 2900 asked, "Think
we'll catch any of them?'' It was an unbending for him—the
easy camaraderie of anticipated action.

"I'd say so. I don't think the CO's had long enough with
the bird to make certain of anything except that their main
force has pulled out of range. I hope so.''

And that's the truth, he thought. Because a good hot
fire-fight would probably do it—round the whole thing out so
I can get out of here.

Every two weeks a helicopter brought supplies and, when
they were needed, replacements. Each trip it also carried a
correspondent whose supposed duty was to interview the
commanders of the camps the copter visited. The reporter's
name was Keith Thomas, and for the past two months he had

been the only human being with whom 2910 could take off his mask.

Thomas carried scribbled pages from the notebook under 2910's air mattress when he left, and each time he came managed to find some corner in which they could speak in private for a few seconds. 2910 read his mail then and gave it back. It embarrassed him to realize that the older reporter viewed him with something not far removed from hero worship.

I can get out of here, he repeated to himself. Write it up and tell Keith we're ready to use the letter.

2900 ordered crisply, "Fall in your squad. I'll get Pinocchio and meet you at the south gate."

"Right." He was suddenly seized with a desire to tell someone, even 2900, about the letter. Keith Thomas had it, and it was really only an undated note, but it was signed by a famous general at Corps Headquarters. Without explanation it directed that number 2910 be detached from his present assignment and placed under the temporary orders of Mr. K. Thomas, Accredited Correspondent. And Keith would use it any time he asked him to. In fact, he had wanted to on his last trip.

He could not remember giving the order, but the squad was falling in, lining up in the rain for his inspection almost as smartly as they had on the drill field back at the crêche. He gave "At Ease" and looked them over while he outlined the objectives of the patrol. As always, their weapons were immaculate despite the dampness, their massive bodies ramrod-straight, their uniforms as clean as conditions permitted.

The L.A. Rams with guns, he thought proudly. Barking "On Phones", he flipped the switch on his helmet that would permit 2900 to knit him and the squad together with Pinocchio in a unified tactical unit. Another order and the HORARS deployed around Pinocchio with the smoothness of repeated drill, the wire closing the south gate was drawn back, and the patrol moved out.

With his turret retracted, Pinocchio the robot tank stood just three feet high, and he was no wider than an automobile; but he was as long as three, so that from a distance he had something of the look of a railroad flatcar. In the jungle his narrow front enabled him to slip between the trunks of the unconquerable giant hardwoods, and the power in his treads could flatten saplings and bamboo. Yet resilient organics and sintered metals had turned the rumble of the old, manned tanks to a soft hiss for Pinocchio. Where the jungle was free of undergrowth he moved as silently as a hospital cart.

His immediate precursor had been named "Punch," apparently in the sort of simpering depreciation which found "Shillelagh" acceptable for a war rocket. "Punch"—a bust in the mouth.

But Punch, which like Pinocchio had possessed a computer brain and no need of a crew (or for that matter room for one except for an exposed vestigial seat on his deck), had required wires to communicate with the infantry around him. Radio had been tried, but the problems posed by static, jamming, and outright enemy forgery of instructions had been too much for Punch.

Then an improved model had done away with those wires and some imaginative officer had remembered that "Mr. Punch" had been a knockabout marionette—and the wireless improvement was suddenly very easy to name. But, like Punch and its fairytale namesake, it was vulnerable if it went out into the world alone.

A brave man (and the Enemy had many) could hide himself until Pinocchio was within touching distance. And a well-instructed one could then place a hand grenade or a bottle of gasoline where it would destroy him. Pinocchio's three-inch-thick armor needed the protection of flesh, and since he cost as much as a small city and could (if properly protected) fight a regiment to a stand, he got it.

Two scouts from 2910's squad preceded him through the jungle, forming the point of the diamond. Flankers moved on either side of him "beating the bush" and, when it seemed advisable, firing a pattern of fletchettes into any suspicious-looking piece of undergrowth. Cheerful, reliable 2909, the assistant squad leader, with one other HORAR formed the rear guard. As patrol leader 2900's position was behind Pinocchio, and as squad leader 2910's was in front.

The jungle was quiet with an eerie stillness, and it was dark under the big trees. "Though I walk in the valley of the shadow . . . ''

Made tiny by the phones, 2900 squeaked in his ear, "Keep the left flankers farther out!" 2910 acknowledged and trotted over to put his own stamp on the correction, although the flankers, 2913, 2914, and 2915, had already heard it and were moving to obey. There was almost no chance of trouble this soon, but that was no excuse for a slovenly formation. As he squeezed between two trees something caught his eye and he halted for a moment to examine it. It was a skull; a skull of bone rather than a smooth HORAR skull of steel, and so probably an Enemy's.

A big "E" Enemy's, he thought to himself. A man to whom the normal HORAR conditioning of exaggerated respect bordering on worship did not apply.

Tiny and tinny, "Something holding you up, 2910?"

"Be right there." He tossed the skull aside. A man whom even a HORAR could disobey; a man even a HORAR could kill. The skull had looked old, but it could not have been old. The ants would have picked it clean in a few days, and in a few weeks it would rot. But it was probably at least seventeen or eighteen years old.

The ornithocopter passed them on flapping wings, flying its own search pattern. The patrol went on.

Casually 2910 asked his helmet mike, "How far are we going? Far as the creek?"

2900's voice squeaked, "We'll work our way down the bank a quarter mile, then cut west," then with noticeable sarcasm added, "if that's okay with you?"

Unexpectedly Lieutenant Kyle's voice came over the phones. "2910's your second in command, 2900. He has a duty to keep himself informed of your plans.''

But 2910, realizing that a real HORAR would not have asked the question, suddenly also realized that he knew more about HORARS than the company commander did. It was not surprising, he ate and slept with them in a way Kyle could not, but it was disquieting. He probably knew more than Brenner, strict biological mechanics excepted, as well.

The scouts had reported that they could see the sluggish jungle stream they called the creek when Lieutenant Kyle's voice came over the phones again. As routinely as he had delivered his mild rebuke to 2900 he announced, ''Situation Red here. An apparent battalion-level attack hitting the North Point. Let's suck it back in, patrol.''

Pinocchio swiveled 180 degrees by locking his right tread, and the squad turned in a clockwise circle around him. Kyle said distantly, ''The recoillesses don't seem to have found the range yet, so I'm going out to give them a hand. Mr. Brenner will be holding down the radio for the next few minutes.''

2900 transmitted, ''We're on our way, sir.''

Then 2910 saw a burst of automatic weapon's fire cut his scouts down. In an instant the jungle was a pandemonium of sound.

Pinocchio's radar had traced the bullets back to their source and his main armament slammed a 155mm shell at it, but crossfire was suddenly slicing in from all around them. The bullets striking Pinocchio's turret screamed away like damned souls. 2910 saw grenades arc out of nowhere and something struck his thigh with terrible force. He made himself say, ''I'm hit, 2909, take the squad,'' before he looked at it. Mortar shells were dropping in now and if his assistant acknowledged, he did not hear.

A bit of jagged metal from a grenade or a mortar round had laid the thigh open, but apparently missed the big artery supplying the lower leg. There was no spurt, only a rapid welling of blood, and shock still held the injury numb. Forcing himself, he pulled apart the lips of the wound to make sure it was clear of foreign matter. It was very deep but the bone was not broken; at least so it seemed.

Keeping as low as he could, he used his trench knife to cut away the cloth of his trousers leg, then rigged a tourniquet with his belt. His aid packet contained a pad of guaze, and tape to hold it in place. When he had finished he lay still, holding his M-19 and looking for a spot where its fire might do some good. Pinocchio was firing his turret machine gun in routine bursts, sanitizing likely-looking patches of jungle; otherwise the fight seemed to have quieted down.

2900's voice in his ear called, "Wounded? We got any wounded?"

He managed to say, "Me. 2910." A HORAR would feel some pain, but not nearly as much as a man. He would have to fake the insensitivity as best he could. Suddenly it occurred to him that he would be invalided out, would not have to use the letter, and he was glad.

"We thought you bought it, 2910. Glad you're still around."

Then Brenner's voice cutting through the transmission jumpy with panic: "We're being overrun here! Get the Pinocchio back at once."

In spite of his pain 2910 felt contempt. Only Brenner would say "*the* Pinocchio." 2900 sent, "Coming, sir," and unexpectedly was standing over him, lifting him up.

He tried to look around for the squad. "We lose many?"

"Four dead and you." Perhaps no other human would have detected the pain in 2900's harsh voice. "You can't walk with that, can you?"

"I couldn't keep up."

"You ride Pinocchio then." With surprising gentleness the platoon leader lifted him into the little seat the robot tank's director used when road speeds made running impractical. What was left of the squad formed a skirmish line ahead. As they began to trot forward he could hear 2900 calling, "Base camp! Base camp! What's your situation there, sir?"

"Lieutenant Kyle's dead," Brenner's voice came back. "3003 just came in and told me Kyle's dead!"

"Are you holding?"

"I don't know." More faintly 2910 could hear him asking, "Are they holding, 3003?"

"Use the periscope, sir. Or if it still works, the bird."

Brenner chattered, "I don't know if we're holding or not. 3003 was hit and now he's dead. I don't think he knew anyway. You've got to hurry."

It was contrary to regulations, but 2910 flipped off his helmet phone to avoid hearing 2900's patient reply. With Brenner no longer gibbering in his ears he could hear not too distantly the sound of explosions which must be coming from the camp. Small arms fire made an almost incessant buzz as a background for the whizz—bang! of incoming shells and the coughing of the camp's own mortars.

Then the jungle was past and the camp lay in front of them. Geysers of mud seemed to be erupting from it everywhere. The squad broke into a full run, and even while he rolled, Pinocchio was firing his 155 in support of the camp.

They faked us out, 2910 reflected. His leg throbbed painfully but distantly and he felt light-headed and dizzy—as though he were an ornithocopter hovering in the misty rain over his own body. With the light-headedness came a strange clarity of mind.

They faked us out. They got us used to little probes that pulled off at sunrise, and then when we sent Pinocchio out they were going to ambush us and take the camp. It suddenly occurred to him that he might find himself still on this exposed seat in the middle of the battle; they were already approaching the edge of the mine field, and the HORARS ahead were moving into squad column so as not to overlap the edges of the cleared lane. "Where are we going, Pinocchio?" he asked, then realized his phone was still off. He reactivated it and repeated the question.

Pinocchio droned, "Injured HORAR personnel will be delivered to the Command Post for Synthetic Biology Service attention," but 2910 was no longer listening. In front of them he could hear what sounded like fifty bugles signaling for another Enemy attack.

The south side of the triangular camp was deserted, as though the remainder of their platoon had been called away to reinforce the First and Second; but with the sweeping illogic of war there was no Enemy where they might have entered unresisted.

"Request assistance from Synthetic Biology Service for injured HORAR personnel," Pinocchio was saying. Talking did not interfere with his firing the 155, but when Brenner did not come out after a minute or more, 2910 managed to swing himself down, catching his weight on his good leg. Pinocchio rolled away at once.

The CP bunker was twisted out of shape, and he could see where several near-misses had come close to knocking it out completely. Brenner's white face appeared in the doorway as he was about to go in. "Who's that?"

"2910. I've been hit—let me come in and lie down."

"They won't send us an air strike. I radioed for one and they say this whole part of the country's socked in; they say they wouldn't be able to find us."

"Get out of the door. I'm hit and I want to come in and lie down." At the last moment he remembered to add, "Sir."

Brenner moved reluctantly aside. It was dim in the bunker but not dark.

"You want me to look at that leg?"

2910 had found an empty stretcher, and he laid himself on it, moving awkwardly to keep from flexing his wound. "You don't have to," he said. "Look after some of the others." It wouldn't do for Brenner to begin poking around. Even rattled as he was he might notice something.

The SBS man went back to his radio instead. His frantic voice sounded remote and faint. It was ecstasy to lie down.

At some vast distance, voices were succeeding voices, argument meeting argument, far off. He wondered where he was.

Then he heard the guns and knew. He tried to roll onto his

side and at the second attempt managed to do it, although the light-headedness was worse than ever. 2893 was lying on the stretcher next to him, and 2893 was dead.

At the other end of the room, the end that was technically the CP, he could hear Brenner talking to 2900. "If there were a chance," Brenner was saying, "you know I'd do it, Platoon Leader."

"What's happening?" he asked. "What's the matter?" He was too dazed to keep up the HORAR role well, but neither of them noticed.

"It's a division," Brenner said. "A whole Enemy division. We can't hold off that kind of force."

He raised himself on his elbow. "What do you mean?"

"I talked to them . . . I raised them on the radio, and it's a whole division. They got one of their officers who could speak English to talk to me. They want us to surrender."

"*They* say it's a division, sir," 2900 put in evenly.

2910 shook his head, trying to clear it. "Even if it were, with Pinocchio . . . "

"The Pinocchio's gone."

2900 said soberly, "We tried to counterattack, 2910, and they knocked Pinocchio out and threw us back. How are you feeling?"

"They've got at least a division," Brenner repeated stubbornly.

2910's mind was racing now, but it was as though it were running endless wind sprints on a treadmill. If Brenner were going to give up, 2900 would never even consider disobeying, no matter how much he might disagree. There were various ways, though, in which he could convince Brenner he was a human being—given time. And Brenner could, Brenner would, tell the Enemy, so that he too would be saved. Eventually the war would be over and he could go home. No one would blame him. If Brenner were going—

Brenner was asking, "How many effectives left?"

"Less than forty, sir." There was nothing in 2900's tone to indicate that a surrender meant certain death to him, but it was true. The Enemy took only human prisoners. (Could

2900 be convinced? Could he make any of the HORARS understand, when they had eaten and joked with him, knew no physiology, and thought all men not Enemy demigods? Would they believe him if he were to try to take command?)

He could see Brenner gnawing at his lower lip. ''I'm going to surrender,'' the SBS man said at last. A big one, mortar or bombardment rocket, exploded near the CP, but he appeared not to notice it. There was a wondering, hesitant note in his voice—as though he were still trying to accustom himself to the idea.

''Sir—'' 2900 began.

''I forbid you to question my orders.'' The SBS man sounded firmer now. ''But I'll ask them to make an exception this time, Platoon Leader. Not to do,'' his voice faltered slightly, ''what they usually do to nonhumans.''

''It's not that,'' 2900 said stolidly. ''It's the folding up. We don't mind dying, sir, but we want to die fighting.''

One of the wounded moaned, and 2910 wondered for a moment, if he, like himself, had been listening.

Brenner's self-control snapped. ''You'll die any damn way I tell you!''

''Wait.'' It was suddenly difficult for 2910 to talk, but he managed to get their attention. ''2900, Mr. Brenner hasn't actually ordered you to surrender yet, and you're needed on the line. Go now and let me talk to him.'' He saw the HORAR leader hesitate and added, ''He can reach you on your helmet phone if he wants to; but go now and fight.''

With a jerky motion 2900 turned and ducked out the narrow bunker door. Brenner, taken by surprise, said, ''What is it, 2910? What's gotten into you?''

He tried to rise, but he was too weak. ''Come here, Mr. Brenner,'' he said. When the SBS man did not move he added, ''I know a way out.''

''Through the jungle?'' Brenner scoffed in his shaken voice, ''that's absurd.'' But he came. He leaned over the stretcher, and before he could catch his balance 2910 had pulled him down.

''What are you doing?''

"Can't you tell? That's the point of my trench knife you feel on your neck."

Brenner tried to struggle, then subsided when the pressure of the knife became too great. "You—can't—do this."

"I can. Because I'm not a HORAR. I'm a man, Bremner, and it's very important for you to understand that." He felt rather than saw the look of incredulity on Brenner's face. "I'm a reporter, and two years ago when the Simulations in this group were ready for activation I was planted among them. I trained with them and now I've fought with them, and if you've been reading the right magazine you must have seen some of the stories I've filed. And since you're a civilian too, with no more right to command than I have, I'm taking charge." He could sense Brenner's swallow.

"Those stories were frauds—it's a trick to gain public acceptance of the HORARS. Even back in Washington everybody in SBS knows about them."

The chuckle hurt, but 2910 chuckled. "Then why've I got this knife at your neck, Mr. Brenner?"

The SBS man was shaking. "Don't you see how it was, 2910? No human could live as a HORAR does, running miles without tiring and only sleeping a couple of hours a night, so we did the next best thing. Believe me, I was briefed on it all when I was assigned to this camp; I know all about you, 2910."

"What do you mean?"

"Damn it, let me go. You're a HORAR, and you can't treat a human like this." He winced as the knife pressed cruelly against his throat, then blurted, "They couldn't make a reporter a HORAR, so they *took* a HORAR. They took you, 2910, and made you a reporter. They implanted all the memories of an actual man in your mind at the same time they ran the regular instinct tapes. They gave you a soul, if you like, but you are a HORAR."

"They must have thought that up as a cover for me, Brenner. That's what they told you so you wouldn't report it or try to deactivate me when I acted unlike the others. I'm a man."

"You couldn't be."

"People are tougher than you think, Brenner; you've never tried."

"I'm telling you—"

"Take the bandage off my leg."

"What?"

He pressed again with the point of the knife. "The bandage. Take it off."

When it was off he directed, "Now spread the lips of the wound." With shaking fingers Brenner did so. "You see the bone? Go deeper if you have to. What is it?"

Brenner twisted his neck to look at him directly, his eyes rolling. "It's stainless steel."

2910 looked then and saw the bright metal at the bottom of the cleft of bleeding flesh; the knife slid into Brenner's throat without resistance, almost as though it moved itself. He wiped the blade on Brenner's dead arm before he sheathed it.

Ten minutes later when 2900 returned to the CP he said nothing; but 2910 saw his eyes and knew that 2900 knew. From his stretcher he said, "You're in full command now."

2900 glanced again at Brenner's body. A second later he said slowly, "He was a sort of Enemy, wasn't he? Because he wanted to surrender, and Lieutenant Kyle would never have done that."

"Yes, he was."

"But I couldn't think of it that way while he was alive." 2900 looked at him thoughtfully. "You know, you have something, 2910. A spark. Something the rest of us lack." For a moment he fingered his chin with one huge hand. "That's why I made you a squad leader; that and to get you out of some work, because sometimes you couldn't keep up. But you've that spark, somehow."

2910 said, "I know. How is it out there?"

"We're still holding. How do you feel?"

"Dizzy. There's a sort of black stuff all around the sides when I see. Listen, will you tell me something, if you can, before you go?"

"Of course."

"If a human's leg is broken very badly, what I believe they call a compound spiral fracture, is it possible for the human doctors to take out a section of the bone and replace it with a metal substitute?"

"I don't know," 2900 answered. "What does it matter?

Vaguely 2910 said, "I think I knew of a football player once they did that to. At least, I seem now to remember it . . . I had forgotten for a moment."

Outside the bugles were blowing again.

Near him the dying HORAR moaned.

An American news magazine sometimes carries, just inside its front cover among the advertisements, a column devoted to news of its own people. Two weeks after a correspondent named Thomas filed the last article of a series which had attracted national and even international attention, the following item appeared there:

> The death of a staffer in war is no unique occurence in the history of this publication, but there is a particular poignancy about that of the young man whose stories, paradoxically, to conceal his number have been signed only with his name (*see* PRESS). The airborne relief force, which arrived too late to save the camp at which he had resigned his humanity to work and fight, reports that he apparently died assisting the assigned SBS specialist in caring for the creatures whose lot he had, as nearly as a human can, made his own. Both he and the specialist were bayonetted when the camp was overrun.

FIREPROOF

Hal Clement

Hart waited a full hour after the last sounds had died away before cautiously opening the cover of his refuge. Even then he did not feel secure for some minutes, until he had made a thorough search of the storage chamber; then a smile of contempt curled his lips.

"The fools!" he muttered. "They do not examine their shipments at all. How do they expect to maintain their zone controls with such incompetents in charge?" He glanced at the analyzers in the forearm of his spacesuit, and revised his opinion a trifle—the air in the chamber was pure carbon dioxide; any man attempting to come as Hart had, but without his own air supply, would not have survived the experiment. Still, the agent felt, they should have searched.

There was, however, no real time for analyzing the actions of others. He had a job to do, and not too long in which to do it. However slack the orgainzation of this launching station might be, there was no chance whatever of reaching any of its vital parts unchallenged; and after the first challenge, success and death would be running a frightfully close race.

He glided back to the crate which had barely contained his doubled-up body, carefully replaced and resealed the cover, and then rearranged the contents of the chamber to minimize the chance of that crate's being opened first. The containers were bulky, but nothing in the free-falling station had any weight, and the job did not take long even for a man unaccustomed to a total lack of apparent gravity. Satisfied with these precautions, Hart approached the door of the storeroom; but before opening it, he stopped to review his plan.

He must, of course, be near the outer shell of the Station.
Central Intelligence had been unable to obtain plans of this
launcher—a fact which should have given him food for
thought—but there was no doubt about its general design.
Storage and living quarters would be just inside the surface of
the sphere; then would come a level of machine shops and
control systems; and at the heart, within the shielding that
represented most of the station's mass, would be the "hot"
section—the chambers containing the fission piles and power
plants, the extractors and the remote-controlled machinery
that loaded the warheads of the torpedoes which were the
main reason for the station's existence.

There were many of these structures circling Earth; every
nation on the globe maintained at least one, and usually
several. Hart had visited one of those belonging to his own
country, partly for technical familiarity and partly to accustom himself to weightlessness. He had studied its plans with
care, and scientists had carefully explained to him the func-
tions of each part, and the ways in which the launchers of the
Western Alliance were likely to differ. Most important, they
had described to him several ways by which such structures
might be destroyed. Hart's smile was wolfish as he thought
of that; these people who preferred the pleasures of personal
liberty to those of efficiency would see what efficiency could
do.

But this delay was not efficient. He had made his plans
long before, and it was more than time to set about their
execution. He must be reasonably near a store of rocket fuel;
and some at least of the air in this station must contain a
breathable percentage of oxygen. Without further deliberation, he opened the door and floated out into the corridor.

He did not go blindly. Tiny detectors built into the wrists
of his suit reacted to the infrared radiations, the water vapor
and carbon dioxide and even the breathing sounds that would
herald the approach of a human being—unless he were wearing a nonmetallic suit similar to Hart's own. Apparently the
personnel of the base did not normally wear these, however,
for twice in the first ten minutes the saboteur was warned into
shelter by the indications of the tiny instruments. In that ten

minutes he covered a good deal of the outer zone.

He learned quickly that the area in which a carbon dioxide atmosphere was maintained was quite limited in extent, and probably constituted either a quarantine zone for newly arrived supplies, or a food storage area. It was surrounded by an uninterrupted corridor lined on one side with airtight doors leading into the CO_2 rooms, and on the other by flimsier portals closing off other storage spaces. Hart wondered briefly at the reason for such a vast amount of storage room; then his attention was taken by another matter. He had been about to launch himself in another long, weightless glide down the corridor in search of branch passages which might lead to the rocket fuel stores, when a tiny spot on one wall caught his eye.

He instantly went to examine it more closely, and as quickly recognized a photoelectric eye. There appeared to be no lens, which suggested a beam-interruption unit; but the beam itself was not visible, nor could he find any projector. That meant a rather interesting and vital problem lay in avoiding the ray. He stopped to think.

In the scanning room on the second level, Dr. Bruce Mayhew chuckled aloud.

"It's wonderful what a superiority complex can do. He's stopped for the first time—didn't seem to have any doubts of his safety until he spotted that eye. The old oil about "decadent democracies' seems to have taken deep hold somewhere, at least. He must be a military agent rather than a scientist."

Warren Floyd nodded. "Let's not pull the same boner, though," he suggested. "Scientist or not, no stupid man would have been chosen for such a job. Do you think he's carrying explosives? One man could hardly have chemicals enough to make a significant number of breaches in the outer shell."

"He may be hoping to get into the core, to set off a war head," replied the older man, "though I don't for the life of me see how he expects to do it. There's a rocket fuel in his neighborhood, of course, but it's just n.v. for the torpedoes—harmless, as far as we're concerned.''

"A fire could be quite embarrassing, even if it weren't an explosion," pointed out his assistant, "particularly since the whole joint is nearly pure magnesium. I know it's sinfully expensive to transport mass away from Earth, but I wish they had built this place out of something a little less responsive to heat and oxygen.''

"I shouldn't worry about that," replied Mayhew. "He won't get a fire started.''

Floyd glanced at the flanking screens which showed armored men keeping pace with the agent in parallel corridors, and nodded. "I suppose not—provided Ben and his crew aren't too slow closing in when we give the signal.''

"You mean when *I* give the signal," returned the other man. "I have reasons for wanting him free as long as possible. The longer he's free, the lower the opinion he'll have of us; when we do take him, he'll be less ready to commit suicide, and the sudden letdown of his self-confidence will make interrogation easier.''

Floyd privately hoped nothing would happen to deflate his superior's own self-confidence, but wisely said nothing; and both men watched Hart's progress almost silently for some minutes. Floyd occasionally transmitted a word or two to the action party to keep them apprised of their quarry's whereabouts, but no other sound interrupted the vigil.

Hart had finally found a corridor which branched away from the one he had been following, and he proceeded cautiously along it. He had learned the intervals at which the photocells were spotted, and now avoided them almost automatically. It did not occur to him that, while the sight of a spacesuited man in the outer corridors might not surprise an observer, the presence of such a man who failed consistently to break the beams of the photocell spotters would be bound to attract attention. The lenses of the scanners were too small and too well hidden for Hart to find easily, and he actually believed that the photocells were the only traps. With his continued ease in avoiding them, his self-confidence and contempt for the Westerners were mounting as Mayhew had foretold.

Several times he encountered air breaks—sliding bulk-heads actuated by automatic pressure-controlled switches, designed to cut off any section with a bad air leak. His action at each of these was the same; from an outer pocket of his armor he would take a small wedge of steel and skillfully jam the door. It was this action which convinced Mayhew that the agent was not a scientist—he was displaying the skill of an experienced burglar or spy. He was apparently well supplied with the wedges, for in the hour before he found what he was seeking he jammed more than twenty of the air breaks. Mayhew and Floyd did not bother to have them cleared at the time, since no one was in the outer level without a spacesuit.

Nearly half of the outer level was thus unified when Hart reached a section of corridor bearing valve handles and hose connections instead of doors, and knew there must be liquids behind the walls. There were code indexes stenciled over the valves, which meant nothing to the spy; but he carefully manipulated one of the two handles to let a little fluid into the corridor, and sniffed at it cautiously through the gingerly cracked face plate of his helmet. He was satisfied with the results; the liquid was one of the low-volatility hydrocarbons used with liquid oxygen as a fuel to provide the moderate acceleration demanded by space launched torpedoes. They were cheap, fairly dense, and their low-vapor pressure simplified the storage problem in open-space stations.

All that Hart really knew about it was that the stuff would burn as long as there was oxygen. Well—he grinned again at the thought—there would be oxygen for a while; until the compressed, blazing combustion gases blew the heat-softened metal of the outer wall into space. After that there would be none, except perhaps in the central core, where the heavy concentration of radioactive matter made it certain there would be no one to breathe it.

At present, of course, the second level and any other intermediate ones were still sealed; but that could and would be remedied. In any case, the blast of the liberated fuel would

probably take care of the relatively flimsy inner walls. He did
not at the time realize that these were of magnesium, or he
would have felt even more sure of the results.

He looked along the corridor. As far as the curvature of the
outer shell permitted him to see, the valves projected from
the wall at intervals of a few yards. Each valve had a small
electric pump, designed to force air into the tank behind it to
drive the liquid out by pressure, since there was no gravity.
Hart did not consider this point at all; a brief test showed him
that the liquid did flow when the valve was on, and that was
enough for him. Hanging poised beside the first handle, he
took an object from still another pocket of his spacesuit, and
checked it carefully, finally clipping it to an outside belt
where it could easily be reached.

At the sight of this item of apparatus, Floyd almost suf-
fered a stroke.

"That's an incendiary bomb!" he gasped aloud. "We
can't possibly take him in time to stop his setting it off—
which he'll do the instant he sees our men! And he already
has free fuel in the corridor!"

He was perfectly correct; the agent was proceeding from
valve to valve in long glides, pausing at each just long
enough to turn it full on and to scatter the balloonlike mass of
escaping liquid with a sweep of his arm. Gobbets and droplets of the inflammable stuff sailed lazily hither and yon
through the air in his wake.

Mayhew calmly lighted a cigarette, unmindful of the
weird appearance of the match flame driven toward his feet
by the draft from the ceiling ventilators, and declined to
move otherwise. "Decidedly, no physicist," he murmured.
"I suppose that's just as well—it's the military information
the army likes anyway. They certainly wouldn't have risked
a researcher on this sort of job, so I never really did have a
chance to get anything I wanted from him."

"But what are we going to do?" Floyd was almost frantic.
"There's enough available energy loose in that corridor now
to blast the whole outer shell off—and gallons more coming
every second. I know you've been here a lot longer than I, but
unless you can tell me how you expect to keep him from

lighting that stuff up, I'm getting into a suit right now!''

"If it blows, a suit won't help you,'' pointed out the older man.

"I know that!'' almost screamed Floyd, "but what other chance is there? Why did you let him get so far?''

"There is still no danger,'' Mayhew said flatly, "whether you believe it or not. However, the fuel does cost money, and there'll be some work recovering it, so I don't see why he should be allowed to empty all the torpedo tanks. He's excited enough now, anyway.'' He turned lanquidly to the appropriate microphone and gave the word to the action squad. "Take him now. He seems to be without hand weapons, but don't count on it. He certainly has at least one incendiary bomb.'' As an afterthought, he reached for another switch, and made sure the ventilators in the outer level were not operating; then he relaxed again and gave his attention to the scanner that showed the agent's activity. Floyd had switched to another pickup that covered a longer section of corridor, and the watchers saw the spacesuited attackers almost as soon as did Hart himself.

The European reacted to the sight at once—too rapidly, in fact, for the shift in his attention caused him to miss his grasp on the valve handle he sought and flounder helplessly through the air until he reached the next. Once anchored, however, he acted as he had planned, ignoring with commendable self-control the four armored figures converging on him. A sharp twist turned the fuel valve full on, sending a stream of oil mushrooming into the corridor; his left hand flashed to his belt, seized the tiny cylinder he had snapped there, jammed its end hard against the adjacent wall, and tossed the bomb gently back down the corridor. In one way his lack of weightless experience betrayed him; he allowed for a gravity pull that was not there. The bomb, in consequence, struck the "ceiling'' a few yards from his hand, and rebounded with a popping noise and a shower of sparks. It drifted on down the corridor toward the floating globules of hydrocarbon, and the glow of the sparks was suddenly replaced by the eye-hurting radiance of thermite.

Floyd winced at the sight, and expected the attacking men to make futile plunges after the blazing thing; but though all were within reach of walls, not one swerved from his course. Hart made no effort to escape or fight; he watched the course of the drifting bomb with satisfaction, and, like Floyd, expected in the next few seconds to be engulfed in a sea of flame that would remove the most powerful of the Western torpedo stations from his country's path of conquest. Unlike Floyd, he was calm about it, even when the men seized him firmly and began removing equipment from his pockets. One unclamped and removed the face plate of his helmet; and even to that he made no resistance—just watched in triumph as his missile drifted toward the nearest globes of fuel.

It did not actually strike the first. It did not have to; while the quantity of heat radiated by burning thermite is relatively small, the temperature of the reaction is notoriously high— and the temperature six inches from the bomb was well above the flash point of the rocket fuel, comparatively non-volatile as it was. Floyd saw the flash as its surface ignited, and closed his eyes.

Mayhew gave him four or five seconds before speaking, judging that that was probably about all the suspense the younger man could stand.

"All right, ostrich," he finally said quietly. "I'm not an angel, in case you were wondering. Why not use your eyes, and the brain behind them?"

Floyd was far too disturbed to take offense at the last remark, but he did cautiously follow Mayhew's advice about looking. He found difficulty, however, in believing what his eyes and the scanner showed him.

The group of five men was unchanged, except for the expression on the captive's now visible face. All were looking down the corridor toward the point where the bomb was still burning; Lang's crew bore expressions of amusement on their faces, while Hart wore a look of utter disbelief. Floyd, seeing what he saw, shared the expression.

The bomb had by now passed close to several of the floating spheres. Each had caught fire, as Floyd had seen—

for a moment only. Now each was surrounded by a spherical, nearly opaque layer of some grayish substance that looked like a mixture of smoke and kerosene vapor; a layer that could not have been half an inch thick, as Floyd recalled the sizes of the original spheres. None was burning; each had effectively smothered itself out, and the young observer slowly realized just how and why as the bomb at last made a direct hit on the drop of fuel fully a foot in diameter.

Like the others, the globe flamed momentarily, and went out; but this time the sphere that appeared and grew around it was lighter in color, and continued to grow for several seconds. Then there was a little, sputtering explosion, and a number of fragments of still burning thermite emerged from the surface of the sphere in several directions, traveled a few feet, and went out. All activity died down, except in the faces of Hart and Floyd.

The saboteur was utterly at a loss, and seemed likely to remain that way; but in the watch room Floyd was already kicking himself mentally for his needless worry. Mayhew, watching the expression on his assistant's face, chuckled quietly.

"Of course you get it now," he said at last.

"I do *now,* certainly," replied Floyd. "I should have seen it earlier—I've certainly noticed you light enough cigarettes, and watched the behavior of the match flame. Apparently our friend is not yet enlightened, though," he nodded toward the screen as he spoke.

He was right; Hart was certainly not enlightened. He belonged to a service in which unpleasant surprises were neither unexpected nor unusual, but he had never in his life been so completely disorganized. The stuff looked like fuel; it smelled like fuel; it had even started to burn—but it refused to carry on with the process. Hart simply relaxed in the grip of the guards, and tried to find something in the situation to serve as an anchor for his whirling thoughts. A spaceman would have understood the situation without thinking, a high school student of reasonable intelligence could probably have worked the matter out in time; but Hart's education had been that of a spy, in a country which considered general education a waste of time. He simply did not have the background to cope with his present environment.

That, at least, was the idea Mayhew acquired after a careful questioning of the prisoner. Not much was learned about his intended mission, though there was little doubt about it under the circumstances. The presence of an alien agent aboard any of the free-floating torpedo launchers of the various national governments bore only one interpretation; and since the destruction of one such station would do little good to anyone, Mayhew at once radioed all other launchers to be on the alert for similar intruders—all others, regardless of nationality. Knowledge by Hart's superiors of his capture might prevent their acting on the assumption that he had succeeded, which would inevitably lead to some highly regrettable incidents. Mayhew's business was to prevent a war, not win one. Hart had not actually admitted the identity of his superiors, but his accent left the matter in little doubt; and since no action was intended, Mayhew did not need proof.

There remained, of course, the problem of what to do with Hart. The structure had no ready-made prison, and it was unlikely that the Western government would indulge in the gesture of a special rocket to take the man off. Personal watch would be tedious, but it was unthinkable merely to deprive a man with the training Hart must have received of his equipment, and then assume he would not have to be watched every second.

The solution, finally suggested by one of the guards, was a small storeroom in the outer shell. It had no locks, but there were welding torches in the machine shops. There was no ventilator either, but an alga tank would take care of that. After consideration, Mayhew decided that this was the best plan, and it was promptly put into effect.

Hart was thoroughly searched, even his clothing being replaced as a precautionary measure. He asked for his

cigarettes and lighter, with a half smile, Mayhew supplied
the man with some of his own, and marked those of the spy
for special investigation. Hart said nothing more after that,
and was incarcerated without further ceremony. Mayhew
was chuckling once more as the guards disappeared with
their charge.

"I hope he gets more good than I out of that lighter," he
remarked. "It's a wick-type my kid sent me as a present, and
the ventilator draft doesn't usually keep it going. Maybe our
friend will learn something, if he fools with it long enough.
He has a pint of lighter fluid to experiment with—the kid had
large ideas."

"I was a little surprised—I thought for a moment you were
giving him a pocket flask," laughed Floyd. "I suppose that's
why you always use matches—they're easier to wave than
that thing. I guess I save myself a lot of trouble not smoking
at all. I suppose you have to put potassium nitrate in your
cigarettes to keep 'em going when you're not pulling on
them." Floyd ducked as he spoke, but Mayhew didn't throw
anything. Hart, of course, was out of hearing by this time,
and would not have profited from the remark in any case.

He probably, in fact, would not have paid much attention.
He knew, of course, that the sciences of physics and chemistry are important; but he thought of them in connection with
great laboratories and factories. The idea that knowledge of
either could be of immediate use to anyone not a chemist or
physicist would have been fantastic to him. While his current
plans for escape were based largely on chemistry, the connection did not occur to him. The only link between those
plans and Mayhew's words or actions gave the spy some
grim amusement; it was the fact that he did not smoke.

The cell, when he finally reached it, was perfectly satisfactory; there were no peepholes which could serve as shot-
holes, no way in which the door could be unsealed
quickly—as Mayhew had said, not even a ventilator. Once
he was in, Hart would not be interrupted without plenty of
notice. Since the place was a storeroom, there was no reason

to expect even a scanner, though, he told himself, there was
no reason to assume there was none, either. He simply
disregarded that possibility, and went to work the moment he
heard the torch start to seal his door.

His first idea did not get far. He spent half an hour trying to
make Mayhew's lighter work, without noticeable success.
Each spin of the "flint" brought a satisfactory shower of
sparks, and about every fourth or fifth try produced a faint
"pop" and a flash of blue fire; but he was completely unable
to make a flame last. He closed the cover at last, and for the
first time made an honest effort to think. The situation had
got beyond the scope of his training.

He dismissed almost at once the matter of the rocket fuel
that had not been ignited by his bomb. Evidently the Westerners stored it with some inhibiting chemical, probably as a
precaution more against accident than sabotage. Such a
chemical would have to be easily removable, but he had no
means of knowing the method, and that line of attack would
have to be abandoned.

But why wouldn't the lighter fuel burn? The more he
thought the matter out, the more Hart felt that Mayhew must
have doctored it deliberately, as a gesture of contempt. Such
an act he could easily understand; and the thought of it roused
again the wolfish hate that was such a prominent part of his
personality. He would show that smart Westerner! There was
certainly some way!

Powerful hands, and a fingernail deliberately hardened
long since to act as a passable screw-driver blade, had the
lighter disassembled in the space of a few minutes. The parts
were disappointingly small in number and variety; but Hart
considered each at length.

The fuel, already evaporating as it was, appeared
useless—he was no chemist, and had satisfied himself the
stuff was incombustible. The case was of magnalium, apparently, and might be useful as a heat source if it could be
lighted; its use in a cigarette lighter did not encourage pursuit
of that thought. The wick might be combustible, if

thoroughly dried. The flint and wheel mechanism was promising—at least one part would be hard enough to cut or wear most metals, and the spring might be decidedly useful.

Elsewhere in the room there was very little. The light was a gas tube, and, since the chamber had no opening whatever, would probably be most useful as a light. The alga tank, of course, had a minute motor and pump which forced air through its liquid, and an ingenious valve and trap system which recovered the air even in the present weightless situation; but Hart, considering the small size of the room, decided that any attempt to dismantle his only source of fresh air would have to be very much of a last resort.

After much thought, and with a grimace of distaste, he took the tiny striker of the lighter and began slowly to abrade a circular area around the latch of the door, using the inside handle for anchorage.

He did not, of course, have any expectation of final escape; he was not in the least worried about his chances of recovering his spacesuit. He expected only to get out of the cell and complete his mission; and if he succeeded, no possible armor would do him any good.

As it happened, there was a scanner in his compartment; but Mayhew had long since grown tired of watching the spy try to ignite the lighter fuel, and had turned his attention elsewhere, so that Hart's actions were unobserved for some time. The door metal was thin and not particularly hard; and he was able without interference and with no worse trouble than severe finger cramp to work out a hole large enough to show him another obstacle—instead of welding the door frame itself, his captors had placed a rectangular steel bar across the portal and fastened it at points well to each side of the frame, out of the prisoner's reach. Hart stopped scraping as soon as he realized the extent of this barrier, and gave his mind to the situation.

He might, conceivably, work a large enough hole through the door to pass his body without actually opening the portal;

but his fingers were already stiff and cramped from the use made of the tiny striker, and it was beyond reason to expect that he would be left alone long enough to accomplish any such feat. Presumably they intended to feed him occasionally.

There was another reason for haste, as well, though he was forgetting it as his nose became accustomed to the taint in the air. The fluid, which he had permitted to escape while disassembling the lighter, was evaporating with fair speed, as it was far more volatile than the rocket fuel; and it was diffusing through the air of the little room. The alga tank removed only carbon dioxide, so that the air of the cell was acquiring an ever greater concentration of hydrocarbon molecules. Prolonged breathing of such vapors is far from healthy, as Hart well knew; and escape from the room was literally the only way to avoid breathing the stuff.

What would eliminate a metal door—quickly? Brute force? He hadn't enough of it. Chemicals? He had none. Heat? The thought was intriguing and discouraging at the same time, after his recent experience with heat sources. Still, even if liquid fuels would not burn perhaps other things would: there was the wicking from the lighter; a little floating cloud of metal particles around the scene of his work on the magnesium door; and the striking mechanism of the lighter.

He plucked the wicking out of the air where it had been floating, and began to unravel it—without fuel, as he realized, it would need every advantage in catching the sparks of the striker.

Then he wadded as much of the metallic dust as he could collect—which was not too much—into the wick, concentrating it heavily at one end and letting it thin out toward the more completely raveled part.

Then he inspected the edges of the hole he had ground in the door, and with the striker roughened them even more on one side, so that a few more shavings of metal projected. To these he pressed the fuse, wedging it between the door and the steel bar just outside the hole, with the "lighting" end projecting into the room. He inspected the work carefully, nodded in satisfaction, and began to reassemble the striker mechanism.

He did not, of course, expect that the steel bar would be melted or seriously weakened by an ounce or so of magnesium, but he did hope that the thin metal of the door itself would ignite.

Hart had the spark mechanism almost ready when his attention was distracted abruptly. Since the hole had been made, a very gentle current of air had been set up in the cell by the corridor ventilators beyond—a current in the nature of an eddy which tended to carry loose objects quite close to the hole. One of the loose objects in the room was a sphere comprised of the remaining lighter fluid, which had not yet evaporated. When Hart noticed the shimmering globe, it was scarcely a foot from his fuse, and drifting steadily nearer.

To him, that sphere of liquid was death to his plan; it would not burn itself, it probably would not let anything else burn either. If it touched and soaked his fuse, he would have to wait until it evaporated; and there might not be time for that. He released the striker with a curse, and swung his open hand at the drop, trying to drive it to one side. He succeeded only partly. It spattered on his hand, breaking up into scores of smaller drops, some of which moved obediently away, while others just drifted, and still others vanished in vapor. None drifted far; and the gentle current had them in control almost at once, and began to bear many of them back toward the hole—and Hart's fuse.

For just a moment the saboteur hung there in agonized indecision, and then his training reasserted itself. With another curse he snatched at the striker, made sure it was ready for action, and turned to the hole in the door. It was at this moment that Mayhew chose to take another look at his captive.

As it happened, the lens of his scanner was so located that Hart's body covered the hole in the door; and since the spy's back was toward him, the watcher could not tell precisely what he was doing. The air of purposefulness about the captive was so outstanding and so impressive, however, that Mayhew was reaching for a microphone to order a direct check on the cell when Hart spun the striker wheel.

Mayhew could not, of course, see just what the man had done, but the consequences were plain enough. The saboteur's body was flung away from the door and toward the scanner lens like a rag doll kicked by a mule. An orange blossom of flame outlined him for an instant; and in practically the same instant the screen went blank as a heavy shock wave shattered its pickup lens.

Mayhew, accustomed as he was to weightless maneuvering, never in his life traveled so rapidly as he did then. Floyd and several other crewmen, who saw him on the way, tried to follow; but he outstripped them all, and when they reached the site of Hart's prison Mayhew was hanging poised outside, staring at the door.

There was no need of removing the welded bar. The thin metal of the door had been split and curled outward fantastically; an opening quite large enough for any man's body yawned in it, though there was nothing more certain than the fact that Hart had not made use of this avenue of escape. His body was still in the cell, against the far wall; and even now the relatively strong currents from the hall ventilators did not move it. Floyd had a pretty good idea of what held it there, and did not care to look closely. He might be right.

Mayhew's voice broke the prolonged silence.

"He never did figure it out."

"Just what let go, anyway?" asked Floyd.

"Well, the only combustible we know of in the cell was the lighter fluid. To blast like that, though, it must have been almost completely vaporized, and mixed with just the right amount of air—possible, I suppose, in a room like this. I don't understand why he let it all out, though."

"He seems to have been using pieces of the lighter,"

Floyd pointed out. "The loose fuel was probably just a by-product of his activities. He was even duller than I, though. It took me long enough to realize that a fire needs air to burn—and can't set up convection currents to keep itself supplied with oxygen, when there is no gravity."

"More accurately, when there is no *weight*," interjected Mayhew. "We are well within Earth's gravity field, but in free fall. Convection currents occur because the heated gas is *lighter* per unit volume than the rest, and rises. With no weight, and no 'up' such currents are impossible."

"In any case, he must have decided we were fooling him with non-combustible liquids."

Mayhew replied slowly: "People are born and brought up in a steady gravity field, and come to take all its manifestations for granted. It's extremely hard to forsee *all* the consequences which will arise when you dispense with it. I've been here for years, practically constantly, and still get caught sometimes when I'm tired or just waking up."

"They should have sent a spaceman to do this fellow's job, I should think."

"How would he have entered the station? A man is either a spy or a spaceman—to be both would mean he was too old for action at all, I should say. Both professions demand years of rigorous training, since habits rather than knowledge are required—habits like the one of always stopping within reach of a wall or other massive object." There was a suspicion of the old chuckle in his voice as Mayhew spoke the final sentence, and it was followed by a roar of laughter from the other men. Floyd looked around, and blushed furiously.

He was, as he had suspected from the older man's humor, suspended helplessly in midair out of reach of every source of traction. Had there been anything solid around, he would probably have used it for concealment instead, anyway. He managed at last to join that laughter; but at its end he glanced once more into Hart's cell, and remarked, "If this is the worst danger that inexperience lands on my head, I don't think I'll complain. Bruce, I want to go with you on your next leave to Earth; I simply must see you in a gravity field. I bet you won't wait for the ladder when we step off the rocket—though I guess it would be more fun to see you drop a dictionary on your toe. As you implied, habits are hard to break.''

BEST-SELLING
Science Fiction
and
Fantasy

MORE SCIENCE FICTION!
ADVENTURE

AWARD-WINNING
Science Fiction!

The following titles are winners of the prestigious Nebula or Hugo Award for excellence in Science Fiction. A must for lovers of good science fiction everywhere!

☐ 47809-3	**THE LEFT HAND OF DARKNESS,** Ursula K. LeGuin	$2.95
☐ 79179-4	**SWORDS AND DEVILTRY,** Fritz Leiber	$2.75
☐ 06223-7	**THE BIG TIME,** Fritz Leiber	$2.50
☐ 16651-2	**THE DRAGON MASTERS,** Jack Vance	$1.95
☐ 16706-3	**THE DREAM MASTER,** Roger Zelazny	$2.25
☐ 24905-1	**FOUR FOR TOMORROW,** Roger Zelazny	$2.25
☐ 80697-X	**THIS IMMORTAL,** Roger Zelazny	$2.50

THE CHILDE CYCLE SERIES

By Gordon R. Dickson

☐ 16012-3	**DORSAI!**	$2.75
☐ 49300-9	**LOST DORSAI**	$2.95
☐ 56851-3	**NECROMANCER**	$2.50
☐ 77420-2	**SOLDIER, ASK NOT**	$2.75
☐ 77804-6	**SPIRIT OF DORSAI**	$2.75
☐ 79972-8	**TACTICS OF MISTAKE**	$2.50

Available at your local bookstore or return this form to: